ISBN: 978-1-942500-77-3
Copyright @ 2021 James Lynch
All Rights Reserved
Boulevard Books
The New Face of Publishing
www.BoulevardBooks.org

"FOR DUTY AND HUMANITY"

by James Lynch

Even though it had been months since it meant anything, Jim still shot up with the Monday morning he 6:30 alarm. 20-plus years of confronting the dreaded Monday morning will do that for a person. Fucking Mondays. Now, truth be told, Mondays weren't half-bad. That happens when you start your own business and you don't have to do the morning dance anymore. His wife, however, wasn't of the same opinion.   He turned and drifted off for another couple minutes while his wife started the ballet of getting ready for the day.

Jim never gloated over it for the fact that she was the only reason he was afforded the opportunity to start his own venture. Being under the umbrella of your spouse's corporate health insurance afforded a great opportunity.

After getting married he decided to branch out on his own. It was time. Now Mondays offered a whole different deal, making money for yourself instead of someone else.

After six months everything was going according to plan......except for the making money part of the deal.

"Are you going to get up?"

"I would imagine so. In good time."

"Whatever."

Jim got up, put on his robe, went to the can and grabbed some coffee.

"Are you going to be busy today?"

God, that question. "Hope so."

"I've got a few things that I need to follow-up on, and I'm waiting to hear back from Sal on a couple of jobs, so I think it should be a good day."

"OK, let's hope."

"Thanks hon."

A quick peck on the lips and she was on her way.

He started the work day by consulting the website job board for Investigators. Until he got some more consistent clients it was what he had to do. The nanny checks he was doing were becoming more sporadic and there was nothing he could rely on as a steady revenue generator. There was one posting about a background check on someone's ex-husband. He put a bid down for $500 for the job. It was better to high-ball the price to leave a little room to haggle. Plus, if he heard back then you pretty much almost had them. This one was right in his wheelhouse.

There were some other promising leads, but the truth of the matter was that he would be finished with all his responsibilities by 8:15, 8:45 if something else came up.

After his wife left and leaving him to his own devices, Jim sipped his coffee for a bit and scanned the net. At about Halfway through an article about the Phillies promising lineup (*"On paper the Phils look great!"*) he got a call.

"Apollo Due Diligence. James O'Neill"

"Is this Apollo?"

"Yes. yes it is."

"Hi, my name is Matt Evans. You put a bid down on the job board about my wife's ex."

"How are you doing? What exactly are you looking for?"

"Well, he's trying to get custody of her kids and he's lying to the court. I know that he's a crook and has a checkered past. I just need to prove it. Is this something you can do?"

"Absolutely. Here is what I would recommend. First, you run a comprehensive criminal check. Where does he live?"

"Somewhere in Long Island, but I know he's moved around a lot in the last couple years."

"OK." New York is a comprehensive statewide check and not county to county. Costs a bit but the information is solid and you get it back in real time."

"OK."

"I'll run him through my databases to find out where else he's lived. From there we can check federal courts, then down to the state and county level, see if he's had any other criminal records, evictions or bankruptcies. If you want, I can check out who else is at the current residence and run them as well."

"What about his credit, can you get credit? How about DMV. I need to know what kind of car he drives."

"No, and no"

"Why not?"

"Because I can't. It's illegal. Unless he signs off on it, but I don't think he would be up for that. As far as DMV is concerned. That's no dice as well. Unless there's a judgment in place or an active order of protection, in which case you would go to the police for that."

"I really want to make sure we get everything on this guy. Why can't you get his DMV information? I thought that's what you guys did."

"Yeah, maybe 20 years ago, but here's the thing. Congress put an end to all that because, well, people started getting all murdery." Hell, even the police themselves now had to account for every plate they ran. "I could risk my license or go to jail if I give that information out." Not that he could even get the information. Well, he could. He used to 'have a guy' that would do all that stuff on the down-low, but only on the condition that the information would never make its way in front of the judge. If you had to explain how you came to possess these records you were screwed. From the way this conversation was going he could guess that it was a risk the client

4

would be willing to take and 'ol Jim would be thrown under the bus. "There's only so much the law will allow. I would also check his media history, both social and print. Sometimes if someone's arrested but the charges were dropped, it may have shown up in the local papers."

"OK, sounds good. I really want to do everything I can for this. What would the cost be for this and how quick can you get it?"

"As I quoted, $500, plus tax is the cost. Usually the turnaround for these reports is about three business days, depending on the response from the state and counties."

"What?"

"$500. The price that I quoted on the site."

"$500? I thought that was a suggested price. You're gonna have to do better than that!"

"Thing is, Mr. Evans, is that I can't do any better than that. I won't do any better than that. I don't think you know what goes into these searches. I've been doing these for over 20 years. I know what is needed for something like this, and I know exactly what you're looking for." The cost of the New York search alone is over $100, out of pocket. Now this asshole wants to nickel and dime me? There would be no haggling with this dick. Fuck this guy.

"I see that I can get a check on line for like $30."

"Then by all means go right ahead." *See what he gets out of that one.*

"I'm just trying to get a good price, that's all. You gotta come down a bit! How about it?"

This jackass is haggling over the price of information for custody of his step-kids. Who knows, maybe his wife was in the room when he called and now he stepped outside. Time to dig in the heels. Normally he would get started in good faith and wait for payment and he hasn't been stiffed yet......yet.

"What I quoted you is the best price I can give. Now there are numerous out of pocket expenses involved on this, so I'm going to need payment up-front. If you want to send a check that's fine, but there is also a PayPal link on my website. If you send a check, I'll get started in good faith, but I'm not releasing any information until payment is made in full." Jim gave him his email address and said that if he wants to go forward then send payment and the details on the person. He hung up knowing that he would never hear from this jerkoff again. If the guy called back, he would raise the price $50. I wonder if this guy's wife knew. Fuck it. Not his problem. Reason number 263 on why he wasn't a good salesman.

Another case of "I want no stone un-turned, you do whatever is takes. Wait, how much was that?"

Upon reflection Jim realized that he was probably correct in his assumption that he stepped outside out of earshot from his wide. In reality this prick most likely wanted nothing to do with the kids, but he had to put up a nice front. Now he could walk back and tell her that he was getting jobbed by someone taking advantage of the situation. Well played. But what a fucking waste of time.

He kind of hoped that the guy would do one of those "*$30 criminal records search on anyone in minutes!*" bullshit ads you see all over the internet. It sounds good, but what they don't notice is that when you sign up, on the 50-page terms of service contract, you agree to pay $30 per month. When the person finds out the charges a couple of months down the road, they tell you to go screw when you ask for your money back. Fuck it. You get what you pay for.

This day was not looking promising, and it wasn't even 10:00.

Back to the job boards. These were the sites for people who for the most part were a bit desperate but had no idea how to navigate the waters. Lots of divorce and cheating spouse cases, which he absolutely refused to do.

Jim never sought out these cases, but people would consult with him from time to time about the possibility. He had a blanket statement, informing them to lawyer up and start writing up the divorce papers because it was over. Once the trust is gone that's it. That most always worked. There were some instances where people just wanted to know for their own edification. These people usually had deep pockets and didn't care about the price, in which case he would pass it on to someone Rigo, a former colleague and one of the best surveillance guys he'd ever worked with. Rigo had no issue handling these cases, and he would usually throw Jim a finders' fee.

What he was looking for were the adoption cases. They were infrequent but were his favorite, something that was right in his area of expertise. Research was his thing, and a good day for him was going through the microfilm section of the New York Public Library, checking birth records, census reports, and old white pages. He's done over a dozen in the past and had met with varying degrees of success. The downside of these cases was the fact that while at times there was a positive conclusion, there was no guarantee that there would be a happy ending. Not that Jim ever followed-up to see how things went, but sometimes it was offered to him. His job was to lead you to the curtain. What was behind it was anyone's guess. His guess was that for the most part, it was probably a good thing that they were given up by their birth parents. Happy endings were always great, and Jim was a complete sucker for one, but there were no guarantees.

Nothing of the sort was found.

At around 3:00 Jim got a call from an unidentified number from a Perth Amboy number. If he didn't know the call, he would usually let it go straight to voicemail, but what the hell, he was on a roll so he answered the call.

"This is James O'Neill."

"Are you a private investigator?"

"Yes, how can I help you?"

"I'm going through a divorce and I think my husband is tracking me and has bugged my phone."

"Why do you think this?"

"He just always seems to know where I am. He's very jealous and wants me to go back with him."

"OK. Let me just say first off that this isn't really my area of expertise."

"Do you think you can help me?"

"I'm not sure, but I'll try. First off. How did you hear about me?"

"I found you on the state's Licensed Private Investigator List."

"Ok, great." I may be of service in this matter, or at least I can help point you in the right direction. Let me ask you first, the phone you're using, whose name is it in?"

"His."

"OK. Based on that you should assume that he is tracking you. Are you calling me from your phone right now?"

"No, I'm using a friends' phone."

OK, at least her head was in the game.

"First up I would suggest that you get what they call a 'burner' phone. It's the kind of phone used by people who don't want to be found, mainly drug dealers. They're untraceable. You just buy blocks of time with it. I would use that when you contact anyone that you don't want your husband to know about. Either that or use your friends' phone."

"OK, I'll look into that. What about my house? I think he may have had it bugged. Can you come by and check? Or maybe send someone."

Shit. Debugging a house. This is when things got tricky. Sure, there were devices for sale on-line, but he had no idea if they actually worked. He did know of a guy who worked time to time at his old company, but he charged a ton. Better to go with one of these guys rather than try himself.

"How big is your house?"

"Why?"

"Well, an on-premises check of an entire house can take some time, and it's not cheap if you want it done right."

"We have a three-bedroom house in Perth Amboy, about 2,000 square feet. I don't have much money to spend though."

Of course not. The best thing to do in an area that he had no real expertise was to…

"I haven't done anything like this in a while, but I used to have a guy who handled these things. Let me reach out to him and see what I can do. What's your name?"

"Tracy."

"OK Tracy. When is a good time to call you back?"

"Anytime. Could you tell him that I think the bugs are in the appliances? Would that help?"

"Sure. In the meantime, do yourself a favor. Go outside for any important conversations or turn on the radio or TV real loud if you have to stay in."

"Would that work?"

Would it work? Sounded good.

"I guess, or I mean, sure."

"Remember, I don't have much money to spend."

"Got it. I'll reach out later Tracy."

"OK, thanks."

He figured he would give it an hour then call back with an unreasonable number, which she would surely turn down. The problem was that *"not much money"* can be drastically different from person to person. How many jobs did he quote thinking that he priced himself out before hearing that my price was much cheaper than they thought? *Always ask for their budget!*

His conscience got the better of him and he checked out his old contact list from his old company. He knew that guys, name, Freddy something. An Italian name. He also knew he was from Staten Island, and was kind of an asshole.

Jim found the list, here it was, Fred "Freddie" Merlino. He used to work for the NYPD, but wasn't a cop. Was that right? He did know that he had all the equipment and wasn't cheap. He found the number."

"Is this Freddie Merlino."

"Who's this?"

"It's Jim O'Neill. I used to work for FSI in New York for Sal and Joe. We used you sometimes for some debugging jobs."

"Oh yeah, how you doin? Still with those guys?"

"No, I left about six years ago and started up my own shop in Jersey City."

"Yeah, how's things?"

"OK I guess. Hey, I wanted to know if you're still doing your thing?"

"I'm kind of retired, but I still do it from time to time. What you got?"

Jim told him of the situation and was told he would do it for $1,500 flat.

"OK, appreciate it. To be honest I don't think that she can afford this but I'll pass it on and see what she has to say. I'll reach out one way or the other"

"OK Jim, I'm pretty much free anytime."

He tried to recall why he thought this guy was a dick when he remembered it wasn't him, it was this old codger who worked with him, Jerry.

So, $1,500 for this guy plus his add-on. Since he would accompany Freddie to the location for this he figured $2,500 total would work.

"Hello Tracy, this is Jim."

"Hi, thanks for getting back!"

"No problem. So I talked to my guy, who's done work for me in the past and is just what you need. We can go to your house as a team and check the entire residence for $2,500."

"Oh dear, I can't afford that!"

"Well, what's your budget?"

"I only have a few hundred dollars."

Yeah, par for the course. "*I need something done quick, but I don't have any means of paying for it*". The problem is that with things such as this is that there really wasn't a set pricing schedule for most of these things. An oil change on your car has a set price. A contracting job usually has a set price. But there was no set menu for any of the services he could offer. Sometimes it worked out for the better, sometimes.....not.

"Well Tracy, unfortunately there's not much I can do for that amount. And I would leave you some advice that anyone who says they can can't, they just want your money."

"I see. Is there anything I can get to check if my appliances have been bugged?"

"Off the top of my head, no. But I would recommend that you use a burner phone from now on and get out of the house as much as possible."

"Isn't there anything else you can do?"

"I'm afraid not. Tracy, I can't say for sure that your ex bugged your house, but I would say that it's highly unlikely. Is this something your ex is capable of?"

"He is a plumber, but he hasn't worked in a while. He is good with his hands, but when I think of it I'm not sure. OK, thanks Jim. You probably think I'm crazy."

Yes, but nothing out of the spectrum.

"No problem Tracy. Good luck"

"Thanks, bye."

"Bye."

He supposed that he could have brought something cheap off the internet and waved it around the house, but he wouldn't be able to sleep at night. There were a bunch of people that would have no problem with it, but it wasn't the way he worked. It was also why he was broke.

At around 4:00 thoughts started shifting to shutting it down for the day and what to do for the evening. Who was working at PJs? Maybe a little happy hour?.....Nah, it was Monday. They were already in there like five nights a week....but still, a couple happy hour pops can't hurt.

"Jimmmy! What's up?" Mike, the owner, said from his perch at the head of the bar.

"Hey Mike. Typical day," He took his seat at the bar and waited for his usual...a glass of house red wine with a side of ice. The Mrs. hated it, what with her Italian upbringing, but for some reason he just liked it. It was kind of his thing

"How's business going?"

"Not bad....Not good, but not bad."

"Cool."

"Where's Lee?"

"She's on her way."

Jim settled into his drink, grabbed a small handful of ice to splash in the wine and went about minding his own business. Where was Doug? He was usually here at this time?

"Anyone see Doug?"

"He was over my office earlier today helping with the books, but he left around three."

Hmm, this was a situation where a simple text would have worked, but sometimes it was more fun to speculate. Before he could even get a though up he walked through the door and plopped himself right next to Jim.

"Hey man, how's things?"

"I'm retired, every day is the same. What day is it anyway?"

"Monday."

"Really? Ok.' Doug ordered his usual, gin and soda, and took his jacket off.

"Any Met's news to share?"

"Other than they suck?"

"Yeah."

Doug was about one thing, the Mets. It was the Mets and only the Mets for Doug. No football, no basketball, no hockey. He respected that.

Doug was a retired tax attorney who crunched all the numbers for wealthy people before hanging things up when he was in his early fifties. A lifelong bachelor, he relegated himself to a quasi-simple lifestyle. A small apartment, no car and little overhead. He could live comfortably on his investments and take nice vacations whenever he saw fit. Jim took affinity to Doug after their mutual admiration for The Three Stooges and the Odd Couple.

"Nope. How are you? Where's Lee, on her way down?"

"Yeah, she should be her in a bit. Things are OK, I guess. Same old same old. Had a few nibbles for jobs today, but no real bites. I think things are trending in the right direction though, hopefully."

"Well that's good. You have to stay optimistic when you have your own business."

"I guess."

They settled into their drinks when the wife walked in, thereby ensuring that further conversation would be limited.

"Hey hon"

"Hey" she planted a small kiss on his cheek? "How was your day?"

"It was ok, nothing major to report."

"Did your friend Sal reach out?"

"No."

"Did you call him?"

"No"

"Why didn't you call him?"

"I don't want to harass this guy. It will come. If he says it's gonna be there it will be. Sometimes things haven't come through on his end. He's never let me down before.....well not really."

"OK. Hi everyone! Hi Doug."

"Hello Lee."

Lee asked how his weekend went.

"Every day is my weekend, Lee. I was just telling Jim about that."

"Oh yeah. Do you have any trips coming up?"

"Yeah, I'm going to Hawaii in two weeks. Staying for ten days."

"That's great. How is Jim going to cope with your absence?"

"We were just talking about that. I may go with him. Hey man, how come you're not hitting up spring training?"

"I did that last year. It was fun, but the airfare to Hawaii was real cheap. I can keep tabs on the Mets from Hawaii as well as here."

The bartender gave Lee her usual glass of sauvignon blanc.

"What do you want to do for dinner tonight?"

"Not sure, Doug?"

"Don't look at me. I ate already."

"I saw a new place just opened on Grove Street by Newark Avenue, looked nice. You want to try it out?"

"What's the name?"

"I'm not sure, looks like a bistro, cute."

"I guess that means you're not cooking tonight."

"Yeah, it's kinda nice out, so let's go for a walk."

"OK, sure."

A couple more drinks and the end of happy hour came and went.

"You ready to go?"

"Yeah. See you boys later."

"Later kids." Doug said as he lifted his drink in a pub-style salute.

The walk-up Grove Street was fairly pleasant. Still a little chilly, but spring was definitely on its' way. Leaves were still bare, but you could notice they were starting to bud. It always seemed the same way every year. You notice some buds on the trees and then bam, everything was in full bloom. Every year Jim took note that he would pay closer attention to the change, but every year he forgot. Not that it mattered in the end as the results were always positive.

"Here it is. Marcos' Bistro."

Jim looked at the menu. It all looked pretty much the same as the others, branzino, grilled chicken, pesto penne pasta, and the ubiquitous bistro burger with .... kale chips?

"Kale chips? The fuck? With a burger? You want to go in here why?"

"You don't have to get the burger. You look puzzled."

"I'm thinking if there's anywhere I can report this. I mean, fucking kale chips on a burger? What the actual fuck?"

"Just shut up and let's go in."

"Ok, I guess I can get something else. Oh Jeeze, look at this."

"What?"

"The servers, they're all dressed as lumberjacks. Think anyone of these manbuns know which side of the axe actually chops the tree? Fucking hipsters."

"What is your problem with hipsters?"

"They think that they're independently minded and go against the norm, but they're nothing but a bunch of followers. Look at the uniforms they wear. I've explained this to you before."

"That's the uniform they have to wear to work."

"No, that's they way they dress."

"You think?"

Absolutely.

The place was typically decorated, a mixture of urban and fam kitsch. Jim ordered the grilled chicken and Lee had the branzino.

After dinner they called it a night. Ahh, growing old. 9:30 and it's time to hit the sack. Tomorrow is another day.

Tuesday, fucking Tuesday. As much as Jim had become a fan of Mondays, Tuesdays were the worst. Monday set the tone for the rest of the week and if Monday sucked, then Tuesday was usually worse.

"Think your old boss will call today?"

"I'm hoping, if I don't hear from him by noon I'll reach out."

"OK." As soon as she walked out the door Jim changed he radio station. God damn, how can she listed to fucking the "Classic Rock" station? How many fucking times can you hear "Captain Jack" and "Stairway to Heaven" in one week? He swore they only played the same 50 songs. Anyway, she was gone and it was time to listen to the local sports. Even though he hated the New York teams, Jim liked to listen anyway, especially when the teams sucked. 10:00 a.m. brought on Benigno and Roberts. They were his favorite. *"Ohh, the pain bro!"*

On to the news. Nothing new on the Hudson County corruption scene, so that was good.

The job board posted the same stuff. Cheating spouses, custody cases, and the occasional "someone is trying to kill me." There was one reply noted in his account for a job he bid on over a week ago. The individual thought she was being followed and wanted someone to follow her throughout the course of the day. He put a bid down for $100 per hour and left it at that. If this person was willing to pay then the least he could do was respond.

"Hello, Julia?"

"Is this Mr. O'Neill?"

"Yes. I'm calling in regards to your request and I'd like to know a little more."

She went on to tell him that she was certain that she was being followed and needed proof. She wanted him to follow her from the time she left in the morning until she came home at 7:00. Boring work, but $100 per hour for nine hours was more than doable.

"Ok, so when I get to your location, I'll give you a call and we'll get started. I'll take down plate numbers and find out who they are. New Jersey has recently changed their laws regarded running plates, but I think in this case they will allow it. I'll get them over to you and we can run from there."

"OK, you're gonna do all that for $100?"

"Per hour, yes."

"What do you mean, *per hour*?"

Fuck

"No, that's per hour. You're looking at over eight hours of work, so that will be $800. I'm going to need half up front as well." This was almost certainly not going to happen.

"But you said that it would be $100."

"Per hour."

"Ok. I don't have that kind of money. Could you do it for $100?"

Shit, here we go. "Per hour, yes." He could go lower, but it was no use. She wasn't even going to go as high as $20 per hour. What a waste of 10 minutes.

"But I don't have that kind of money."

"Sorry about that."

"So, you won't do it then?"

"No, sorry. Maybe you could have a friend help you out."

"But I need this done quickly. Could you please do it for me?"

"Look, I'm not a charitable organization. I'm over an hour away and it would end up costing me money to do this. God luck to you though."

What a waste of fucking time. Everybody needed something but nobody wanted to pay. People looked at what he did as a novelty, until they needed something.

Sal didn't call by noon, so Jim made the call.

"Hey Jim, what's doin'?"

"Nothing Sal, just wanted to follow up on your last call. Anything come of that?"

"Yeah, this could be a haymaker. I'm waiting to hear back before I get you in on it. I want you to nail this down."

"So what are we dealing with?"

"It's a company in Jersey. They never ran background checks on their employees before, and I guess some shit went down."

"Great, waddya got?"

Jim got the contact information and said goodbye. Shit, this could be good.

The company manufactured something or other and they have locations all over the country. Apparently, they never ran background checks and one of their workers in Florida was just collared by his probation officer. They never ran checks on these guys or anyone else at the company."

"Ok, great. Well, not great that one of their workers was locked up, but, oh, you know what I mean."

"Yeah, I get it."

Sal gave him the contact info and advised him to call as soon as possible.

Shit, hopefully this could be a big one.

"Hello, Chris, this is Jim O'Neill, from Apollo Due Diligence, I understand that you're in need of some backgrounds. Sal referred me to you."

"Oh, hi Jim. Thanks for calling. What we have is that one of our workers at our Houston plant was arrested for a sex offense. Apparently, this wasn't his first time either. We have a couple hundred employees nationwide and we need to check every one of them. Can you do that?"

Can he do that? Holy shit! "Yeah, I handle things like this all the time. What is your time frame."

"Well, as soon as possible."

"Ok, but here's what we have. The response time for criminal checks varies on the state and county of residence. Some are immediate. Some can take several days. It's a physical check of records, so we're dealing with actual people and not checking a database. It's just not up to me. Anyone that says they can get an instant criminal check is lying to you."

"That's fine. I want to be as thorough as possible."

"Great."

They worked out the final details and Jim sent the contract over. This was a mother-lode case. A "Haymaker" as Sal would call it. Over 200 employees at $95 per person. Almost $20k. Less Expenses he would net about $13k. Not bad.

An hour later he got a couple more checks from another client. He was going from a standstill to over a hundred miles an hour, all in the span of a couple of hours. Such is the business. Some help may be in order.

___

Later that day at the bar he explained to Lee the sudden windfall in work and tried to couple it with an idea that he knew she would not be too keen about.

"So I think I have to hire someone."

"Why"

"I think it would make sense. Pay some kid $15 bucks an hour to handle my skip traces and basic backgrounds. This is a big job coming up and I could use someone. It would also free me up to go pursue other endeavors."

"Let's get your company's bank account in order first. Maybe when you get to over a thousand dollars."

"I'd hire some college kid, a part timer. Someone who can work a couple hours a day with no real set hours. I can always pay the kid in cash on the side. Some lickspittle who will do my bidding. I can mold them in my image. Plus it's nice to have someone I can throw under the bus."

"You going to show him how you to talk to Doug about baseball and the Three Stooges at PJs every other night?"

"Maybe."

She was right in the sense that he didn't want to bring someone on just for the sake of saying he had an employee. He had to get this one right. He worked for people in the past who came up empty in the pay department and he would be the last guy to do that.

"Look, this client needs this done quickly, and there's no way I could do it myself. I could farm it out, but I would lose most of the profit. If I bring in someone, just for a month or so, it would be a good thing."

"Well, if it's just for a month or so. Until this job is done."

"Promise."

They sat in silence for most of the dinner as Jim's thoughts were preoccupied with the hiring process. Bringing someone on to teach the ropes was going to be a gas.

Since he had no real office, he set up some interviews through a client he sometimes did work for. She had a bank of offices for small companies and she let him have a conference room for a couple of hours in exchange for some criminal checks on prospective tenants.

He put an ad on Craigslist under the writing/editing category. 80% of the job would be summarizing and writing up reports so the client can understand.

Three days later he had over 40 resumes, about eight of which were worth a look. Of the 40, 30 were way overqualified and he was sure that they'd be difficult. The other two he was sure were a joke. Of the eight, he thought he had a good chance. Besides, he only had the room for two hours.

Contestant number one was a young woman, well dressed, and seemingly prepared for the interview. He greeted her and they sat down in the room. Upon sitting down, he noticed that she placed her phone right next to her resume. After the basic greetings there was a moment of silence where Jim was preparing the next question, her phone rang. Their eyes met for a moment before she glanced down at the phone.

"Oh, it's my friend. Do you mind if I answer it?"

"By all means, go right ahead."

She answered the phone and gave the one finger, the *wait a sec* motion. Holy shit! Did anyone tell this girl what not to do in an interview? What the flying fuck did she think would come from this?

She hung up the phone and explained that her friend is in the promotions business and needed some velvet rope for an upcoming event.

"Do you know anyone?"

"Um, no."

"Was it wrong that I answered my phone during the interview?"

"You tell me."

"I'm sorry if it did, but my friend needed my help. Besides, I think my resume is strong enough to stand alone."

They spoke for another five minutes before he led her out.

"Good luck with your friend." Jesus Christ. Hopefully someone would tell her that she fucked up. Wasn't going to be him though.

Contestant two was a local kid on the waiting list for the JCPD. He wanted a job where he would be doing something similar.

This was a conundrum. You want to help this kid out, if only for the reason that if you don't and two years down the road he pulls you over, you're fucked. If you do and he gets called into the academy in a month you have to start all over again. Jim told the kid that he would like to help him out, but he was looking for someone long term, someone to maybe take over the business someday. He understood and went on his way.

Applicant number three was a real whopper. He sat in his chair and rocked slowly back and forth. He could tell he was on the verge of losing his shit and he felt for the kid. "Gordon, right?" Jim reached out his hand to greet him and was met with something similar to gripping a fat, wet, warm sponge. And the hair. A beautiful, wiry mess that went perfect with his glasses.

Gordon Peralta was a 22-year-old college student at Hudson County Community College.

"Hey man, how you doing?"

"Ok Sir."

"Hold on, I'll be right back." Jim went and got a cup of water to bring back to the kid.

"Here, drink this. Take five minutes and collect yourself. Take some deep breaths. I'll be back and we'll do the interview."

"Ok, thanks."

Jim left him in the room to recover.

Damn, this kid was a mess. He was most assuredly unpopular, and it looked like he hadn't exercised since he was in third grade. He had zero self-confidence and most assuredly still a virgin. On the plus side he was willing to bet the farm that this kid was good with computers.

Jim could taste his sense of desperation, which was good because he wouldn't be able to pay him much. Plus, he had the best quality in an assistant should they ever go out in the field. He could outrun this kid should shit hit the fan.

"So tell me, what are you looking for."

"I want to find a job."

"OK, that's a given. Looks like you don't have much work history."

"No sir."

"You live in the Heights. You have roommates, parents, or live by yourself?"

"I live with my Mom and younger sister."

"OK, here's what I'm looking for. I need someone to work about 15-20 hours a week when needed. Most of the work is home based, but in the beginning we can meet up here so I can show you the ropes. There may be times where I ask you to go to the local court to dig up some records. It says here you're currently in school?"

"Yes. I'm going to Hudson County Community College for business."

"That's cool. I can work around your schedule." "You think that's something you would like to do?"

"I think so, I guess."

"Love your spirit! This company is a private detective agency, but that's not who we are. We do records searches, phone interviews, locate people, and background checks. We don't do surveillance, no insurance fraud stuff, or follow around cheating spouses. The most field work we do is maybe every year or so knock on a door and serve some papers. But one never knows what's going to happen. For the right money, I'll take on anything as long it's legal. What I won't do is compromise myself or others. My company exists solely to get to the bottom of things, and that's mostly public records and such. You OK with that?"

"I guess."

"Are you OK with computers?"

"Pretty good, I guess. I know Word, Excel, Powerpoint, and photoshop."

"OK. So what are you looking for in life Gordon?"

"Well, I would like to get my degree at some point, but I also need the work."

"OK, Gordon, I just have one more thing for you to do. Here's a pen and paper. I want you to describe your commute here and describe what the secretary who walked you into this room. I'll be back in ten."

"OK."

This was a good exercise. It gave you a bit of insight into his writing skills and memory.

It was also a spot check, to see how they did on a moment's notice. He's worked with people before who had great pedigrees from good schools only to find that they had no idea how to construct a sentence. Some of these kids were screwed out of a basic education along the way. Some were just not very bright. At one point they just gave up. But there were other kids, college graduates, who obviously had someone else write all their papers. Just too fucking lazy to do it themselves. That was more infuriating.

Jim let him be for about ten minutes before returning.

"Let's see what you have here."

"This morning I took the Kennedy Avenue bus to the Path train station in Journal Square. I got on the Path for one stop and got off at Grove Street. I walked across the street and got on the elevator to the 5th floor to get here. I was greeted by a young woman wearing a red top and a black skirt. She showed me into the room where I sat down and I waited for the interview."

Perfect.

Jim looked out the door and noted what the secretary was wearing.

"Hmmm. Not quite."

"What?"

"You described the secretary as wearing a red top. It's clearly burgundy. I'm sorry."

"What?"

"Kidding. The pay is $15 per hour, plus any expenses that you have. If we work together, I pay all the expenses. I do want to tell you that you absolutely do not want to do this as a career. Long term, this job is not for you and I'm not kidding. You only want to be here about a year, maybe two tops. What it will provide you is some analytical and research skills that may come in handy in the future. A bright side to the job is that you can tell chicks that you're a private eye. They dig that. Is this something you may be willing to do?"

"I guess so."

"OK, great. I have a couple more people on the list, but I have a feeling I'll be reaching out."

"OK, sir."

"None of that sir, shit. At least not when we're alone."

"OK."

"Alright, take it easy then."

"OK, thanks."

This kid was perfect for the job. Everything about him was unremarkable. He could come and go into just about any place and be immediately forgotten two minutes later. That was the problem with overly good-looking people. You hired a pretty girl to go somewhere and scout a place, they will be immediately remembered. This one was such a non-descript dud that he could come and go with minimal notice. *Kid Cellophane.*

After Gordon he interviewed a couple others to round things off. Two of them were older than he was and from the looks of things, they could have used the work more than the kid. It was more depressing than anything. Things took a wrong turn somewhere in their lives. Not that it was any of his business.

With that part of the day done it was time to retire to PJs, have a few, and wait for the Mrs.

"Hey hon, how did it go today?"

"Not bad, I think I found a kid."

"OK, good." She gave a quick peck on the cheek.

"You're gonna have to get a load of this kid. A complete zero. The worst."

"And you hired him?"

"Not yet, but he was clearly the best one I interviewed. Not that the bar was set high. Had some real winners come through."

"Why him?"

"I just told you, but I'll elaborate over dinner."

"OK. Glass of sauvignon blanc."

"So how was your day?" It was more of a courtesy him asking her that question. Every time she started telling him about what she did during her day his brain went into immediate shutdown. She worked as a business manager and handled such things as coding and developing flow charts for bank projects. As soon as she started talking his brain shut down. Nothing but old Bugs Bunny cartoons on playback. Sometimes he got through a whole episode before she stopped talking. Not to mock her work. She did a good job, was well-paid, and her work was the only reason he was even in business, but just talking about the daily minutia of her work his brain fell out.

"Another glass of cabernet Jim?"

"Sure."

"Let's have one more and grab a bite. Where do you want to go?"

"Want to try out the new joint?"

"I don't know. Latham work?"

"Sure. Their scallops are great."

"Perfect. Let's go say hi to Dan and Kris."

Dinner was mostly eaten in silence, aside from Jim cementing his opinion that this kid was the right way to go. On the way home he was going to reach out, but it was after nine. Better let it to sit overnight.

The next morning Jim called him to let him know the news first thing.

"Hey, this Gordon?"

"Yes. Mr. O'Neill?"

"Yes. How you doing?"

'Fine."

"So I wanted to let you know that the job is yours if you want it. Like I said, the hours are flexible, maybe about 15-20 a week. Pay is $15 an hour and any expenses that you may incur along the way. So what do you say?"

"I think I can do that, but my Mom has a few questions. Hold on for a sec."

"Hello Mr. O'Neill, this is Rose Peralta, Gordon's Mom."

"Hello Mrs. Peralta. How are you?"

"I wanted to ask you some questions about what he'll be doing for your agency."

Jim could see where this was going. Here was a person who got all the information they know about private investigators from TV.

"Mrs. Peralta, I'd like to hire your son to do some part time research for me. I do background checks, locate reports, and skip tracing. The work he'll be doing is from his computer. I may ask him to go to city hall to check some records, but nothing more."

"That's it?"

"Pretty much."

"OK. So no surveillance or anything like that? No cheating husbands or insurance cases? Do you do anything like that?"

"Not really, but there may be some instances. I don't really do surveillance or anything like that. There may be some witness interviews, but for now I just want him to get to know the research. He doesn't even have to leave home."

"Ok. I just worry about my son."

He liked this woman immediately. "Mrs. Peralta, I want to hire your son because I saw something in him (nothing) that I didn't see in any of the other people I interviewed. He seems to be smart and responsible enough to handle what I have in mind for him. As he learns I'll give him some more responsibilities as they come. But I do want to make one thing clear. This is only a temporary thing for him before he gets a better job. This will be good experience for him, but I certainly don't want him to make a career out of this."

"Really?"

"You have to believe me on this one. I am the poster child of why you shouldn't make a career of this. That doesn't mean to say he won't be picking up some valuable skills that will help him down the road."

"OK. I'll have to take your word for it. As far as I'm concerned, I think it would be a good experience for him, but I worry."

"I understand completely."

"Hold on, here he is."

"Hi."

"So, you in?"

"Sure. When do you want me to start?"

"Give me a couple days to get things set up. I also need for you to get fingerprinted to make sure you're not a wanted man or a sex pervert or anything."

'I'm not."

"Great. I'll reach out to you tomorrow and I'll give you a start date."

"Great. Thanks. Looking forward to the call."

He had Gordon come over to his house two days later to get him up and running. The fingerprint appointment was set up and he could get to work while it was being processed. Finally, an employee! Jim tidied up the house. No awards or such to place in order to impress the kid, just a copy of his PI license on the wall. He needed more shit.

4:00 right on the dot Gordon rang the bell. Jim saw him in, got him a chair, and they got started.

"OK Gordon, here's the deal. First off, what do you want to be called?"

"Gordon is fine."

"Gordy"

"No."

"Gordman?"

"No."

He could tell not even to suggest Gordo. He could bet that he was probably called that his entire life. No need to dig that up. Nicknames were stupid anyway.

"OK Gordon. This is what I want you to get to know. This system is known as WestSearch. To get on this system you have to be a licensed private investigator. This has a bunch of information that the general public doesn't have access to. You can get names, addresses, dates of birth, relatives, assets, phone numbers, judgments, liens, and criminal records. Each search costs a bit different, so we start at the bare minimum and work our way up. We'll start with skip traces. Skip tracing is a fancy term for finding deadbeats and people who don't want to be found. It's usually people who owe money, people who skipped out on rent or major bills, hence the skip."

"OK, cool"

"The only thing I have to tell you right off the bat is that you're going to be dealing with some sensitive information. Please don't log on and start dicking around looking for old girlfriends or childhood buddies."

"No problem there."

"OK, good. If you really want to look up someone on the fly, the just ask me. Sometimes I get audited on these searches and I could lose my license." That was bullshit, but it would work in the meantime.

"I also use it to track down witnesses. Usually when we get one of these jobs, we get their name and last known address. So I'm just gonna give you one I got today. This is from my client down in Freehold. A law firm that pays on time, which is nice."

"Gotcha."

"So after we log on we get to plug in the information, see?"

"Ok"

"Here you go. Henry DeMasco. Last known address, Keansburg, NJ. Approximately 63 years old. This is good for us."

"Why?"

"Well, think about it. If this guy was Bill Jones, we'd have a problem. There are probably about 40 Bill Jones in Freehold alone. I want to show you, but each search costs cash. The odder the name, the better it is for us."

"So here we go, I have a new address on this guy. Looks like he moved to Asbury Park back in July."

"How do you get these addresses?"

"Good question. They nail down these people through credit headings. If there's anything in this person's name, like utility bills, credit cards, cable, voting records, etcetera, then it goes to this system. 99 per cent of the people have something in their names. There is the one per cent that don't want to be found though. These people are off the grid. Nothing in their names, burner phones, zip."

"How do you find these people?"

"Not easy, but it can be done. Usually I just go to their last address and check them for relatives. Relatives can be of help, but it depends on the reason you're looking for them. If it's because they owe money, then I don't bother. No reason to bring their family into their fuckups. There are plenty of companies that have no compunction whatsoever in going through their family for these guys fuckups. I don't play that way. It's not their fault. There are a lot of placed that don't give a shit about stepping over that line, some places that I worked for, but I told myself that I would never do that if I opened up my own shop. So now that I'm calling the shots I won't do it. I may have lost a few bucks, but at least I get to sleep at night. I'll let the other guys handle that stuff. If I can't find the person directly, then I stop there. And the one main thing I don't do is misrepresent myself, unless absolutely necessary."

"Waddya mean?"

"There may come a time that you have to use a fake name, but it's a rare occasion. You'll probably never have the opportunity. In the past I had to use a fake name in order to tape one of those self-help conferences for a copyright infringement case.. I used my alternate name, Larry Talbot, *The Wolfman*. Now that I told you I have to get you to pledge your secrecy on that one."

"OK." He had no idea what he was talking about.

"Ok."

"So what I've got for you is a couple of locates. I want to do a few with you before I let you go on your own."

"Cool. Say, what do you do about stalkers and creeps and such?"

"I get a lot of those. It started as some friends who wanted to get back in touch with old girlfriends and such, nothing more. I did those for free because I know they'll never reach out. When I give them the

information they take it home and stare at it.
Inevitably they decide against it. Never had one tell
me they reached out. What I think is that they realize
that they had nothing to say to them after all these
years. I just try it to let them know that I can pretty
much find anyone, anywhere.....within reason."

"Within reason?"

"Yeah. If they skipped town I can find them more
often than not. If they skipped the country it would
make it a bit harder."

"Ever not be able to find anyone?"

"Sure, but it's rare. When I get a case where
someone I don't know wants to find someone and I'm
not certain about their intentions I inform them that my
policy is to let the person know first that they are
looking for them. If they're ok with it I go through with
it, but more often than not they never follow-up."

"Oh, that sounds reasonable."

"Yeah, some companies don't give a shit, and there
were some instances where people have been killed,
so I don't like to go there. Not worth it."

Jim sat with Gordon for the next hour going over the
ropes. Before he left Jim gave him the pricing sheets
to show what each search cost.

"OK, beat it. You good to get home?"

"It's 7:00. I think I can take care of this."

"I just don't want to get on your Mom's bad side. Take it easy kid. I got you down for three hours, right?"

"Right."

"So what is that, like $30."

"$45"

"Oh, right, OK." Fuck, this kid remembered. Wait, was it 7:00? Why the hell wasn't his wife breathing down his neck? He called.

"Guess where I am?" He heard enough in the background to know.

"Why didn't you reach out?"

"I knew that you were with your new guy, so I figured I would leave you alone."

This was a first. "Oh, OK. I'll see you in a few."

It was after 7:00. . Oh, well. Anyway, it was a good day overall.

As promised, the background checks started to roll in. Jim set up a cloud account for Gordon to use. It took a few weeks to get the kid up to snuff, but he took to it well. He got good at the research and making them look pretty. All's Jim had to do was go over it one more time, send them out, and submit the invoice.

This is what he envisioned when he opened up Apollo Due Diligence. He knew better than to hang his hat on it though. Things could turn to shit tomorrow. Conversely, they could get ten times better tomorrow too. The only surety is that you never know.

Once a week they would get together and Jim would take him out for a burger while they went over some cases.

On one particular April evening he asked Gordon about maybe upping his game now that school was finishing up.

"What are your plans for the summer, kid?"

"I don't know. We're supposed to go to my Grandmother's summer place at the shore some time."

"That's cool. You don't sound too excited about it though."

"I don't really like the beach."

Jim noted his physique and knew. This kid was a bowl of jelly, fuck, he probably wore his t-shirt in the water. Jim understood that one. He was a short fat bastard when he was a kid too. But puberty took care of that when he grew 10 inches in a year and a half. After that he noticed that girls looked at him a bit differently, in a good way, which was nice.

The puberty train did not come to a full stop at this kids station. Maybe it slowed down enough to throw some eggs, but that would have been it. The cheeseburgers and milkshakes along with a mostly sedentary lifestyle didn't help either. Shame too. This kid had something in him. He could really use a self-confidence boost. Wasn't his job though.

"Yeah, it can be a drag sometimes I guess. I love it though. Some of my best memories are from my days living at the shore. Good times, good friends, beautiful women, late nights and bad decisions. Where does your grandmother live?"

"Near Asbury Park. It's ok I guess. My sister likes it more than me."

"What about the chicks? Nice, huh?"

"Yeah, I guess." Jim noticed him shift in his seat. He was obviously uneasy about the line of questioning.

"You're a good kid, you do your work, and I'm glad I hired you. But every time I bring up the topic of women you clam up."

"It's cool. I guess I never thought about it because, well, I don't have to spell it out, do I?"

Kid had a point. This kid broke out into a sweat eating French fries.

"Ah, that's horseshit. What does your Dad say about it?"

"I don't know, I haven't seen him in about ten years."

Shit.

"That sucks. I'm sorry man, no really. No kid should have to go through that. Is he dead?"

"He may as well be. He walked out on us when I was eleven. My Grandmother and my uncle helped out with us after that. She says we we're better off without him."

"You know where he is?"

"Not really. Pennsylvania, I think."

"You want me to help find him? I mean, that's what I do."

"I know. I don't think so."

"Look, I'm not going to pressure you into this, but just give the word. Time heals a lot of this stuff. Also, you are an adult now, so you don't have to consult with anyone. At the end of the day it's none of my business, so I'll just leave it at that."

"OK"

Jim picked up the bill and set the kid on his way until next week. Even though it was none of his business he dwelled on this kid's father and how a man could walk out on his family. Fuck it, none of his business.

If the kid wanted to talk about it he would let him, but don't bring it up unsolicited.

Next weeks' meeting went off without a hitch. No talk about family or anything else much for that matter. As Jim looked at the check he leaned into the table.

"Hey, I have a new assignment for you."

"What?"

"I want you to take a couple hours in the next week, I'll pay you, to look up anyone that could use our services. I'll leave the rest up to you."

"I bet. Listen, when you get the chance and you're dicking around on the net, see what you can find and we'll talk about it next week."

"Sure thing. Later."

"Later Gordon."

Jim hoped that by giving him a little assignment it would get his head in a different place.

Next week went by without a hitch. It was the middle of May and the Phillies were already 10 games under 500. At least this year they had the courtesy and not get his hopes up for the summer.

Jim went to meet up at the diner across the street as usual, only today was a real perk because *she* was working. By she Jim meant that the usual daytime hostess, damn, he didn't even know her name. Jim just referred to her as "*Kitten.*" She was in her early 20s with an exaggerated body found mostly in superhero comics and teenage boys doodles. Her smoky-eyes and a fondness for tight sweaters and yoga pants were gravy. She was always friendly and usually had a slight grin on her face that acknowledged that she knew what she had. She knew.

Not that Jim would ever act upon it. To her he was just another old man leering at her ample assets. Even Jim's wife acknowledged she oozed more than once, which prompted Jim to go into fantasy mode, with was immediately quashed by the Mrs.

"You know that even on your best day when you were single, you would never stand a chance with that one."

"You really know how to hurt a guy."

"I do, don't I?"

Kitten sat Jim and he asked her if she would be kind enough to look for a short, chubby kid with freaky hair and glasses before handing her a fiver.

"Thanks and yeah, I've seen you two together here before. What are you, his Uncle or something?"

"No, he works for me. Mainly computer stuff, but once a week we meet here to discuss business."

"What do you do?"

"We're Private Investigators, but not the kind of stuff you think."

"Really? I think I'd be good at that."

"I'm sure you would."

"Why don't you hire me? I bet I'd be good at it"

He would hire her at $50 per hour just to read his mail. His mind wandered for a moment, thinking about having her for a girl Friday, but they quickly evaporated when reality reared its ugly head. Oh, and he was married.

"I wish I could, but I'm kind of fully staffed right now."

"OK, let me know though."

"Will do. Say when this kid comes in could you send him back?"

"Ok."

Minutes later Jim saw that kids head through the door. Afro, giant glasses, and pasty face. This kid had to be the whitest Puerto Rican kid he ever saw. Looked like he was walking up to give his Bar Mitzvah recital.

The hostess made good on her promise and walked him back. They seemed to have a brief exchange on the way back.

"Found him." She looked at Gordon and asked "Are you guys really PIs?"

"Yeah. This is Gordon, or as I like to call him, *The Bloodhound.* Fucking kid is relentless when it comes to tracking people down. You ever see "Dog the Bounty Hunter?"

"Yeah! I love that show."

Of course she did.

"Well, it's all bullshit. This kid is the real deal. Nothing gets by him. Amirite Bloodhound?"

"Um, yeah, I guess," he said while looking straight down at his placemat, cheeks flushed.

"This kid, he's so humble. Humble, and relentless. He may not look it, but he is extremely talented when it comes to these matters."

"Ok, whatever. See ya." And the waitress was on her way.

"What was that all about?"

"Nothing. You see the cans on that one?"

"Um, yeah, she's pretty, I guess."

"You guess? Christ. When I was your age..." *shit, don't even go there Jim.* "Sorry. So what do you have. Did you do your homework?"

"Yep. Look at this." He showed Jim his phone

"It's this organization that was looking for private eyes to help find missing people."

"Interesting. Tell me more."

"Let me show you." Gordon showed him the link to "Helpfindourmissing.org"

"OK, let's take a look."

Jim looked at the site and took note that all of the people listed as "Missing" looked to be fully functioning adults.

"You know what the problem with this is?"

"What?"

"These people aren't missing. One is not missing if they know exactly where they are."

"On the top, it just doesn't sound right. I hate to sound cynical, but more often than not these things are a scam. They inhale the donations stemming from people with good intentions who think it's a worthy cause, then they make a shitty website to show the world what good they're doing for the world. Let's take a look. OK, let's check out the missing. You can barely read these things. Oh wait, here's one. Jacob Williams, missing since November 2016. Last seen at an ATM Machine in Oswego, NY. Look at this. It says that he's an avid outdoorsman and has been known to live in the woods for periods of time. Where do you think he is?

"The woods?"

"You're good. You think this guy wants to be found?"

"Probably not."

"No. He probably just said fuck it to the world and split. If only... .."

"It says here that his wife misses him and wants him home."

"She's probably the reason why he's in the woods. Poor fucker... unless."

"Unless what?"

"Unless they're all in on it. Hmm.." Jim thought about it for a second but decided to drop the notion all together.

"Look, here's another one. Cindy Jacobus, age 19, a runaway. Not much you can do about that one. While they identify her as a runaway, she's not. She's fucking 19, an adult in the eyes of the law. Old enough to make her own decisions. I know it bites, but I bet most of these people left for a reason. As far as children are concerned, there's a thing called the FBI and police. We wouldn't be able to do anything anyway. We can only find people who have some kind of footprint. These people probably left a shitty home life and just up and got the hell out. Hopefully she found a safe environment that encourages her to grow, but most likely not. Some are probably fucked up in the first place and that sucks, but it's none of my concern. The people running this organization would ask for us to work for free just to show on the books that they actually tried to do something. Get a write off and ask for donations. My guess is that there would be some kind of church or religious nuts behind all this.

I like the fact that you're trying. On the surface it looked promising and you did nothing wrong, but this ain't happening. Anything else?"

"I found this on a job board this morning. This could be good for us" Gordon showed him the message, which was a request to find out who a potential suitor was all about. She added that her potential mate was currently working on an oil rig in Alaska.

"Oh, Jeez. I wonder how much money this woman gave to this guy." He read through a bit further and decided that this would be good practice.

"You know what, let's reach out to this one and see what she has to say. Probably won't take it, but it can't hurt to look into it."

He logged into the site and bid $150 for the job, which he was sure would be the lowest bid.

"Why did you bid so low? You're not going to make any money."

"Yeah, I know. This one is going to be For Duty and Humanity."

"What's that?"

It's a Three Stooges reference. My old boss coined it for a case where you're not going to make any money, but it's for a greater good. Kinda stuck in my head. Help a fellow human being out if you're in the position to do so.

This woman has probably lost some serious cash. I bet she's desperately lonely and was willing to believe anything. Some predator spotted her in some dating forum and took her down. Most of the time these people are too ashamed they were duped, lick their wounds, and go back to their lives. At least this one is asking for some help. This is good practice." He left the bid with his contact information and picked up the menu.

Ten minutes later he got a call.

"Hi, this is Anne Cabrera. I'm the one who wants you to check out someone for me."

"Okay, tell me a bit about why you want this person located." You always had to check that they were trying to track down a person for legitimate reasons.

"I feel so stupid, it's kind of embarrassing." Fuck. Of all the things he's heard, *I feel so stupid* was probably the worst. How much money did she send this guy?

"I met this man on Facebook, and we started an online relationship, and well, one thing lead to another and...." Jim cut her off before she could say another word. "How much money did you give him?"

"Oh, I didn't give it to him, it was a loan. He promised me he would return it as soon as he got back from the oil rig he's working on in Alaska. It was for $10,000. He said he was going to give me back $20,000. He sent me flowers! He said he loved me!"

Shit, he thought for a second that he was in the wrong line of business. What made these women such easy

targets for these scumbags? He guessed it was the loneliness thing. Lack of companionship will make a person do stupid things, like get send money to a complete stranger, or worse, get married.
Unfortunately there were predators out there more than willing to separate them from their money.

He was glad that he didn't quote a larger fee as he immediately knew that there was virtually no chance that he would track this guy down. In the ensuing of conversation he would discover that this woman had never met him in person. This was a case of some dirtbag sitting at a terminal in Lagos or Volgograd sending out a wide net of proposals to people. Most would immediately smell a rat, some may show a little interest until they came to their senses, and some just would fall for it, like this one. She seemed like an erstwhile intelligent woman. Good job, well spoken, a little unfortunate looking, but nothing horrific. He listened to the rest of the story and told her that while it was a long shot, he would take the case.

She asked why he asked for such a low fee.

"Anne, there is a very slim chance that this guy exists. And even if he does I can all but guarantee you that you will never see a nickel of that money again."

The small fee was for what he could offer, an address trace, reverse phone number check, and a name search. Maybe he would send a letter to see if he could flush anyone out. Little to no profit, but most of the service was for his time, which was something that he could spare at the moment. It would also be good practice for the kid. This woman was just run over the coals and she didn't need another predator reaching into her purse. The low price allowed him to walk away when they started to get too demanding, which they almost always did.

She gave Jim the guy's name James Parker (fake), phone number (fake), some pictures (fake), a copy of his oil rig contract (fake), and addresses in Long Island and Texas. The Texas address was where she wired a good portion of the money.

It was the addresses that provided a glimmer of hope. He would start there. The address in Texas even had a name attached to it. It was rare to get a physical address. Most of the time it was PO Boxes.

"Well Eudora, I see a good jumping-off point."

"I want to find this guy.."

"First off, I don't think that this guy is even in the United States, but I am intrigued by the addresses. Let me get to work on it and I'll get back to you with the initial results."

When he ran the address in Long Island he found the number of the current owners. Jim left a message on their voicemail and left it at that. The next day he got a response.

"Is this James O'Neill?"

"Yeah, what can I do for you?"

"I'm Mr. Clarkson, you left me a message at my house yesterday."

"Oh yeah, thanks for getting back. I'm a private investigator and was recently hired to check something that involved your address. My client….."

"Did your client get scammed out of money by a guy names James Parker?"

"Yeah." He was glad that he didn't have to offer up the information.

"Yeah, we get a lot of stuff sent here under his name. We have no idea who this guy is. You should see some of the stuff they send this guy. Nice shit, too. I've started keeping some of it. Most of it is love letters, but some woman have sent flowers, candies, and scented candles and shit."

"I can imagine. So you have no idea who this guy is, do you?"

"Man, I've never heard of this guy."

Jim believed him. He offered too much information. He even got back in touch. If need be, he would offer Helen the option of putting a surveillance guy on the property for a day or two, but this was when the cost of the case would skyrocket. Put a guy on the property for a couple days, running license plates, and doing additional research would be at least a couple grand. Even then he could practically guarantee that no positive results would come to surface.

"Okay, thanks."

"Could you do me a favor?"

"Sure, what's up?"

"If you could give me a call when you wrap things up to let me know what happened I would appreciate it"

"Sure, no problem."

"Thanks and good luck."

The address in Plano Texas proved to be a more promising lead. He ran the name at the address and was surprised to find an actual human being attached to it, with a Social Security Number and date of birth.

He ran her SSN and found that she was born in California and had an extensive address history. A phone number check on her found one number that was out of service.

Fuck it, he thought. The thing to do in this case was to send the letter. He wrote up one on his stationary, where he informed that his company was hired to contact her regarding a fraudulent transaction. He advised her to contact his office before the proper authorities were contacted. Jim knew how to write threatening letters as he was the recipient of numerous of them from various agencies.

The letter was sent. Other than that, there was nothing much else he could do.

He updated Anne and advised her to contact him should she hear from this guy.

"He called me yesterday. He asked for another $10,000."

"Tell me you didn't send it."

"Not yet, but I think I'm going to."

Dear God. "Please, do not send him the money."

"But he said that he needed it to free up the $10,000 that he owes me. He said that he felt real bad that he had to ask me, but he was in a tough position."

"Anne, listen to me. For the love of God, do not send him any more money."

"You think? I wanted to ask you before I did."

"This guy will try to take all your money. The fact that you've never met him in person should raise a few flags to begin with. Right?"

"But he's on an oil rig."

"Anne, this guy is not on an oil rig. I think you know that by now. You're being played. Please, just sit tight and wait it out until I get a response."

"Okay, if you say so."

Christ, the thought of going over to the dark side was looking better and better.

A week later he got a text message from a guy stating the he was the Texas woman's husband.

*Hello James O'Neill, how are you doing today? I am
so sorry to you for the late response, I will try to write
you a kindly email tomorrow on behalf of my wife.*

Who is this?

You will know when I mail you, good night from UK.

He left it at that and decided to wait for the email,
which never came. A couple days later he got
another text stating the he was the husband of the
Texas woman and that they had no idea who James
Parker was. When asked why the was money
directed into his wife's account, he stated that he has
written to the bank for a statement regarding the
transaction.

He heard nothing again from them after that.

While there was definitely something there, with
physical addresses and names, it went way beyond
the $150 fee. Now it was her turn to do some work.

Jim contacted Anne and gave her the information,
adding that there was enough to warrant further
investigation, but she would have to contact the
proper authorities.

"Oh, I don't want to get him in trouble, I just want my
money back. I thought that you would do all this for
me."

"It doesn't work this way. I've exhausted all my
means in this one. What you need to do is to contact
the authorities in Collin County Texas and Suffolk
County New York and present them with the

information I gave you. I feel that you have enough for them to at least take a look. If they have any questions I'll be glad to answer them."

"Will he get in any trouble?"

Sheesh. He really wanted to feel bad for this one, but it was getting harder by the minute. "Anne, this man is not who you think he was. He does not work on an oil rig. The certificate he gave you is fake. Everything he said to you is a lie. You're a nice woman and I feel for you, but you've been scammed, plain and simple. He will never be coming through the door to sweep you off your feet, ever. He will take every last dime from you and move on to the next person. The fact that I may have found some possible accomplices is important because if the authorities can prove that they're a part of a larger criminal organization, then it just might help prevent the next person from losing their hard earned money to these garbage people.

"Why can't you do this? I don't want to look like that bad guy here."

For the love of God. "I can't do this because I wasn't the victim. You are. This is entirely up to you. I've taken this as far as I can. I can't tell you what to do, but I strongly suggest you take my advice."

"Well, can't you take a look out by the place in Long Island? Maybe see if he's there? I sent you his picture, remember?"

"Anne, my work is done here. You paid me $150 for what I did. You have to know that this person does not exist. The sooner you realize that the better.

There are some truly horrible people on this planet who love nothing better than to take advantage of people's giving nature. They are predators, and when they are done picking the carcass of their last victim they go on to the next one. This is what they do."

"But, he said he was going to call. He said he loved me."

"I'm going to hang up now Anne. I sincerely hope you do the right thing. I think that you know that I'm right."

"He sent me flowers."

"Anne, do you have children?"

"Yes, I have a son. He's 33 and he's going to be married soon."

"Have you talked about this with him?"

"No."

"I strongly suggest that you should. I'm gonna have to say goodbye now. If you want to have your son call me I'd be happy to talk with him. Goodbye Anne, and good luck. I really hope things work out for you. If you want to have your son call me feel free to give him my number and we can talk it over."

Jesus. That was pathetic. What a pigeon. And these fuckheads know exactly how to target these mopes.

Jim hoped that his son would reach out, maybe stage an intervention. At least the son would have a more vested interest, seeing that it could be his inheritance she pissed away into the hands of these garbage people.

May turned to June and things were going as well as they could be. The background checks were coming in consistently and Gordon was doing about 20 hours a week when he could.

It was early afternoon on what was another fine summer day when Jim was out on his front veranda sipping an iced tea and counting the traffic infractions at the corner of Jersey and Grand Street. He was up to five when he got a call from a 415-area code. He left it go to voicemail rather than hear another robocall.

It turned out to be a law firm out in San Francisco. They were handling a divorce case there and learned one of the petitioners was previously divorced in Hudson County. They wanted any records they could get. They settled on a price, $75 per hour, four hour minimum, plus expenses. A quick $300 for what would seem to be an easy job….*Seem.*

Any time you have to deal with court clerks, *any time,* it was always a crapshoot. Better bring in the kid and baptize him in this side of the business. The kid was on summer break and he would most likely be available. What else did this kid have to do?

He called him and he picked it up on the first ring.

"Hey dude, what's the word?"

"Nothing, what's up?"

"You free tomorrow morning?"

"Yeah, I think so. I've got some stuff to do with my sister later in the afternoon, but I can make it.

"Meet me at the coffee shop across from the Hudson County Courthouse tomorrow at 9:30."

"OK, what are we gonna do?"

"Tomorrow is going to be a special day for you. Tomorrow you become a man....metaphorically speaking. Some court records to research. Fun stuff!"

"I know where the coffee shop it, in fact......"

Jim cut him short "9:30 then?"

"OK. See you then."

Poor kid. Jim knew that this kid had no idea what was in store, for he was going to meet with the brick wall that was the Hudson County Court Clerk's Office. Many a man greater than Jim were brought to their knees by the stifling bureaucracy that is the court clerk. It would be a great learning experience for the kid, and the hope was that he may be able to put that part of the job off on the him, which would be nice.

Tuesday at 9:30 came and Gordon showed up as expected. It was just so nice to have a kid actually show up on time. He knew he sounded like an old shit, but damn, having someone show up on time was worth its weight in gold.

"Hey Gordon, over here."

"Hi Mr. O'Neill, er, I mean Jim. What's going on?"

"Nothing, just have to go into the clerk's office to look up some court cases is all."

Jim handed him a $10 and told him to get whatever he wanted. He came back with a cruller and a chocolate milk and handed Jim the change.

"No coffee for you, huh?"

"No. I tried it a couple of times, but I don't like it all that much."

"That will probably change down the road, but anyway, here's the deal. I have a client that needs to find judgments and records from a divorce proceeding back in 1993."

"How long can this take."

"Days, maybe weeks, who knows. The court clerk is the only thing that stands between us and the information we need.

There is a quest before us, Gordon, and this task is wrought with peril, for the Court Clerk must not be underestimated. Should you find it in your heart that you are up to the quest, then finish your cruller and we'll head in. You're going to need your strength."

"I think I might be able to....."

"You can't help here, Gordon. I'm gonna show you how cruel an unforgiving this world can be. You'll see, finish your cruller."

After going through the metal detectors they headed for the elevator.

"Gordon, I don't care what stories you've heard, but on the third floor lies the clerk's office. You ever meet a court clerk?"

"Well I...."

"See, we're here at ten. It's the time of the day they kind of decide that they might actually do some work. From nine to ten they talk about what tv show they saw the night before. At 11 they start talking about what they're going to have for lunch, so they shut down. After lunch they get back to their desks around one. From one to two they talk about what they had for lunch. At about 3:30 they talk about what where they're going after work, so things are done for the day.

[In his best Quint voice] '*You ever see a court clerk up close Mr. Peralta? Remorseless creatures they are. Y'know the thing about a clerk, she's got... lifeless eyes, black eyes, like a doll's eyes.*' They are civil servants, Gordon. They don't care and they can't be fired."

"Why were you talking like that?"

"It's from 'Jaws.' Quint's speech on the Orca before the shark attacked. You've seen it.....right? Tell me you've seen it."

"Yeah, that old movie. I remember that my dad liked it."

"Good stuff, huh?"

"I guess."

They walked out of the elevator and into the clerks' office.

"OK, here we go. Let me handle this."

"Good morning!"

Clerk doesn't even look up. "Yes?"

"I need any information on a couple of civil cases."

Without looking up she slid the papers under the window. "You have to fill out these request forms. When you're done come back to the window."

He took the paperwork and filled it out.

"See, when you get a request from a client, always try to get the case number. If they don't have it then we have to look it up. If they don't have the case number they're going to have to look it up by the name, which can take some time. Always try to fill in every detail."

Jim filled it and handed it back.

Without looking up "This will take some time. Come back later today or tomorrow, if we have it."

"Well, can we check to see if you have it first before I come back? Maybe I can get a number to call?"

"No honey. You're gonna have to come back."

"I did this before and was given a number."

"I don't know who did that, but they were wrong. We don't do that here, honey."

"But I was just in here a couple of months ago and they gave me a number."

"No they didn't."

"Are you....." This is where they got you. It didn't matter what actually happened the last time, the clerk's version was always the right one. Just accept defeat. It was better that way.

"OK, I get it. I'll come back later."

"Mr. O'Neill, this case looks to be a divorce case. We do not release information on divorce cases."

"But this is a final judgment, it has nothing to do with any aspect of the case that may be sealed. I received this information from here last time...."

"I don't think you did."

"But..." Damn. He knew he was right, but what the fuck did that matter.

"Mr. O'Neill, you have people waiting behind you, please come back..." She looked up and dropped her glasses and looked straight at Gordon.

"Aren't you Gordon, Agnes' grandchild?"

"Yes ma'am."

"Well I'll be! I remember you from when you was just a child. You've grown. I'll never forget that beautiful head of hair!"

"OK, then, I guess we'll be on our way. There is a line after all."

"Gordon, are you with this man?"

"Yes ma'am. He's my boss."

"Well why didn't you say so? You come back in the office and I'll see what I can do."

"What about the line of people?"

She met Jim with a glance and summoned another clerk. "Judy, can you take the window for a bit? Thanks"

Judy looked a touch annoyed as she was most likely talking about her upcoming lunch.

A side door was opened and they were ushered into the back office. For the first time in his professional life Jim had made it past the impenetrable barrier of the clerk's office.

"Tell me son, how are you? How's your Mom and your sister?"

"They're good, I guess."

"Look at you, a fine young man. Lord! I used to work with your Grandmother here in the court building. We both started out here as clerks. She always had her sights set on something bigger, but I was perfectly happy here."

"Thank you."

"Now, let me see what you need." She looked entered the case numbers into the computer and asked what we needed.

"Anything that's available."

"OK, I'll be right back."

A couple minutes go by and she comes back with a file full of copies.

"Do you think I can make copies of this?"

"Oh, no dear. These are the copies! Here you go. I think this should be everything." She handed the file over to Gordon. Jim thought that it was a kind of slight, but what did he care. He got the information.

"Thank you, I'm sorry, I never got your name?"

"Stella. Stella Goodwyn. Your Mom might remember me. Anyway, you have a good day son and if you ever need anything else you come and ask *me.* You understand?"

"OK, Stella, that's great." Jim interjected. He was met with a quick, cold glance from her.

"I was talking to Gordon."

"OK, gotcha. Thanks for all your help, Stella."

"Yes, and thank you."

Walking back to the elevator "We have to talk."

"I gotta head home. I've got something to do with my sister."

"Next time. Man. That was great. Good job today!"

"Thanks, later."

Jim walked back down Newark Avenue and headed home. There was a time in his life that he would have popped his head into a local joint or two to see if he saw any friendly faces, but things change over time. Also, it wasn't even noon. Plus, who the hell was this kid and who the fuck was his grandmother?

He made it home, forwarded the paperwork, and put in the invoice. This was a pretty good day so far. A quick check of emails saw two new backgrounds come through the pipeline. Even better. This was what he envisioned when he started out on this venture.

At around 4 he was starting to wind things down for the day when he got a text from Doug asking if he'd be around for a couple before he went to the Mets game. It wasn't completely out of the question, but it was only Tuesday. Oh, what the fuck.

When he met Doug at PJs he figured he had about 45 minutes before his wife plopped down next to him.

They sat in silence for a couple minutes with their heads craned to the TV. CNN had a bit on about hoaxers harassing the aggrieved families of the latest mass-homicide. It was an all-too-common occurrence and there were usually two camps in the hoaxer brigade; either it didn't happen or it was a "*False Flag*" staged government plot to take your guns away. This one focused on the latter. And with the anonymity of the internet, they had free run to attack whomever they pleased with no fear of reprisal.

"How low of a piece of shit do you have to be to do something like that? What kind of person would do this?" Jim asked to no one in particular.

Doug had no reply, just a shrug.

"These fuckers hide behind an internet persona and inject nothing but misery into the world!"

"It's sick, but what can you do? There are just people like this in the world. Maybe it's one of those senses of belonging things. These people are pretty much mostly outcasts and they cling together in their own little forums on the internet. You can't deny someone their opinion, no matter how sick."

"I get it, but having an opinion is one thing. Harassing grief stricken people crosses the line! They need to be put on notice."

Rick, the IT guy sitting across the bar chimed in "You can't doxx them and you can't confront them head on.

There is nothing you can say that will change their minds."

"I've done some work for old clients in the media. Some dirtbags would send filthy anonymous emails to their on-air talent. I mean some sick shit. I could never look at the person it was directed at the same way again after reading them. Some would get bolder as time went on because there were no repercussions. What I would do is keep an eye on the emails to see if there was anyone else they were harassing. A couple times they would put out some identifying snippets, like their hometown or a first name. Editorials were the best. It wasn't often, but I did identify several people. From there we would hire a local agency to send some goons by to knock on their door with copies of all the emails along with a stern message to cut the shit. Never heard a peep out of them again. As far as I know that wasn't illegal. It was just an accumulation of information. These shitheads identified themselves."

"Just don't feed the trolls. They thrive on that."

"I get it."

Jim noted the name of the leader of the latest victims coalition, Stan Gershwin. He was sure he could find at least a contact for him.

Talk turned to who was on the hill for the Mets (Matts), and if they had a chance against the Cardinals tonight. Jim and Doug disagreed, which was the usual case when it came to this, but it didn't matter. It was friendly banter.

Doug split to go head to Citifield just as Lee walked in.

"Hey hon, how was your day?" she asked as she kissed his cheek.

"Not bad. This kid I hired knocked it out of the park today. Got me through the gator swamp that is the court clerk's office. This kid is the fucking clerk whisperer, which is worth its' weight in gold. I'm gonna give this kid a raise."

"Slow down, wait until you get ahead a bit."

"Yeah, you're right. I get ahead of myself sometimes. Thanks for reeling me back in. But I'm telling you this kid is a great pickup. Maybe I won't give him a raise, just a promotion. Vice president, maybe. No stock options though."

"Right, whatever. What do you want to do for dinner?"

"I picked up a steak for myself and some swordfish for you."

"OK, great."

They had a couple more drinks and headed home.

After dinner Jim jumped back on his computer with two questions in his head, finding contact information for Stan Gershwin and who the fuck was Gordon's grandmother?

Locating Gershwin took about five minutes. Jim sent a carefully worded email explaining his area of expertise and his willingness to volunteer his services.

Finding who this kids grandmother was would prove to be a bit different. What was her name? Agatha, Aggie, Agnes? Agnes, that was it.

What about the last name? Fuck. At least the first name was a bit unique. He typed in the name of Agnes Peralta, which was a start.

Several names came up, but nothing identifiable. A search of Agnes and "Jersey City" was a bit broad, but hell, when you have nothing but time on your hands it wasn't a big deal. Still nothing came up. Agnes plus Jersey City plus Asbury Park paid off.

"Agnes Hughes," retired Hudson County Department of Family Services Director, Ocean Grove, NJ."
Boom.

Now the conundrum of how deep should he go. He put it down and decided to go no further until he got clearance from Gordon.

Wednesday morning, he got a call, he noted that it was an unidentified number with a 412-area code. Pittsburgh? Fuck it, let it go to voicemail.

A couple minutes later he saw that a voicemail was left. Unusual for what he thought was a robocall. The voicemail check was from Stan Gershwin. He wanted to talk. Jim dialed him back immediately.

"Hello, Stan, this is James O'Neill. Sorry I missed your call. Thanks for reaching out."

They talked for several minutes before Jim agreed to help out. Jim asked for a couple of the top perpetrators and any information they had.

"Jim, I just want to let you know that some of these emails are obscene and quite disturbing, and are extremely personal."

"Got it. They will go no further than me."

:"Thank you, I appreciate the help."

"No problem, I just want to help out if I can. I'm limited in by capacity, but I do have some experience in this. If I can expose a few of these people for you it would be my pleasure."

"Thank you so much."

You could hear the pain in his voice. Jim could not imagine the grief this guy had to go through on a daily basis. He had no children, so he could not identify with him on that level, but as a human being he could relate.

He got to the diner early and ordered an iced tea. The hostess took him to his seat while giving a flirty glance. He took note of the glance and thought the better of acting upon it before popping open his laptop and checking his messages. Stan had sent him the information for the worst of the people harassing them, with more to follow.

Gordon walked in shortly after and ordered a ginger ale and a cheeseburger. Jim only had a salad seeing that he would be eating again in 2 hours.

"So you mind if I ask who your Grandmother is?"

"She's retired down the shore. She used to work for Jersey City before going to the county and taking her job as the head of family services."

"I guess she had some gumption, to go from being a clerk to head of family services."

"I guess."

Maybe she just knew the right people, or had something on them. Even though Jim was never a public servant, he still knew that there weren't many people who could take that jump.

"So what's her name?"

"Agnes Hughes."

Damn Jim was good.

"She's a Hughes and you're Peralta?"

"Yeah, my father's name is Peralta. She wanted us to go back to my Mom's maiden name after my Dad split, but Mom wouldn't do it "

"That sucks…..I mean your Dad leaving. Growing up without a father must have been rough."

"It was ok, I guess."

"Maybe it's for the better. Some fathers are not the greatest people in the world."

So, how was your Dad?"

"What?"

"Your father, was he a good guy?"

Jim thought that one over for a moment. "I guess. I mean, he was ok. I'm the youngest of seven, so by the time I came around he was just in it for the yelling."

"What do you mean?"

"Growing up I saw what he had to deal with and I tried to keep a low profile. My siblings took a lot of gas out of the guy and towards the end he was kinda spent, on cruise control. We just minded our own business for the most part and as long as I stayed out of trouble, I was good. Overall, I guess he was OK. He did like to take us places on vacation and to the shore, where we would go fishing or crabbing."

"At least your dad took you somewhere."

One thing Jim could say about his dad is that he was around. He was yelling most of the time, but he was around.

"Anyway, so dig this. I have a new thing going on. I reached out to an individual who's getting harassed by some hoaxers."

"Since this is a pro-bono job, I think I've gotta do this mostly by myself. Not sure I can pay you. The out of pocket expenses are minimal, it's just mostly time so it's no big deal. Also....*fuck these people*."

"For Duty and Humanity?"

"Exactly. Someone's been listening!"

"Cool. Don't devote too much time on this one. I'll feel guilty.....Well, not really

"Thanks man, you're a good kid."

Jim motioned for Gordon to scoot over and he showed him what information was available.

"So here's what he have. We'll start with this fucker, he's merciless on this guy and his family. He's attacking him saying that not only was your child not murdered, but that he never existed. What, the actual fuck?"

"What it is with these people, Jim?"

"I dunno. Maybe it's a sense of "I know something you don't know." These shitheads parrot the latest drivel spewing from the likes of these bloated gas bags down in Texas and the like. Real human garbage. And apparently they have quite the following."

"Put your tinfoil hats because this shits gonna get weird. But here's the rub….What do we do if we find one of these fuckers? You can't engage them in conversation and tell them they're wrong. Subjecting them to public scrutiny will send them back in their hidey-holes, and doxxing them will get you……., I mean us, arrested."

"What can we do?"

"Well, let's worry about that when we get there. Maybe we can just hand over the info to the client and see what they do with it. What we do have to make sure of is that whatever we find can be found on any public forum. No home addresses, relatives, or license plates."

"Gotcha."

"So here's what we're gonna do. I'll get to work on some of these and I'll send you over a couple as well. OK?"

"Yeah, got it."

"Alright then. I'll send over some other stuff as well. Should give you about four to five hours work."

"Ok, cool."

"Oh, also, I know this is getting into the personal zone. Have you ever thought about looking up your Father, to see where he is?"

"What? You'd do that?"

"Sure. It is what I do?"

"I'd have to think about that. I think the last I heard was that he was out somewhere in western Jersey or Pennsylvania. I'd have to think about it."

"Talk it over with your Mom. Look, I don't want to poke around where I have no business, but I'd be happy to do it."

"Ok, thanks."

"Ok, later."

"Later."

Jim finished his iced tea before putting his laptop away and calling it a day.

"Gentlemen!"

"Hey Jim!"

"What's the good word?"

Jim just got some muffled grunts in return as Carla poured his wine.

"Thanks Carla. How are you?"

"Fine thanks!"

No Doug. He should be around. After all, the Mets were off today. He fired off a text before settling in. Jim got a response that Doug was down in Delaware visiting his mother. Damn. That meant that he'd have to pay attention to his wife, a labor that on the surface didn't sound so bad, but having Doug there made it much easier.

"Hey hon!" Speak of the Devil. Jim finished his text to Doug letting him know how selfish he was before leaning in for a kiss.

"What's going on?"

"Nothing. I decided I would help this guy out."

"The man you were talking about?"

"Yeah. I have to try and help. Even though my resources are limited, anything I can do to help. Expose these fuckers."

"OK. Just don't get carried away. I know how you get. You're not getting paid for this, right?"

"Yeah."

"Don't go crazy then."

"I hear you."

Several glasses of wine led to the inevitable conversation of where to eat. Jim didn't really care, just as long as it wasn't a hipster place.

"How about I go pick up stuff for burgers."

"You're going to grill?"

"Sure, why not."

They drained a couple more before Jim went off to pick up the food while Lee got replenished the wine supply. It was a good routine as they both knew what each other liked and how to go about it. Jim though it was better as well so he could do some work right after. He was going to go down the Rabbit Hole later on and having a full stomach and a pleasant wine buzz was going to be necessary

---

After three hours of research Jim called it a night. His brain was filled with the absolute nonsense spewed by these people, but he did reach one conclusion.....these people were nuts.

Jim narrowed the scope of his investigation down to two people. One, Montotone259, had an extensive Youtube presence as well as being an avid poster on the fringe message boards. From what he could initially glean was that he was somewhere in Colorado and his first name was Dan.

Contestant number two, Chemtrailz42, seemed to be based somewhere out of eastern Pennsylvania. Fuck, he hoped the number was tied to an address rather than being the 42nd shithead with that handle. While Montotone was more aggressive in his theories, Chemtrailz42 seemed to be a bit more subdued, a least on the surface. He was more concerned about his beloved Chemtrails, with hundreds of videos to prove it. He was quite concerned about what they were coating the earth with. Not that he wasn't without his other charms. He looked at his posting history and noted that within 12 hours of any mass shooting or other disaster, he would post that it was all staged. Either that or it was caused by Government manipulating the weather through......... Chemtrails. Also of note was outer space wasn't real, Hillary Clinton was actually Shirley Jones from the Partridge Family, and Donald Trump was actually actor .....Ron Masak, who played Sheriff Mort Metzger from "*Murder She Wrote*." What the actual fuck.

Tossing in bed Jim could not but help to think about these people. What was the chemtrail thing all about? He knew that the idea started a long time ago. But, after 20 years you'd think they would have something to hang their hat on. What was the end game for these idiots? He that the reason these people went down these roads was to get the feeling that *they know something that no one else does'* in order to feel superior. Made sense.

He recalled one of the few things he actually learned in college. His abnormal psych professor from Stockton relayed a story of one of his past patients who was convinced he was dead. The professor asked him if he thought that dead people bleed. The patient replied no, that was ridiculous. The doctor then pricked him with a needle, drawing a small amount of blood. The patient responded "Well what do you know, dead people do bleed."

He knew that he couldn't get into their heads because it would be pointless. No, he just had to focus on just identifying who the hell these people were. Nothing more.

Jim woke up to a text from Gordon asking to call him. After getting a cup of coffee and checking the incoming mail he gave him a call.

"Hey man, what's up?"

"Hold on a second, here's my Mom."

This was not going to be good.

"Mr. O'Neill?"

"Yes?"

"Where do you get the nerve to fill my son's head with such nonsense as finding his father?"

"Hold on..."

"No, you listen to me. He's better off without that bastard in his life."

"OK, I get it. But listen to me. Let's get something straight. It was simply a topic of discussion, nothing more. We were just talking about our fathers' and where we came from. He mentioned that he hasn't seen his father in over ten years. If I was an accountant or a taxidermist I wouldn't have asked any questions, but the nature of my work dictates that I ask some questions."

"I get it, I'm sorry for erupting like that. It's just a sensitive issue. Did he tell you what happened?"

"No."

"Did you look into it?"

"I file things like this under 'none of my goddamn business'."

"As well you should!" A moment went by before he heard her talk to her son as if she had her hand over the phone. Gordon. I need to talk to him in private for a second, OK?"

"So, can I ask you something? Do people know when they're being investigated?"

"No. All the records and database checks I do are completely discreet. It's mainly public record. I just know where to look."

"Interesting. Is this the best number to contact you at?"

"Yes."

"Ok. I have to go, here's Gordon." Jim could tell she was on a fishing expedition.

"Whatup?"

"Sorry about that. My Mom is a bit overprotective."

"No worries, I get it. Hey, I've got some work to send over. Work work, not the other stuff. Should be a couple of hours' worth. If you want to check the job boards again tack on another hour for yourself."

"OK, cool."

"Alright, I'll talk to you later." Jim disconnected and went back to the emails. About nine checks came through. Jim could handle most if not all of them, but he had to keep this kid in the loop.

"See you tomorrow?"

"Sure. I can make it over after 3:00. Oh, and I think I might have something for you."

Two hours later Jim got a call from an unidentified number, looked to be local. He went against his better judgment and answered.

"Apollo, can I help you?"

"Jim?"

"Yes. Is this Mrs. Peralta?"

"Rose. Call me Rose."

"I have a sister names Rose. how can I help you?"

"I'd like to speak with you about the situation with Gordon's Father. I also have a confession to make. When I initially heard where Gordon was going to be working I was a bit apprehensive, now I see it as kind of a sign."

"Ok."

"Do you have any free time later today to possibly meet? I'm afraid it's a bit complicated."

"I can meet up later this afternoon, like 2ish?"

"Ok. Where do you want to meet?"

"Do you know the Starbucks at the Grove Street Path Plaza?"

"Yeah."

"OK." Before disconnecting Jim realized he had no idea what she looked like. Kind of hard to meet up with someone when you don't know such a thing.

"Oh, Mrs. Peralta, or Rose. I'll be wearing a blue polo shirt and jeans. I have brown hair and am six feet tall. Or give me a ring when you get in and I'll wave you over"

"Why are you telling me this? Oh, OK, I get it. Duh, I never met you."

"See you later today." Jim hung up and thought how much this was going to cost him. There was no way he could accept payment. He surmised that she was interested in locating her ex-husband. He could eat that cost, no problem. If talk came to more expensive details he would steer her away. Start at the basics and go from there.

Jim went back to work and had things basically finished up for the day by 12:00. Back to the Hoaxers. He was starting to get a sense of their overall personalities. While Monty was aggressive, old Chemtrailz seemed just to be going along with the zeitgeist. As far as Jim was concerned they were both colostomy bags, but at least he saw them on different levels. Neither of these guys would be open to the suggestion of cutting it out, so he had to go a different route. *"Don't feed the trolls!"* kept resonating in his head.

After several rounds of cross-referencing and media searches it was revealed that Chemtrailz was one Walter Blackstone of Easton, Pennsylvania. Jim found his Facebook profile, which was public. Pages and pages of youtube videos and pictures of his beloved chemtrails. A google street view of his home was exactly what he thought it would be, a small, one-story house, maybe 1,000 square feet, with broken siding and an old Lincoln up on blocks in his yard.

Jim left it at that and hopped in the shower before his meeting.

Jim got to the Starbucks early, ordered an iced tea, and sat at a table near the door. At 2:05 a lady came in and immediately started looking around. Mid 40's, dark hair, trim figure, but a bit "Momish" looking. Which stood to reason, seeing that she was a mom. Nice rack. She passed him over, so Jim dialed her phone. When she looked down Jim called out to her "Hello Rose."

"Oh, hi!" She came over and sat down.

"Do you want anything to drink?"

"What are you having? "

"Iced tea."

"I'll get one of those. I'll be right back."

"I've got this."

"Are you sure. Thank you!"

Jim got another iced tea and brought it back.

"So, Rose, what can I do for you? You know I have a sister named Rose."

"I know, you told me. First off, please don't tell Gordon about our meeting. I'm still not sure what to do about this."

"I'm guessing this is about your ex-husband."

"Yes, did you look anything up?"

"No. I don't like looking into anything like this until I get the green light. So what's the deal?"

"Well, where to start?"

"You're really conflicted on this. Let's just start with what do you want my services for? I'm guessing that you want me to locate your ex-husband. Am I close?"

"Kind of. He left us under difficult circumstances. It was a real big mess. He was a good father and a decent man, but something happened that proved to be unforgivable."

"I don't need to hear what happened, unless you want to tell me."

"OK. So here goes. My husband was a building inspector for the county. He worked there for years and did well by us, but things went bad real fast. Long story short, he came home one night stumbling drunk after a work Christmas party. He wasn't much of a drinker so this was kinda weird. He came home and we got into an argument, which woke up the children. He went to pick up my daughter to take her back to bed and he ended up falling on her, dislocating her shoulder. A neighbor heard the screams and called the cops. They came and arrested him. My mother, who was the head of Youth and Family Services took it from there. Also, at the same time, it was exposed that he took some bribes in order to clear unsafe buildings for occupancy. He always maintained his innocence, but I listened to my Mother and he was out of our lives. The divorce was quick and he was granted no visitation rights. My mother made sure of that. I was so certain he was guilty for such a long period that I never gave it a second thought, but now that I think about it, I may not be so sure. The main thing I think about is the fact that he was never a heavy drinker. Maybe a beer here and there, but nothing more. I also think that my brother may have been involved. Over the last couple of years he's made some comments about it at family events. He even laughed about it. You know that when you see people across the room talking and they then both looked directly at you?"

"Yeah, it's unsettling."

"It is. He's basically my mother's footstool. After she retired he left the Sheriff's department. He left as soon as his pension kicked in. I'm guessing he was told to pack his bags after Mom left her post. My Mom had a lot of influence in Hudson County, and I don't have to tell you how corrupt it is."

"Yeah. I remember Brendan Byrne said that when he died he wanted to be buried in Hudson County so he could continue to vote Democrat."

"Yeah, that's it. I was so under my Mom's spell that I refused to look at things objectively. Oh God, if I'm wrong on this one I'll never forgive myself."

Jim though that this must be tearing her up. To think that if she was wrong, fuck. Having these kids grow up without a father because she may have sided with the wrong team would be crushing.

"I just want to know if he's OK."

"He never reached out?"

"No, the fact that he hurt his daughter devastated him. He never forgave himself. That and his reputation was ruined in this city."

"I get it. So you want me to locate him?"

"I guess. How much would that cost?"

"Nothing. I can't charge you for this."

"I'm afraid I'm going to have to insist."

"I got this. I'd be happy to help out. This one is on me. I'll find him and get some of his contact information, phone number, address, and the such. What you do with the information is up to you."

"OK, thank you. But please, don't tell Gordon we met."

"Gotcha. No problem. You have a good kid there."

"Thanks. he's special. He just needs to spread his wings a bit. That's why I'm glad he's working for you and not in some dead-end job."

"This is a dead-end job. Please, if he ever gets designs on doing this for a living, then for the love of god tell me and I'll fire him. This is not something you want to do long-term. Granted, he is learning some basic skills that may help him in the long run, but for the love of god don't allow him to do this for a living. Trust me. It sucks."

"Umm, OK."

Jim took the vitals on the husband before they finished their iced teas and said good day. It was only 3:30, so he had about an hour and a half. Time to get home and do some digging.

Jim looked at his phone and saw a missed text from Doug. He knew what it said before he read it and was out the door a couple minutes later.

"Hey man!"

"Hey Jim."

"What's new."

"Real skullduggery going on. Fun stuff though."

"Who's throwing the rock tonight?"

"Syndergaard. No, wait. Colon."

"Oh, cool. I like Colon. I mean, as far as I can like someone who plays for the Mets."

"I get it."

A couple minutes later Mike walked in with Chris and they took their seats at the head of the bar. Shortly after that Bob and Mary came in. He hadn't seen them in a couple of weeks and was happy to see them. Mary told Jim that she was in Spring Lake last weekend and ran a 5K.

"How did you do? It was hot as hell up here, was it any better down the shore?"

 "It was fucking hot, but I did OK. It was more of a walk/run, for charity, so we took our time"

"So we were about a half mile from the finish line when a guy right in front of me had a heart attack. He wasn't in good shape to begin with, but damn. I heard later that he died."

"Did you know who he was?"

"No. Poor guy, he never crossed the finish line."

"Well, he kinda did."

"Did what?"

"Reach the finish line. In a mortal sense."

"What? Oh, shit Jim!"

"Sorry, couldn't help myself. How's things?"

"Not bad. Too hot, but that's OK."

"I'll take it over too cold, any day. You get any fishing in yet?"

"No, not yet. The boat's still on land. Hopefully soon."

"Gotcha."

Unremarkable banter followed until Lee walked in.

"Hey hon, how was your day?"

"Pretty good. I'll fill you in later."

"OK."

"How was yours?"

"Fine, I guess."

They had another couple of drinks before the usual "What are we going to do for dinner?" discussion ensued. They both agreed on the Vietnamese place they frequented, where Lee got the seared tuna and Jim had the rainbow trout. They were treated very well there.

During dinner Jim filled Lee in on his day, but he kept the meeting with Rose to himself. It wasn't that he couldn't trust her to keep it to herself because, who was she going to tell?

It was more of an issue that she would ask 50 questions that had no answer. At least, not immediately.

This thing was in its' infancy and there were lots of avenues to walk down before he could even start connecting the dots. He wanted the discussion to center on the hoaxers and what to do. Even though he would never admit it, he knew that she was smarter than he was. Not exactly smarter, but she had a different way of thinking. Years of programming experience and project management gave her a different mindset. More structured and pragmatic. Sure he bristled any time she offered a suggestion, he took it all down for further review.

"So what are you going to do?"

"Not sure. I have a couple of guys in my sights, but the more I look into them, the more I'm convinced that they just don't give a shit. These people are so far gone that I don't think there's any coming back."

"I get it."

"I'm thinking a visit might be in order."

"What? Remember you're not getting paid for any of this! Slow it down. Christ! I hate it when you do this! Sure these people are monsters, but as we were just talking, nothing you can do will stop them."

"I know, I know. I never said I was going to do it. It's just an idea. Don't worry, it's cool."

On the way back home they popped into PJs to see if anyone was around. Big Joe was in there watching the Mets, so Jim saw it as a reason to stop in for a nightcap, which Lee never had a problem with.

Joe was the only person Jim knew of who could hold an in-depth conversation while drinking bourbon and texting constantly. He was another Mets fan, a defect Jim was willing to look past.

Two wines later they headed home and packed it in for the night.

Wednesday was unremarkable other than the fact that the heat broke a bit and it was a spectacular day. Jim texted Gordon and told him to meet at his place instead of the diner.

3:30 rolled around and Gordon was at the door. Jim showed him through to the back patio and brought him a glass of lemonade. After going through the days' work they looked at the two individuals targeted by Jim. He was confident enough that he had them both identified and was ready to pass the information on to Stuart. He showed Gordon listened intently as Jim described the steps he went through and why he came to this conclusion. It was really nothing more than connecting some dots and looking things up through the right database. This wasn't an instance where he had them dead to rights with a "Smoking Gun," but rather a sum of the parts that could not be denied.

"So what do we do?"

"I think I'm just going to pass it on and see what they have. Remember, this is pro-bono work."

"What's that?"

"It means we're not charging any money."

"Gotcha."

"So you said you might have something?"

"Yeah. Check this out."

Gordon typed a link into Jim's laptop.

It was an open call for investigators to locate individuals who had unclaimed assets coming to them. They were going by region, and the northern New Jersey area was up for grabs.

"This is in the zone. Good fucking job man!"

"I know, right."

Further reading revealed that the company as a startup based in Atlanta that promised to expedite the process of relieving unclaimed assets to people who were supposedly completely unaware.

"Can't hurt to send out an email, right? I wonder what the take is on our end?"

Jim sent the email before finishing up with Gordon and calling it a day.

An hour later Jim got a call, 404 area code, where was that, Atlanta? Jim answered on the third ring.

"Apollo Due Diligence, James O'Neill."

"Mr. O'Neill, this is Lamar Gibson from Prime Asset Recovery Services. I'm responding to your email."

"Yeah, thanks for calling back so quick. I'd like to know a little more."

"Mr. O'Neill, my company identifies unclaimed assets for people throughout the country. Many of these people have significant sums of money coming to them, however they are proving hard to locate. We are looking for partners in different regions to do some more in-depth research. We would pay you for your time and research expenses and will add a bonus of $500 per person you get to sign with us."

"OK, what information do you have on these people?"

"We have their names, last known address, and their phone numbers"

He could definitely swing this.

"What I would like to do is give you a list of about ten people. I'm giving other lists to other investigators in the area and will see who does the best job."

"What are you paying for the initial research?"

"What do you charge?"

He wanted to keep it low, but he still had to make a decent profit.

"$50 per person, plus $45 per hour if I have to leave the immediate area for travel time and .65 per mile?"

"That's fine. We can do that. You will be paid after we get the information."

"OK, that's fine." Even if he got stiffed it would be no great loss.

"Excellent. I'll have my secretary send you over the information. You are where again?"

"Jersey City, NJ."

"That's right. I have so many territories to fill I have a hard time keeping on top. Pleasure to speak with you and hope to hear from you soon. Have a blessed day Mr. O'Neill."

"OK, Thanks." Blessed day. Oh fuck.

He thought this looked promising, but his goodbye left Jim uneasy. Sounded like a backwater preacher. One of these guys who drains every last penny from the poorest of the poor in the name of Jesus before moving on to the next hustle. Left him feeling dirty. The last thing he wanted was to be a cog in one of these shake-down organizations.

A quick check of the company revealed that it was recently incorporated, with Lamar Gibson as the CEO. Lamar Gibson's linkedin page showed that he was involved in several startups before opening Prime Asset. He looked to be active within the community and church, and chronicled all of his good deeds. This guy really liked to pat his own back. It's one thing to do it after a few scotches at the bar, but writing about how wonderful you are on your own linkedin posting was too much. The bullshit meter was running high with this one. Better to keep it at arms' reach.

After doing some research Jim realized that it was indeed a thing, but as predicted, there were predatory outfits out there. This guy just jumped on board. Even looked like he was charging a lower rate.

The information came through and Jim went right to work. Out of the ten people he got, only five were shown have new addresses. Several had new numbers and there were a few with a couple of email addresses.

Jim updated the information through the company's site and called it a day.

Initial research showed addresses were in Union City, Newark, and West New York. Not exactly Park Place and Boardwalk, but what the fuck. It was local enough that he could just hop on the Path or the light rail.

The research showed that all the addresses were up to date. He wrote up some letters and set them aside. Jim decided to put it under his clients' company and just added himself as the contact just in case they turned out to be crooks, which was a distinct possibility.

How hard could this be? After all, he was locating the people to tell them good news. He was fucking Ed McMahon doing Publishers Clearinghouse Shit! This was after all the Lords work.

He was explaining the new opportunity to his wife over dinner that night.

"This could be big, honey."

"So, explain this to me again."

OK, so this company locates unclaimed assets found in peoples' names. You know, like bank accounts, tax payment overages, and the like. Those people that are owed at least $30k that they can't find directly are led out to me. I lead them over to this company and they expedite the return. I get a commission for each person."

"How much? "

"Five hundred per person."

"When do you get the money?"

"When the person gets the money."

"How long is that?"

"I was told about six to eight weeks.

"How can you be sure that you're going to get paid?"

"Look honey. I had them sign a contract, which I know really doesn't mean shit, but I have to take them at their word. I get paid for travel and research. I'll send the initial bill out and if I don't get immediate payment I'll shut it down.

"I just want to see that you're paid for your work."

"Yes, getting paid for work is good. We can both agree on that. Look, the searches only take me three to five minutes. From there it's all phone calls. No heavy lifting, nothing more than tracking down people and informing them that they've got some cash that they didn't know about. Should be a slam dunk." His wife asked too many god damned questions.

"Just seems weird to me."

"What do you know about this business anyway, other than what I tell you. This isn't Chase. For Christ sake, you have to put some trust in them that they'll pay up."

"I just want to make sure you get paid."

"Gotta have faith. I've got to get back to a little work, so I will be taking my wine in the study."

"Oh Christ. Well, at least you're busy."

Jim mapped out a route and decided that it would be better just to take a Zipcar the next day. The mileage and hours he charged would more than take care of that expense.

Jim actually got up with his wife on Thursday. He decided that he should at least dress a little professional, dockers and a polo would do. He had his coffee, kissed his wife goodbye, grabbed the paperwork and headed off. Almost felt like he was working a regular job again. Almost.

First stop was Union City. A bit rundown, but par for the course for this neighborhood. This should be easy. Yeah, right.

The front door was open a creek so he could kind of nudge himself into the foyer. He looked down and saw there was a pile of mail on the floor. Upon further inspection he saw that the majority of these letters were addressed to the person he was looking for. Maybe they split town? He waited for someone to leave and piggy-backed in. Being an ordinary looking white guy had its advantages in these situations.

He made his way up to the apartment, 3B. He stood outside for a couple of minutes before knocking. Didn't hear a thing. After knocking a few times, he taped a letter to his door and took a quick picture for his client to see. No way he would miss that.

The next address looked a bit more promising. The building was well maintained and he got his hopes up a bit.

Luck was with him again as he caught someone entering at the same time. The person even held the door open for him to get through the foyer and inside.

He walked up the stairs and found the apartment. No answer so he did another tape job. As he was doing this a neighbor opened her door.

"Excuse me, but do you know if Anne Curtis is currently residing here?"

"Who are you?"

Jim handed her his card. "My name is James O'Neill. I've been hired by an agency to contact Ms. Curtis. I have some information for her that she would like to hear."

"Yeah, a lot of people are looking for her."

"What do you mean?"

She said nothing and shut her door.

The other two residences where more of the same. Shitty buildings, no positive IDs on the residents, zilch. More tape, pics, and he was done by noon.

Upon returning home he did some more research. He was convinced that two of the people had returned to their respective countries and one may be a guest of the state. He found some phone numbers for relatives of Anne Curtis and reached out. The first one looked to be an in-law in New Hampshire. When he identified himself and what the nature of the search was, he just said "well good luck finding her. I didn't think that she had two nickels to rub together. I'll pass on the information if I hear from her, but she'll never call you."

Jim found another number. From the name and age range he supposed it may be her daughter. Anne was 63 years old and the woman who came up in the relative search was 32.

When he identified himself and said that he would like to contact her mother. He didn't let on about the assets this time. Maybe he could tell her it was good news and just leave the contact info. Jim could tell that just the name of her mother got her agitated.

"I never want to talk to that woman again in my life and don't call here again!"

What the actual fuck? 0-for-four, and he was pretty sure he ruined the last one's day. How toxic could these people be?

This was getting to be a bit depressing. Time to put it aside, do the billing, and call it a day. A drink was sounding pretty good right about now, but it was only 2:30. Had to wait, so he got back into some shorts and a t-shirt and went for a walk. A little waterfront contemplating sounded pretty good right about now.

At 3:00 he got a call. Another unidentified number. He went against his better judgment and answered it anyway as he really wasn't doing anything at the moment.

"Apollo, James O'Neill."

"Hello Mr. O'Neill. This is Tracy Thompson. We talked a while back about my husband bugging my house."

Oh shit. He thought that the price he quoted had ended any further need for assistance. She probably wanted some more free advice.

"Yes Tracy. How are you?"

"Not good. My husband is still harassing me."

"Have you gone to the police?"

"No, because I can't prove it. Not yet anyway."

"OK, what do you need from, me?"

"I wanted to ask you if it's possible to bug appliances."

"Appliances, like toasters and coffee makers? I believe we discussed this and it's a highly unlikely possibility."

"I think he's bugged my refrigerator."

"Why do you think that? Is it new?"

"No, but it's been making some noises lately."

"Anything else. Have you been having conversations in your kitchen that he knows about? Can you recall anything specific?"

"Well, not really, but..."

"Are you still using the phone he's paying for?"

"No. I brought one of those 'burner' phones. The phone he's paying for is back at the house in a drawer with the battery out. Someone suggested that I do that."

"Good. Here's what you do. When you get home call a friend and make some things up. Better yet, talk like you're making a date with someone. Ask them to meet up at a certain location later that evening. Give a specific time. Make sure it's a place your husband knows about but would rarely go on his own. Show up about 15 minutes past your given time and check out the place. If his car is in the parking lot then there then something's up."

"You think that would work?"

"Well, it would be the most cost-effective. Try that and let me know what happens."

"OK, but do you think that you might be able to come by and check out the refrigerator?"

"Tracy, this is what I would advise. I know you're going through a rough time, but it will get better. I really don't think that your husband bugged any of your appliances, but try it this way."

"OK. I'll try it."

"Good luck Tracy."

"Thank you, Mr. O'Neill."

He disconnected and decided to head over to the bar. He thought that any one of a dozen other agencies would have seen her as a mark and taken her for what she had. He could have at least gotten a couple hundred, but he liked to sleep at night. It was also a major reason why he was broke.

He plopped down in his usual seat. Jim was eager to talk about just about anything that didn't involve his day.

Bob and Mary came in shortly after, which was always a welcome sight. Michelle and Joe came in shortly after, followed by Mike and Chris. Lee started a conversation with Mary while Jim talked with Michelle and Joe. Michelle asked what was going on and Jim informed her of the hoaxer situation.

"I just don't know how to deal with these fuckers. I mean, you can't expose them because I'll get locked up. There is no arguing with them because in their reality they're the enlightened ones."

"Yeah. You can't un-fuck a mind once it embraces the crazy."

"Yeah. I gotta think outside the box on this one. Last Saturday you guys were ready to roll. So how'd you end up?"

"On her back" muttered Joe.

The normal reaction would have been a rap upside the head, but Michelle just gave a small giggle and an eye roll. These guys knew each other all too well.

"We ended up at the Keyhole. Nothing out of the ordinary"

"Cool. I believe I left you here then we went to that new hipster joint on Columbus."

"The one with the mustache sign?"

"Yeah."

"Why?"

"I don't really know. It was the only place that didn't have a line through the door. I had the chicken. Nothing great but not too bad. Lee had the salmon." Lee always had the salmon.

"How's work treating you, Joe?"

"It's there. Pays ok, but I still have to bartend to keep ahead. You still pulling shifts at your brother's place?"

"After the summer. There's no reason to open early on Saturdays during the summer. If Rob's stuck I'll fill in every once in a while. Lee hates it when I bartend and I understand why, but it's nice to have some walkin' around money in your pocket. Plus I really don't mind the work. As long as it's not a regular gig."

"I get it. The shit you have to put up with if you're doing it full time ain't worth it."

"I get you, but when I'm at my brother's place I have a very low tolerance to that type of bullshit. It's not like I have to consult with a manager before I get the ok to toss   someone."

"Yeah, that's nice."

Conversation flowed and before anyone knew it was after eight. It was time to get something to eat, but this was one of those nights that you just didn't want to end. It was a spontaneous party but no one really noticed. Eight to ten good friends, having a few snorts, shooting the shit, plenty of ball-busting, and enough laughter to last a week. Fuck it. We'll just pick at some shit at home. Lee was in agreement. This was one of those nights where if you left early and missed something you would regret it. One thing was for sure, not much work was going to get done tomorrow.

Before he blinked, there were two weeks left until Labor Day. Summers just went faster and faster the older you got, and it sucked. One day you're toasting Memorial Day Weekend, and the next thing you know you're scrambling for plans for Labor Day. He remembered that as a kid the very last sign of the summer was the Jerry Lewis telethon. God how he hated to see that. The one thing that took the sting out of it all was that football season was starting soon and for the first time in a while, the Eagles were shaping up to be somewhat decent this year. The Phils were 30 games under 500, so it was time to look forward to having a different team from another sport let you down. The endless cycle of futility rolls on.

The pro-bono job working on the hoaxers proved to be overwhelming. He settled on his chemtrail guy in Easton, PA, checking in on him now and then to see any new activity and if the number of his followers was getting any larger. At times Jim thought that old Walt was a harmless crackpot, but then he would post some heinous stuff denying everything about what was happening around him, except his beloved chemtrails. He desperately wanted to ask him just one question, "What's the end game? When is the earth coated enough with the chemtrail residue that they can finally make their move? Who is they?

Working with the new client locating the people with unclaimed assets was proving to be more difficult than he ever would have thought. The people that did actually respond were reaching out to Jim that the company wasn't living up to their end of their promise that they would streamline the process for them. He would reach out every now and then to one of the people who he got on board, John Tchu from Bloomfield. He talked to him one day out of sheet curiosity to see if these guys were holding up their end of the bargain. He was told that they pretty much evaporated after he signed the paperwork. "They don't seem to give a shit" was how he put it. You would think that since they were taking %18 off the top they would do a little more.

When Jim reached out he was told that it was all up to the courts and they couldn't do anything and that they should stop bitching about it.

So that was that. They signed the paperwork ensuring they would get their cut. Fuck them after that. How Christian.

Jim went back to the contact list and circled one individual that he thought could really use the money, Randy Olson of Manchester Township, right in the middle of the Pine Barrens. The money that his mother, Rhonda, had put away for him specifically was in an account that he had no idea existed. Her obit showed that she was a lifelong waitress in town. Fucking lady probably lived day to day, but still managed to put something away for her son. Randy had $35 grand coming to him. Looking at his social media Jim was sure that he would blow it on truck tires and mud-bogging equipment, but what the fuck did he care.

Randy never answered his letter, not even certified mail, and the cell phone number he found for him, even though it was active, went straight to voicemail, which was full and not accepting any messages.

Maybe is was time for a road trip.

A quick look showed that Manchester Township was about a half hour from where he grew up in Medford Lakes. If he did go down he would have to stop by and see Mom. This would have to wait until Gordon got back from his grandmother's at the shore.

The advantage of downtime is that it gives you some time to revisit some back burner issues.

He decided it was time to do a more in-depth check on the Gordman's dad, Max Peralta.

Federal court records showed that he only had one Bankruptcy, which was a short time after his life fell apart. A county check showed nothing in the judgment, lien, or civil suit category before or after the incident. Criminal check came up empty.

He had been living at his current address for over ten years, tucked away in Philipsburg. A check of other residents at his address came up empty. Just him. Guess he never got remarried.

Media research showed a bunch of stuff.

Jersey Journal, November 24th, 2004, "Hudson County Building Inspector Accused of Domestic Abuse."

Star Ledger, December 4th, 2004, "Hudson County Building Inspector, currently under Investigation for domestic abuse, charged with accepting kickbacks."

Man, how did this guy's life go to shit so fast? Maybe he had it coming, who knows.

Further reading revealed that the police were called to an altercation at the Peralta residence, where they found the father intoxicated and their daughter injured. They arrested him on suspicion of child abuse and locked him up for a couple days. Fast forward ten days and he was brought up on charges of taking kickbacks for clearing buildings for occupancy when they were not up to code. An envelope with $20k in cash in his vehicle that was linked to Sterling Corporation, the company that owned the building that was cleared.

Who the fuck would forget an envelope with $20 grand? Plus the fact that he was hit with both charges in the same week didn't sound right.

A check of Sterling Corp. revealed that it was a Delaware based corporation with no discernable footprint in New Jersey. Nothing unusual there. A check with Manta and Bloomberg didn't reveal much more. Their website was fairly generic. He could spend all day on this one. Time to pivot. Let's see what Grandma was all about.

Agnes Hughes, Ocean Grove, NJ, D.O.B. 04/13/1944, Ocean Grove NJ, two children, Rose Peralta (Nee: Hughes), and Norman Hughes Jr. Owner of the residence at 42 Hector Avenue, Ocean Grove, NJ, as well as condos in Jersey City Heights and Bayonne. Current residents of the condos were the kids. while it must be nice not to have the overhead of rent or a mortgage, it was probably a power play on Mom's part.

Courts came up empty. Media didn't reveal anything out of the ordinary, other than her role with the county. Nothing scandalous, at least on the surface.

Norman Hughes looked to be a different matter. Numerous judgments right off the top. Looks like he was not in good standing with the Ford Motor Corporation. Also looked like other creditors were not happy with him as well. Two Bankruptcies on top of that kind of put together what kind of guy this was.

A business database check on him revealed that he was the principal of Alpha Security agency in Bayonne. Looks like he started the business shortly after he was ushered out of the Sheriff's Department. The rest was par for the course for a retired Law Enforcement Officer.

Elite's website was as basic as it got. Made his own website look advanced by comparison. His name was nowhere to be found on the site. He bet that he probably got some decent contracts through his county connections and he was sure that Mom helped him out as well. Must be nice.

He had a basically solid write up on both, but whatever he could find on line would pale in comparison to asking Rose a few questions. But that would have to wait. Plus, cocktails.

Jim got to PJs and sat down next to Mike. Being Jersey City royalty, he knew just about everyone in the right places. What the hell, it was worth a shot. He motioned for the bartender for his usual and to back Mike up.

"Hey man, you know anyone from the Sheriff's Department?"

"Not really. I did know one guy, Dave Fogerty, but he retired years ago and lives in Fort Lauderdale."

"What about Agnes Hughes? She was pretty big with Health and Human Services."

"Yeah, I didn't really know her, I'm more in tune with the City and not the County. I do remember her from a few functions way back when. She had a bit of a reputation as a real ball-buster from what I recall. Jeff Leary knew her pretty well. He worked with her at the County, but he moved to West Palm Beach after he retired."

"Gotcha. You know Norman Hughes? Her son?"

"Don't think so."

"Ok, thanks."

"Why are you asking?"

"Ah, nothing. Just doing some digging and some things are not adding up."

"Who's the client?"

"No client. Just for my own edification. A favor."

"For who."

"No one you know."

"Ok."

After that the talked shifted to what everyone's plans were for Labor Day coupled with the anticipation of the upcoming football season. It was the best time of the year to speculate. Every team was tied and there was plenty of optimism to go around. PJs was definitely a Giants bar, so Jim was in the distinct minority since he was an Eagles fan, but Jim was used to it. There were a couple of Eagles bars in Hoboken, but why would he want to go there? Jim would rather surround himself with Giants fans that were his friends over being in a room with a bunch of Eagles fans that he didn't know. Eagles fans had a reputation for being a bit.....difficult.

Lee and Doug showed up shortly after and the evening was getting off to a good start. It was decided early that tonight would be a burger night, so there would be no drama in that matter. They invited Doug along, but he politely declined.

Over burgers Lee started peppering Jim with questions about the cases. Jim found it annoying as hell at times, but at the end of the day it was good to bounce some ideas around. Jim decided not to tell her about the most recent foray into the Hughes family and keep it to work that he was actually getting paid for.

"So I think these guys are crooks. I feel so slimy that I even worked with them."

"You didn't know. How could you know?"

"Yeah, but still. I'm thinking of just telling these people, well this one person, about the money he's got coming to him and leaving it at that."

"Where is it?"

"I got this guy down in Manchester Township. His Mom died a couple of years ago. She was a lifelong waitress, but apparently there was some money set aside, like $40 grand. He has no idea it's there. I sent him a couple of letters, tried calling, and even sent an email. Nothing. This looks like an in-person job. I think I have to do this to cleanse my soul. And also, fuck these guys."

"Isn't that near Barnegat?"

"Close, but I think it's in Burlington County. Right in the heart of the Pine Barrens. You should see this guys' Facebook page. This guy is a Piney through and through. It's about twenty minutes from Mom. I could swing down and check in on the old lady at the same time. I think I might bring Gordon with me."

"Why? You're not getting paid for this, so why should you bring him?"

"I'll wrap it around a paying gig. I think it's good to go. Just waiting on final word."

"OK, as long as you're getting paid. You know you do this all the time. You have to remember that the reason you're in business is to make money. You can't do this shit just because you feel you have to. Make your money first, then you can go out and do this shit. We have a mortgage to pay. Goddammit!"

"I get it. I get it."

"I don't think you do."

"Look, I've got this. I know what you're talking about. I've got plenty of business rolling in, enough that I can take him with me. Gordon has been kicking ass for me and I thought I'd take him on a field trip. I figure that I can go see this guy, maybe stop in on Mom, and be on my way." He left out the side excursion. She didn't need to know about that. He didn't count this one as lying as it was more of a protecting her from the truth issue.

"You're bringing him to meet your Mom? Why?"

"Because the guy we're going to see is less than 20 miles from her. I can't not go and see her. I'll just pop in, maybe give her some scratchers and see how she's doing. She's and old woman for fucks sake. I shouldn't need to have a reason to see her if I'm close by."

"That's fine."

"Thanks for giving me permission to see my Mom."

"You know what I mean."

I know. Jim drained the last of his Malbec and eyed another bottle sitting on the bar.

"You want to split another one?"

"Only if you do."

"Great, leave it up to me." Jim got up and headed to the bar. What the hell. It was a nice night and they had gotten their argument over with. The next half hour or so should be filled with mutual admiration and niceties before calling it a night.

Jim got to the Enterprise on Washington Street in Newark earlier than his slotted time. It was important that he get the right car for this trip.

"Hi, may I help you?"

Jim handed the clerk his drivers' license and credit card. "I called yesterday and tried to reserve the black Impala. I was told that there were no guarantees that it would be there, but it was probable."

"OK, let me check Mr. O'Neill."

"Thanks."

The clerk clattered away at her keyboard before delivering the news.

"We do have the Impala in the lot Mr. O'Neill, but it will be $15 extra for the day."

"Great, but I usually get the free upgrade. I do have a corporate account."

"Hold on." More clattering.

"I mean, it's no big deal." Jim hated to ask for this shit. It was only $15, but screw it. That was an hour of Gordon's pay.

"No bother. Sure, you can get the Impala at no extra charge."

"Great, thanks!"

They pulled around the Impala and after scrutinizing the vehicle for a moment he was on his way. Black car, black suit, dark sunglasses. Let's roll.

He circled back to Jersey City heights to pick up Gordon, who was waiting outside his door.

"Dude, I thought I asked for you to wear a black suit. What the fuck is that?"

"I only have one suit for weddings and funerals. My Mom said it's not clean. This is the best I could do."

He was wearing gray khakis and a white shirt and what looked to be black sweater vest.

He looked like the last-minute invite to a sweet-16 party and had no idea what to wear. Just thrown together with no rhyme or reason. It would have to be fixed in order to get the desired results.

"Ok, we'll work with what you have. Get in." Maybe they could find a Goodwill so he could buy the kid a $5.00 jacket to throw on him..

"So what are we going to do today?"

"What aren't we going to do, my friend. We're going across the board. Couple of stops. Should be back by the afternoon."

"Where to first?"

"Manchester Township, NJ. I got a little traveling music." When they hit the turnpike Jim hit Pandora to the Devo Channel. *Through Being Cool* was the first on cue.

"Who's this?"

"Devo, bitch. You ever hear of them?" Jim knew the answer to that one before it ever left his mouth.

"Nope."

"Didn't think so."

"So who are these guys?"

"They're a band from the late 70's, early 80's. A bunch of Dadaist art students from Ohio who put a techno band together in the 70's. They had a sound and an attitude that I liked. They were weird and they knew it. Didn't give a fuck. Really resonated with me when I was a nerd way back when."

"I get it. This isn't so bad."

"So, what kind of music do you like there young fella? You like the rap music?"

"Not really."

"Metal?"

"A little bit. I remember my Dad liked it. I used to listen to some of his music after he left. Metallica, Rage Against the Machine, Black Sabbath."

"Ok, so that's something to go on. Anything else. You've got some Irish in you. You listen to any of that stuff? Or do you go the other way with the Puerto Rican and island stuff?"

"I don't mind the Irish stuff. I don't seek it out or anything, but my grandmother likes it. Especially around St. Patricks' Day. My sister took step-dancing."

"Ok. That's cool, I guess. I think that music should ultimately be something that you seek out. Sure you get some nudges here and there growing up, but you've gotta figure it out for yourself. Don't go along just because everyone else seems to dig it. Or unless you notice that girls like to jiggle around to it. I spent a week on a Grateful Dead tour for that one. No regrets though."

The Ramones came on after Devo and instead of talking over it, Jim just decided to let this kid take it in for a bit.

'So you never told me where we're going."

"First stop, Manchester, New Jersey. You ever been to south Jersey that wasn't the shore?"

"I went to Great Adventure once when I was a kid."

"Ok, that's in the zone. Did you do the safari?"

"Yeah."

"OK, well, it's kind of the same. Keep your hands inside the windows at all times and try not to stare."

"What?"

"Just kidding. It's a lot different. Sometimes you'd think you're in backwater Alabama when you're 20 miles outside of Philadelphia. Most of it's good. Shit. I grew up down there. Went to college there too. I was never a full-fledged Piney, as they're called. This dude were stepping is a true-blue one. Doesn't make him a bad guy. It's just another way of life. The kind of life that you would never think existed in the great Garden State."

"So who's this guy we're looking for?"

"He's one of these guys we were hired to let know they had money coming to them. His cellphone wasn't accepting incoming calls, and I don't think he even has an email address. I picked this guy because he wasn't the one who lost the money, like most of the others. Besides, I think he could use it the most."

"Is he poor?"

"I'm sure he is, but that's all relative. I just hope this guy isn't a fucking skinhead or anything. There are plenty of them down there. Guys who never made it or barely made it out of high school, with severely limited prospects. Some of them get groomed by dickheads that tell them that it's not their fault, it's because of the immigrants that come here to take their jobs."

"Really? Think he might be?"

"Don't know. We'll find out."
"So were you poor growing up?"

"Not really, but we weren't people of means. My dad worked as an immigration officer and probably never made over $30k a year with seven kids. Back then a house was $17k and things were much cheaper, so it worked. When I was old enough my mom went back to work as a nurse so we were OK. Not great, but OK. Never had the greatest cuts of meat or the good cereals, but we were good."

"I see.."

"I had to go to my friends house for the good stuff like Captain Crunch or Lucky Charms."

'Got.."

"No, we had that fucking Lucky Charms that came in one of those giant bags. What was it called?"

"I don't.."

"Kaboom! That was it. There was a picture of some pathetic clown on the bag, and it was all distorted since it was you know, a bag."

"Can we…"

"That fucking clown. I remember sitting there at breakfasts with that thing staring at me. There was no back of the box to read with any games. Just that clown, looking at me. Mocking me. He knew we were poor….So yeah, we were good….I guess."

"Ok then."
The ride went on in silence for a half hour while Jim regained himself.

"So can I ask you a question?"

"Sure, what's up?"

"How did you get into this line of work?"

"Kinda by accident. It started with Casino Control Commission down in Atlantic City. I cut my teeth updating the blacklist book. All the people with mob connections who were banned from entering casinos. I did that for a bit before I was laid off. After that I dicked around there until I got my shit together and moved up to Brooklyn. I got a job with a company doing background checks and although it was a drudge, I got pretty good at it. I burned out there and quit to travel for a year before I landed a job with another company. These were my old bosses that I talk about from time to time. Good guys, retired NYPD detectives. I ended up running the show there, running executive protections jobs, surveillance, scheduling, and background checks. It was there that I realized that the PI business is a demanding mistress, and if you could get by doing mainly background checks and the occasional job like this, then you're good to go.

I'm a lazy man. If I can make a couple of grand a week without even putting shoes on, then that's the job for me. My wife is cool with it too......for now."

"I see. Was there any specific reason? Any time that you said, fuck this, I'm out?"

"Yeah. The first time it entered my head was when I testified as an expert witness on a missing person's

138

case. After that it was the burnout from the executive protection jobs. We provided drivers, retired cops, to chauffer multi-millionaires and their families around town. For the most part it was fine, but it became too much. I would get calls at midnight demanding a driver at 2:00 a.m. to pick up their daughter at her prep-school in New Hampshire because she had a nervous breakdown. It got too much that I couldn't take a shit without having three missed calls from harried personal assistants needing someone immediately because their boss is coming back from his business trip to Frankfurt on his private jet early. I couldn't blame the assistants because they were just relaying their bosses demands. These were people who weren't told 'No.' You ever see "The Devil Wears Prada?"

"Yeah. I saw it with my Mom."

"Pretty accurate. Only I wasn't getting paid shit. It became stressful and it effected a lot of other things in my life. Didn't need it so I quit. Left on good terms and still keep in touch with them.

An hour later they pulled off the Parkway at Toms River and headed west to Manchester. Jim took note that Gordon was tapping his hands a bit to the 80's nu-wave along the way, which was nice.

The main road leading in had the usual. Target gave way to Walmart, which gave was to TGI Fridays, which led to Golden Corral. After the last strip mall (Great Wall Chinese, Tom's Liquors, Rent-a-Center) they took a left onto Gateway Estates Trailer Park.

"Don't look these people in the eye. They know their situation and are well aware."

"OK, it's not gonna be easy."

"I know.'

The streets were active, much more than they should have been for 11:00 a.m. on a Tuesday. Not that these people had anywhere to go."

"Man, I couldn't imagine living here."

"It's not all that bad. This is where strippers come from."

"What?"

"Look around. Most of the locals around here are fine with they way they are. Getting out never came across their minds. There are plenty of young women who grow up in these dumps. Too smart for school, probably take up smoking by 13 or so, drinking and partying a short time later. I can't be certain but I'm sure there are plenty of predators around here more than willing to take advantage of them in order to give them at least a smidgeon of self-worth. By the time they're 18, if they haven't been knocked up, they're well on their way to the nearest pole. Maybe they make it down to Atlantic City, Philly, or New York. Maybe they don't, but at the very least, at least they had an idea to get the fuck out of here."

They pulled up to Randy's trailer, 18 Mallard Court. His trailer looked to be better maintained than the others, which gave him a bit of hope. Trouble was that his truck was nowhere to be found. From this guys' Facebook posts he was never more than 20 feet away from the thing.

"Let's take a quick drive around and come back, maybe around lunch hour."

They drove back to be main road and Jim pulled in to the liquor store and told Gordon to wait. Five minutes later he came back with a couple of splits of champagne and some scratchers.

"What are these for?"

"Well, I figure I could try to wine and dine the guy if he first refuses."

Pulling out of the lot he saw Randy's truck drive by in all its' glory. A metallic blue Ford F-150 with lifts and oversized tires. The car was most-likely worth more than his house, but who the hell was he to judge.

'Shit, there he is! Excellent. This never happens like this."

The truck pulled into the trailer park road and Jim followed. Driving in Jim realized his mistake of wearing a black suit and driving a dark car. He stood out like a fucking law officer beacon. Why not just ring the dinner bell. Jim gave him a half-block lead and passed him when he pulled in. This was a time to act. Jim parked the car and got out with the letter.

"Hey, are you Randy Olson?" Jim shouted.

He was halfway in the door and turned his head.

"Who wants to know."

"Dude, I'm not a cop or anything. I was just hired by someone to find you. I sent you a couple of letters regarding the matter of some money you have coming your way."

"Oh yeah, I got those. I thought it was a big joke." Randy looked to let his guard down and turned to come back to Jim.

"It's not dude. You got a minute?"

"Yeah, a minute."

Jim went on to explain about the situation and why he was hired.

"So you got all dressed up just to come down here and tell me this?"

"Not really. This is our first stop. I grew up around here."

He was relieved that this guy was a seemingly rational human being. Jim couldn't answer the question of where the money came from, only that it was there.

"So I have to reach out to these people and they'll get me my money? That's great, but what's the catch? None of this shit comes without some strings attached."

"Yeah, you're right, this is what I need to tell you."

"What?"

"These people who hired me. They're crooks. They don't give a fuck about you. They'll give you a great story as to how they're looking out for you, but they don't give a fuck. They're going to take %18 off the top and file it with the courts like everyone else. They don't expedite anything for shit. No matter what they say. Do yourself a favor and do it yourself. Find a local lawyer you can trust who will charge a flat rate. If you can't find anyone I think I can help"

"What do you get out of it?"

"Nothing. I'm just trying to do someone a solid. Maybe right a few wrongs. I didn't know your Mom, but it looks like she really wanted to set you up as best she could. I can dig that.

If anyone asks, we never spoke of this. I mean it. I'm sure these assholes will come after me, but I'll deal with that. Take care of it yourself and maybe pay it forward down the line."

"Ok man!"

"Just do me a favor and shake your fist or yell something when I get back in the car."

"OK."

He was going to give him his card but thought better of it. Better not to leave a trail. He looked in his in the rearview mirror and saw Randy give him the finger and shouting what could be put in the "Go fuck yourself" category.

"Did you get him to sign on?"

"Nah. These Pineys don't know whether they're coming or going. Fucking rednecks." He smiled to himself as they drove towards Route 70 West.

The ride was silent for most of the way until they reached the entrance for Leisuretown, his mother's retirement home. They used to call it "Seisuretown" when they were kids. Funny back then. Now, not so much.

"48 Walston Way, please."

"OK, go ahead."

"You never told me where we were going."

"You're in for a treat. We're going to see my Mother. Only for a couple though. I don't make it down here too often and I can't not see my mom when I'm down. She's 94. A good 94, but 94 nonetheless. I can't not check in. You're coming with me. I have to show her that I actually have an employee. She's gonna dig it."

"Ok, I guess."

"Fuck dude, you're still on the clock. She's a pretty awesome person. Plus, she's a Jersey City girl too. Grew up on Pavonia Avenue in the 1920s. Think about that for a second."

"That's cool."

"OK. Grab the scratchers and the champagne. She'll like it if you give her this stuff."

"OK."

Trouble with these retirement villages is that they all look the exact same. He was 90 percent sure he entered they right place, but called out her name first. No response. Upon entering the place he saw the family pictures. Right place.

"Mom?"

No response.

"Lady?"

No response. Jim turned and shrugged at Gordon, who looked perplexed.

Upon entering the living room he saw her there, sleeping. At least he hoped she was sleeping. Half-upright in her chair with her mouth agape. Jim went to her and placed his finger under her nose. Still breathing. Now it was time.

"MOM!" Jim shouted.

She snapped out of her slumber and looked not at Jim, but right at Gordon.

"Who the hell are you?"

"I'm Gordon. I work for your son."

"Which son?"

'Me, Mom. Hi, how are you. I was in the neighborhood and thought I'd drop by."

"Oh, thank you. Don't you look nice. Did you get dressed up just for me?"

"Yep."

"Yeah, baloney!"

"Mom, I'd like to introduce you to Gordon. He works for me."

"You work for my son? What's he paying you. Not enough I'm sure."

"He pays me fine, Mrs. O'Neill. Here. He got this for you" and he handed her the booze and scratchers.

'Oh, thank you. I need my drinking cup. I only have my coffee mug. Be a dear and get me my glass."

"Not so fast. You eat today?"

"I had half a muffin earlier."

"Maureen said there was some leftover chicken in the fridge. You good with that?"

"I suppose."

Jim went back and fixed her a plate. Roast chicken, broccoli, and some rice.

Here you go lady.

"Where's my glass?"

"It's right here." Jim placed her glass next to her and poured some Prosecco.

"Hand me the scratchers."

"Not until you eat your broccoli."

"Go to hell." She gave Jim the stink-eye before choking down her veggies. After all these years, the worm had completely turned.

"So, is Maureen treating you well?"

"Not really."

"Is she still beating you?"

"Yes, but only in places that don't leave bruises."

"I guess I'm the only one that loves you."

"You're the only one here."

"Sure, but that counts for something, right?"

"I suppose. So what do you do for my son?"

"I do background checks, and sometimes this."

"We're in the middle of two cases today. The first one was about 20 miles away. I wouldn't be able to live with myself without coming by."

"Oh boy. What do you want?"

"Nothing more than to spend some time with my Mother."

"Yeah, like blazes."

"Have some more Prosecco. Did you know that Gordon here is a Jersey City kid?"

"Oh yeah? What Parish?"

"Excuse me?"

"What parish? That's how we identified where we were from back in the 30s."

"The 1830's?"

"Shut up." His Mom shot Jim the old 'shit on you' sign; thumb touching nose creating a right angle with the rest of the fingers waving back and forth.

"You still got it, Mom!"

"Yeah, says you. I grew up in St. Michaels parish on Pavonia Avenue."

"I'm from St. Nicholas on Ferry Street."

"Oh, that's nice. Do you still go to church? I know this one doesn't. You know it wouldn't kill you you know."

"Yeah, yeah."

"I'm afraid we don't go as often as we should. We're Christmas and Easter Catholics, Mrs. O'Neill."

149

"Well, it's more than this one."

"I get it, Mom. Still not going to happen. Are you going to eat, for Christ sake? Your foods getting cold."

"I'm not hungry."

Jim examined the plate further and it looked like she ate half of it, which was the best it was going to get. He took the plate and laid down the $20 worth of tickets. He got the crossword ones, which she liked the best since they took the most time. Time was one thing she had in abundance.

Jim took her plate and did the dishes. Coming back in the room he motioned for Gordon that they had to go.

"OK lady, we're outta here."

"You're leaving me?"

"Sorry, but I have to get back to work."

"Well, it was good to see you."

"Take care lady." Jim reached and gave her a hug goodbye.

"Goodbye Mrs. O'Neill. Nice meeting you."

"Where are you going?"

"Next stop. Easton, PA."

"What's going on there?"

"Just a wellness check. You think you're the only person that I stop in on to give them scratchers and champagne?"

"You mean there's somebody else?"

"No one could ever replace you, Mother."

"Bye Mrs. O'Neill. Nice to meet you?"

"OK, goodbye."

"She seemed nice."

"Yeah, she's OK." She was more than OK. Jim aced out when it came to Mothers. She wasn't your stay at home Mom growing up. When Jim was in third grade she went back to work as a nurse. Jim pretty much grew up as a latch key kid, which was fine. Jim was doing his own laundry shortly after and made his own lunch as well when she wasn't around. Not your traditional house, what with seven kids and four teenage girls running amok, but it was all he knew.

"OK, next stop, Goodwill. I think there's one on Church Road."

"What are you getting?"

"Need to get you a bit more dressed up."

They found the Goodwill store and headed in, passing through one of the most depressing sites known to man, the Goodwill toy section. Just keep your eye on the prize, the young adult formal wear section. He took a quick glance at Gordon and thought "Husky" size would do. Jim was no stranger to that section. Growing up his brother never let him forget it.

Jim had in mind to get this kid as properly dressed as possible, maybe he could pass off as a Junior G-Man, but looking at this kid, his age and size made Jim realize that he would never be able to pull it off. Time to pivot.

"Gordon, hold up for a second."

Gordon stopped and turned around. No, this kid would do better as a basement shut-in who knew too much.

"Your hair, how crazy can you get it?"

"What?"

"How much can you afro it out?"

"It can get pretty big." He rubbed his hands in his hair and there it was. Man, this kid had a rug of hair on him.

"Dude, that mane is going to treat you well in the future. You may not know it yet, but it will."

"I hate it."

"Hate it? I would kill for that rug. Look at what I have to work with!"

"What, you look good."

"Well, thank you, but you never got to see the top look." Jim bent over and showed Gordon his thinning top and growing monks-cap.

"Oh, I get it."

"Listen, you're going to have to trust me. Come here." Jim went over to the shirt section. "Ahh, here it is! Only three dollars too."

Jim pulled an orange and white paisley shirt from the rack and held it up to Gordon the way a mother would their child when school clothes shopping.

"What do you think?"

"I don't like it."

"Perfect. Now we just have to make sure it's ill-fitting just enough. No time for a changing room, just try it on."

Gordon reluctantly put on the shirt and gave a turn.

"Ohh, perfect. Ok. Let's roll."

"But I look like an idiot."

"Yes you do. Take it off for now. I promise the only person to see you wearing this shirt is me, and maybe some people in Easton, PA. You know anyone in Easton, PA?"

"No, or I don't think so."

"Good."

Jim picked up an empty spray bottle on sale for a quarter before checking out.

"What's that for?"

"Nothing. You'll find out later."

"What are you planning for me."

"I'm not quite sure, but I will guarantee that you won't be put in harms way."

They pulled out of the lot and headed to 295 North, destination, Easton, PA.

They stopped for lunch on the way and had some burgers for lunch at a Chilis in Clinton. Jim gave him a bit more insight to the overall plan and Gordon was on board. More than that, he was into it.

"Ever been to Pennsylvania?"

"No. I only left New Jersey a couple of times. I went to Disneyland when I was a kid and to Washington DC on a class trip. I mostly go to the shore."

"Pennsylvania's OK. Philly is one of my favorite cities. Some of them have a superiority complex about us The irony is that they choke our roads headed to the beaches every chance they get during the summer. They act like they don't like being there though. I've got an idea. Why not go to the beautiful Pennsylvania beaches of Lake Erie? Have at it, suckholes!"

"Why do people have a problem with New Jersey?" Gordon asked as he was bathing his curly fries in a bath of ketchup.

"I don't know. Jersey gets shit on anywhere you go. I've been in the fucking Himalayas and have gotten my balls busted about it. My theory is that most people only know Jersey by their view from a cab going from Newark Airport to New York City. Not a pretty sight, I'll admit, but refineries have to go somewhere. You know what? Fuck 'em. Remember one thing. Wherever your life takes you always be proud to be from Jersey. Shout it from the hills. Being from New Jersey gives you an iron hide, wear it proud."

Upon reaching Easton they headed to their final destination, 235 Dogwood Terrace, home of Walter Blackstone. They gave the property a pass before settling in on a space where he could keep an eye on the driveway. There was the ubiquitous pickup truck on blocks and an old black Buick Grand National parked in the driveway. He looked to be home, which was a plus.

"Reach into my back and grab me that pin."

Gordon reached into Jim's bag and pulled out a lapel pin.

'What's this?"

"It's a Free Mason pin. It's like kryptonite to these idiots." Jim grabbed the pin and placed it on his lapel before putting on his sunglasses.

"Well, how do I look?"

"Pretty cheesy!"

"Wait until they get a load of you!"

They camped outside his house for about a half hour before he saw the door open."

"Get down dude! Can't see you. Put your seat all the way back."

A white male, mid 50's to early 60s, short-cropped white hair, medium build, exited the building. This was the guy, matched his Facebook page pic. No doubt about it.

He exited his one story, not dilapidated but could definitely use some work, white house with his garbage in hand. Normally the protocol is not to be identified when on a surveillance, but Jim only had one day. On his way out to the garbage Walt noticed Jim in the Impala. Jim stared right at him and never broke a glance. Walt looked away as he put his garbage in the receptacle, then stared back. Perfect. He had this douchebags' attention. Walt walked backward while maintaining eye contact. Jim made a motion as if he were talking into a microphone, making him stop in his tracks. Jim then put the car in gear and drove away, slowing to a crawl as he passed his house before pulling away.

The thing about doing a surveillance is that it's 98 percent sitting idle and two percent pure adrenaline. No matter what the situation, the moment you had your mark on sight, it was met with sweaty palms and an accelerated heart rate. At least, that's what happened with Jim. He never bothered to ask other PIs. Mostly because he never found himself in their company. He was the only one he knew, which was good enough for him. He turned to Gordon and told him to get up.

"We did good. Sorry about that. Need to maintain the illusion."

"I get it. What happened?"

"I got a make on his car and let him know that he's being watched. Right now this shithead is on line with his cabal of conspiracy nutjobs letting them know that to Government is on to him. I guarantee it." Jim drove around the neighborhood until he found the most likely exit point for this guy to take. He took up residence halfway down the block and settled in.

"I'm still not sure why you're doing this."

"Well, here's the deal. Since you can go to jail for outing these shitheads, and you can't meet them head on in their own domains, chatrooms, and social media, since it only seems to empower them, 'feeding the trolls' as it's known., I thought, what the fuck, let's overfeed the trolls. Force feed them, gorge 'em. Give them what they crave in an enormous dose. I hope this guy is shitting himself right now. Fucking tin foil hat crowd. They don't care who they destroy, as long as it fits with their narrative. Grieving families, people who lost children, 9-11 victims, they are all fair game. I figure what the fuck, let's give a little back. It beats choking them out, which I'm told is illegal. Hopefully we're not done."

"And you're not getting paid for this, right?"

"Nah, just don't let my wife know if she asks."

"OK. I'm glad to be a part of this."

"We're not done yet. Put on that stupid shirt and poof your hair out just in case."

Gordon complied and shortly the outfit was complete.

"Man, you look pathetic. Absolutely perfect! Now let's just wait a while and see if he makes a move. I'm guessing he does."

Jim thought that he may be close enough to Philly to get some of their radio stations. It was afternoon, so maybe he could find Mike Missanelli somewhere and hear any updates on the Eagles.

As the clock turned three Jim was starting to lose hope. He had to get the car back by six or he would be charged for another day. He figured that he would have to hit the road by four just to be safe.

"Let's give it another 25 to 30 before we call it. You have anywhere to be?"

"No, my Mom is working late so I've got nothing going on."

"OK, cool.....Oh shit!" Before he finished the sentence he saw the black Grand National pull up to the stop sign before making a left.

"Oh, this is good. This never happens." This is the tricky part. He's on to us, so we have to keep a loose tail."

"You mean keep a distance?"

"Yeah." Jim put the car in gear and made the left down Davis Avenue. He noted that the Buick was about four or five cars ahead, so he should be good. Jim was just glad his car stuck out. If he were in Seaside Heights in the 1980s he would have been screwed, but this day he was lucky.

He saw that the car made a slight left at the end of the road and entered a large parking lot. The pulled to the side and hoped that they could find his car in the lot, if that was where he was. If he did that to lose the tail he was screwed. The only plus to that would be not having to explain to a client that he lost them. That's why he didn't do it anymore.

They waited a minute before going into the lot. Easton Foods and a pizza joint. The did an up and down of the lot and found the Buick. Damn, this never happened. Of course this happened though, he wasn't getting paid for this one. He parked the Impala five rows over and headed into the supermarket.

"You're on dude. Oh, wait a minute." Jim grabbed the spray bottle. "Take off your glasses." Jim gave him a good spray on his face and armpits. Not too much. Just wanted to give the look of a kid who walking up the stairs from his mother's basement counted as cardio.

"You know what to do?"

"Got it."

"Just remember, don't get close to this guy. He's a coward, but even a coward can be dangerous when backed into a corner. Also, I'm pretty sure your mom would murder me if anything happened to you on my watch."

"Ok."

Gordon went into the market and Jim followed a minute later.

They moved in sequence, Gordon at the far and Jim at the near on the side of the registers. They found him in the third aisle in the frozen food section. Jim gave Gordon the nod and he was on his way. He didn't miss a beat as he headed right up to him.

"Excuse me. Are you Chemtrailz42?"

"What?"

"Chemtrailz? It's you, isn't it?"

"How, what…what's going on?" Jim was standing 20 feet away but he could tell this guy was visibly agitated. Keep your distance, dude.

"I don't have any time. I just want you to know that you're close! They're on to you!" From 20 feet away Jim could tell that the kid sold him on it.

"Close on what?"

"So close......oh shit! They're here! No time to talk! No, it can't be! It's him! Oh crap oh crap oh crap!" Gordon made a point to stare right at Jim before releasing an exasperated squeal and running in the opposite direction. He had to note that the kid added a nice touch by waving his arms in the air while running away.

Jim walked briskly up the aisle but paid him no mind. He had Walt on his left, so he could see the Free Mason lapel pin.

"What the hell is going on? Who the fuck are you? Why are you following me?"

"This doesn't concern you, Mr. Blackstone. Not at the moment." Jim stared right at him, and what he saw was a man who was dead in his tracks. Just stood there motionless as his mind tried to process just what the hell was going on.

Jim walked up the aisle and spoke into his imaginary microphone in his sleeve. He made a quick left at the end of the aisle before tearing down the fourth aisle and double-timing it to the door. He never looked behind, just hoped he lost the guy. Jim hoped that he was still in the frozen food section with an exploded head.

He made it out of the store and made his way back to the car. Gordon was by the drivers' side laying low, just as he was told. He clicked the fob and they got in.

"Get back down until we hit the highway."

"Ok." Gordon got back in and assumed the position.

Leaving the way they came in, Jim caught a glimpse of his car still in the lot. He exhaled and they headed to Route 22 East to Philipsburg. In no time they were back in Jersey and it was over.

"So, what did you think?"

"That was fucking great!"

"Yeah, it was pretty cool! You see the look on his face? There was nothing there."

"Yeah, it was classic. I came up to him and when I gave him his internet handle his face went white! He was all like......Duuurrrr, what's going on? Who are you?"

"Tee Hee! I fucking love that stuff! You killed it today! Good fucking job!"

"Thanks."

"You pumped up or what?"

"Yeah man. I feel great."

"Just remember, most of the time this shit happens we'd be driving back in silence. Defeated silence. We should be back to drop off the car in about an hour. You said you have a little time. My brother owns a bar right near where I have to drop this off. He has an Irish Pub with really good food. You like tacos?" Who was he kidding, of course this kid loved tacos.

"Yeah, I like tacos. What kind of place is it?"

"Typical Irish Pub. Mostly local regulars, some college professors, civil servants, musicians and other miscreants."

"OK, sounds good."

"Cool. We'll drop this off and head over for some food. I'll send you back in an Uber after."

"Works for me."

"Cool."

"What do you think this guy is doing now?"

"Hopefully he's locked back in his little hidey hole. If the world is lucky he's gone silent", but he had serious doubts for that conclusion. This was going to be a good litmus test about handling trolls. The warning sign was not to feed them as it only makes them stronger. There was no reasoning with them on any level as they had it in their minds that they had all the answers and everything else was drinking the government kool-aid.

"Do you think he got our license plate number? Think he could find us?"

"I seriously doubt that he would get a plate, and even if he did there is little chance that he would have been able to do anything with it. DMV has shut that stuff down. Even if he did, it would come back as a rental car, which is a dead-end. Oooh, that would be great! Let's hope this guy used some resources and spent a decent amount of cash only to find that it comes back to Enterprise."

The rest of the drive back was uneventful backslapping. It was a good day and they did the Lords' work. Time for cocktails.

After dropping off the car they walked up Central Avenue to the Alehouse. It was after five so his brother would probably be home getting ready to come back for the night shift. He wasn't going to bother to call him. He had enough on his plate and didn't want him to come running down just because he was there. Not that he would anyway.

Upon entering he saw Rich behind the bar, which was always a good sight. A couple of seats were open and they took their seats. Rich instinctively grabbed a bottle of Malbec and came over.

"Hey man, how you doing?"

"Not bad, just tending to the usual suspects. Ed's well on his way."

"Has he started biting yet?"

"No, but he's getting there. He's on the grabby stage."

"Noted. Rich, this is Gordon. He's been working for me for the last couple of months as an investigator."

Rich extended his hand. "Hello Gordon, how do you like working for this guy?"

"It's OK."

"OK? Just OK? He's just shy. Get this kid a sarsaparilla, it's on me. We hit the road today for a couple of jobs. He performed admirably. I may even pay him for it this time."

"What are you drinking?"

"I'll have a coke please."

"And a couple of menus when you get the chance."
Jim looked down the bar and saw some familiar
faces. "I'll be back in a couple minutes, I just have to
say hello to some people. Get whatever you want. I
told you that tacos are great, but everything else is
good too. The wings kick ass." Jim walked down to
the end of the bar to say hello to the regulars, which
today consisted of Ed and 68 Mike. He caught the tail
end of the conversation which ended with Ed calling
Mike a Commie for being in a workers union.

"Hey guys, what's up?"

"Hey Jim, what brings you here today?"

"Had a job down in South Jersey and Pennsylvania so
I picked up a rental at Enterprise on Newark Avenue.
Just dropped it off and came here to take my
employee over for some grub."

"You have a worker?" Asked Ed. "Have you crushed
his spirit yet?"

"Working on it. I'm breaking him down
psychologically at the moment. The beatings start
later, then the rebuild starts."

"Good. How's business?"

"Can't complain. I have some steady work coming in right now, so I was able to hire someone part time so I can be freed up to work on some other shit."

"Good. Good."

Jim looked down the bar and saw Gordon looking straight ahead.

"I gotta jump. I'll be back in a couple."

Jim walked back to his seat at the bar. "You know what you want?"

"I guess. Can I get some wings and chicken tacos?"

"Sure. How do you like your wings? They go from mild to chef's revenge. How spicy do you like them? You like the heat?"

"I guess, but not too much."

"Let's go with hot. Hey Rich, when you get the chance we're gonna have one order of chicken tacos, one blackened chicken tacos, and an order of hot wings."

"OK. You want them all together or the wings first?"

"I don't think it matters. Just bring them all out at once."

Jim took his seat next to Gordon and commiserated a little more about their good fortunes on the day before small talk and baseball took over the conversation before the food came out. Jim took a wing and ate a taco before he noticed his brother walk in.

"Hey man, what brings you here?"

"Had a surveillance job and dropped off the rental at Enterprise down the block. Got a side trip to Mom in too. She told me to tell you you're an asshole."

"Sounds like something she'd say. How'd she look?"

"Pretty good. Gave her some scratchers and booze, so she was in a good place."

"I get it. Where'd you go?"

"We started out down in the sticks. You remember Bass River State Park? Around there first, then we stopped by Mom before heading to Easton PA to check in on another crackpot."

"We?"

"Oh shit, I'm sorry. Rob, this is Gordon, my employee. This is the kid I was telling you about who started working for me a couple months ago."

"How you doing Gordon." Rob extended his hand, but Gordon's were currently covered in blue cheese and hot sauce, preventing the completion of the handshake."

"Fine thanks. Please to meet you. Great wings here."

"Thanks. So you met my Mom? Did she smack you around?"

"I'm sorry, what?"

"Smack you around? You know, call you in close to tell you something before popping you one."

"She lit him up emotionally. We got there early, so I'm pretty sure she hadn't started drinking yet. I brought her the goods though. She's probably all worked up about now.

"Oh, OK. So Gordon, how do you like working for this idiot?"

"I like it."

"See? Told you."

"I'll go into detail later, but this kid kicked ass today."

"Cool. I gotta take care of some stuff, but I'll be back. You staying for a bit?"

"I will be."

"OK. I'll talk later."

"Later."

"So if you don't mind me asking, what was he talking about when he was talking about your Mom hitting me?"

"Ah, nothing. She just gets a little punchy after a couple. Brings her back to when we were kids."

169

"Really? I'm sorry to hear about that."

He realized the kid was buying to that theory. "Of course, we're kidding. My mother would never do anything of the sort. We just kinda joke around about it. It makes up for all the emotional damage she caused"

After they ate Gordon ordered another coke when a guy Jim didn't recognize as a regular come headed straight to Gordon. They locked eyes and there was a familiarity resonating from the both of them.

"You're Max's kid, aren't you? Gordon, right?"

"I'm sorry, do I know you?"

"I'm Jerry Feeley, how you doing? I used to work in the same office as your Dad. I met you a couple of work outings. You grew up, but I remember that head of hair."

"Oh, hi." Gordon extended a limp-wristed hand out. He leaned over to Jim and told him he'd like to leave. Gordon tensed up, almost recoiled.

"I got it." Jim started to dial up an Uber for the kid.

"I just gotta say, your old man got railroaded."

"When is the car gonna get here?"

"Says about four minutes."

I'm just gonna wait outside. Nice meeting you."
Gordon excused himself and started towards the
door. Jim followed him out.

"You OK?"

"Yeah, I'm fine. Just wasn't expecting that."

"I don't think he meant any harm. He sounded
genuine."

"I know, I just want to go home. He doesn't know
what happened."

"Maybe he does. I mean, not to you, but on the other
side."

"YOU DON'T KNOW!"

"Ok dude. Sorry man. Cool down a minute. Just
remember we're all on your side. Don't forget that.
OK?"

"Ok, I'm sorry. It's just....."

"No worries man. Totally cool. You've got some shit
you need to sort out. Remember dude. We got you."

They waited in silence until mercifully the car pulled
up to take him home.

"Look, I just want to tell you one more time. You
kicked ass today and thanks."

"Thanks Jim."

"Ok, I'll reach out tomorrow."

"OK, take care dude."

His ride took off and Jim turned back to the bar, filled with questions.

Jim entered the bar to see Jerry Feely talking to Rob.

"Hey man, no offense. I didn't mean to get the kid worked up. I'm Jerry Feely. I used to work in the same office as his old man."

"Jim O'Neill. It's cool. I guess you caught this kid off-guard."

"Jerry is in the Hibernians with me" Rob said. "He's a retired surveyor with the county. What freaked this kid out?"

"Jerry, you would be able to tell us a little bit more about it. I've caught snippets from the kid and read a blurb or two, but other than that I'm in the dark." Jim made no mention of the meeting with Rose.

"His father was in the buildings department. Worked in compliance department handling Certificate of Occupancy approval. Most of those guys were a bunch of scumbags who couldn't take a bribe fast enough. His father was different. Never took a dime. Never ratted anyone out, but he still ruffled a lot of feathers. Anyway, he did the best he could, but he pissed off too many people. Anyway, there was a Christmas party one night at Casa Dante in Journal Square. He never had a reputation for drinking and I never saw him at any of the watering holes near the office. But that night, out of nowhere we all saw him stumbling around, completely out of his mind sauced. We managed to finally pour him in a cab home. Read about what happened the next day. Two days later they hit him with the bribery charge. This poor fuckers' life was obliterated in the span of two days.

173

He was run out of town on a rail and three months it was like he never existed. There were rumblings around the office that his mother in law had a hand in it, but no one dared to mention it. What a cunt that one was. I remember seeing her son there. Douchebag worked for the Sheriff's department. Complete waste of oxygen. Perfect case of public service nepotism at its' finest. I remember that after the mother in law retired he was quietly asked to call it a career as well. Kills me to think that roided out dirtbag actually got a pension."

"Wow. So you think this kid has been walking around for the past six years without his father in his life just because he was an honest man? And on top of that his own grandmother may have had a hand in it? Fuck me."

"Yeah. Makes you sick."

The more they talked the more Jim realized that this guy Feeley was a decent guy. Problem with that is that a lot of the time, although it's genuine and no harm is meant, the timing is essential. Aside from that, Jim wanted to know more about the Uncle. Seemed to Jim that this guy knew exactly what happened. It was just a matter of how to get the information.

"This kids' Uncle was a complete douche. He was one of those guys who screened people at the entrance to court buildings. Not sure what the guy looks like know, but he was juiced up then. Most of those guys were. Just what you want when you enter a government building, a bunch of hooched up gorillas trying to intimidate everyone who walks through the door. He was clearly the king of douchebaggery at his location, and it pissed a lot of people off. No one could really do much about it because of who his mother was. I wouldn't be surprised if this guy had a hand in taking out that poor kids father."

"Think he was roofied or something?"

"I dunno, but you never fucking know. This kids father wasn't a teetotaler, but in the four or five times I associated with him the most I've seen him drink was a couple of beers, tops."

"If this guy was on steroids he probably knew how to get his hands on some other shit. Makes sense."

"Hey man, I'm not accusing this guy of anything, but let me just say it makes sense."

"I got it. Hey Rich, do me a favor and get this guy a drink. What are you having?"

"I was on my way out, so maybe a shot of Jameson?"

"Sounds good. Two shots of Jamo when you get the chance."

Rich poured the drinks and Jim raised his glass to the guy before draining it."

"Thanks for the information dude."

"Mind if I ask you something?"

"Anything."

"How did you come to hire this kid?"

"I put an ad out on Craigslist and when I interviewed him I found that he fit all I was looking for. Plus it looked like the kid could use a break."

"I want to know how you knew who this kid was."

"That giant head of his is hard to miss. Plus I remember his Mom.....nice tits."

"I get it. Good luck." They shook hands and parted ways. Jim looked at the clock and noted that it was past six. Lee should have called him an hour ago. Maybe she was working late. Jim went ahead with preemptive strike and dialed her. Straight to voicemail. Oh well, he tried. Jim figured he could hand for another half hour before the issue arose again.

Ten minutes later she called back and notified that she was going out with her friend Eileen in the city and that he should fend for himself for the night. No problem there.

Since it was so rare that this happened, Jim felt that he had to make it count. If he were near home this would have amounted to eating hot dogs in front of the tv while watching baseball, but hanging in Newark at his brother's bar would have to do. He walked back to the end of the bar and picked up the conversation with Ed and Mike. Jim had done some work for Ed in the past, which was always welcome because he paid in cash, immediately. Usually it was people who owed him money, and there were many.

Ed owned about ten blocks in downtown Newark as well as real estate on college campuses around the country. He hit 70 and was selling off his holdings so he could enjoy the piles of money he accrued for the rest of his life. Ed was a self-made man and liked the fact that Jim took a chance and started out on his own.

"So you have an employee? Good for you!"

"Yeah. I have some steady work coming in, enough to warrant me hiring this kid part time. I took him out on a run today since he's been doing a good job for me."

"You put an ad with the local AV Club?" Mike asked.

Jim laughed and nodded. "Yeah, the kid looks like a dud, but he's got a good head on his shoulders."

"His head's a virtual planetoid."

"That's my fault."

"You could have hired anyone, and you chose that kid?"

"Yeah man. A kid likes that needs a break. Sure I could have hired a chick his age with great tits, but where would that take me? It would be a constant struggle and I'm sure it would end badly. Also, let me ask you something. Was he wearing glasses?"

Mike thought for a second. "I'm not sure, was he? Yeah he was, wait."

"Exactly. If that was some hot young chick, you would have remembered everything from her eye shadow, to what perfume she was wearing, to her wrist size to note how tight you should put the handcuffs when you chain her to your radiator. This kid is practically invisible. He can come and go and you would never notice him. That's what you want in this business. Most of the work this kid does for me is from his home, but it's good to have a kid like this when needed. I'm too pretty. I go noticed." Jim got Rich's attention and Jim motioned to buy the next round for Ed and Mike.

Banter ensued for the next half hour before the night shift arrived in the form of two night time regulars, Bub and JoJo. Bub was a local landlord, having brought several buildings in the neighborhood before the area became somewhat gentrified. He had a steady income stream and hasn't had to work in years.

Jojo was a native citizen of Newark who worked as a caretaker of the local church. He was much smarter than even he gave himself credit for and was the author of some of the most repeated one-liners in the bars' existence.

"How was work today Jojo?"

"I did it."

"Works for me. Rich, get the boys from Bub on down a round on me."

Jim looked down at his watch and it was going on 8. Shit, he should get home. If he got into an Uber now he could make it home before the Mrs., in which case she wouldn't call him down to PJs for a nightcap. Sometimes it was just better to go home. He dialed up and Uber and hit the road. He did the classic Irish exit. Got up to go to the bathroom before exiting out the side door. It was better this way. When you don't say goodbye it means that no one can get you "One for the road," in which case you would be there for another half hour.

He slipped into the car just as he got the call from Lee. He declined to answer it, opting for calling when he was safe at home.

He got through the door and it wasn't even 8:30. Still time to go out for a nightcap, but seeing as it was Wednesday, he thought he would be a little responsible. He immediately got changed to his house clothes, thereby cementing his decision to stay put. When you kept your pants on there was always a chance you could be goaded into going back out. When the house shorts were on, the decision has been made. He decided to check on the wife, who true to form was still in the city with her friend. He declined to meet her at PJs and said he would be waiting for her at home. Besides, his head was filled with questions about his earlier conversation at the bar. Plus, there was still a half bottle of Malbec sitting on the counter from the night before. He poured himself a glass, grabbed a few ice cubes, and headed to his office.

When he went to log on to the system he was bumped out, with the notification that someone using his ID was logged on. That could only mean that Gordon was on the site. Jim determined that he probably wasn't doing anything for work, but rather doing the same thing Jim had intended.

Jim let it go and made a note to address it in the morning. He saw exactly what he was doing and he couldn't blame the kid. He had the tools in his hand that could answer a lot of questions.

Fuck it, no more work tonight. He grabbed the remote and settled in for some bad television.

It was a good day. Truly the Lords' work has been served.

The next morning, after seeing his wife out the door, Jim tended to the garden for a minute before settling in. Logging on the search site Jim saw that the account activity confirmed his suspicion.

Search Activity:

Max Peralta, Philipsburg, NJ.

Comprehensive Search (address history, relatives, people at work, criminal, judgments & liens).

Looked like Gordon's search only cost about $12. Negligible, but it would have to be brought up.

He didn't think that this kid had the cajones, or the resources, to head out to Philipsburg himself, but you never knew. Although for all intents and purposes, this kid was one of the most passive people he ever met, but that shit can change on a dime.

Jim decided he would just go about his business and would reach out to him later today.

He sent Gordon an email with the day's work and got the confirmation that he received it and nothing else.

As Jim was going over the daily checks to see if there was anything missed, he got another call from Sal, which usually meant a new client, which was always nice.

"Hey Jim, what's doin?"

"Hey Sal, what's going on?"

"So I got something for you, one of my old clients. Has a bank in New Jersey and we used to run checks for them. Good client, pays on time."

"That's always nice. Do I know them?"

"Maybe, you remember Pete Lombardi?"

"Yeah, I remember him. Niagara Bank?"

"So you do know him, great."

Sal gave him the information and Jim said he would follow-up. He remembered the client from years ago and although it was only a couple of checks a year, they paid almost immediately.

Jim reached out to Pete and they picked up where they left off years ago. They were hiring two new people in accounting and wanted the full-boat check on both at $650 per person. Pete was a good guy, but wasn't much for small-talk, which was kind of refreshing. Most matter of fact stuff. Jim hung up and prepared some releases to send over and he would get going.

Looked like another good day was on the horizon. It was jobs like this that offered him the luxury of going off on these completely pointless endeavors such as yesterday.

As soon as he got the info he went to the search engine, which was clear, meaning that Gordon wasn't on line. He didn't want to do it, but he had to send a message. He opted on the security notifications to send a text code every time someone logs on.

The two checks went without any great revelations. The good thing about accountants was that the client only wanted fiduciary checks done. Bankruptcies, judgments, liens, credit, license check, and criminal. The standard operating procedure was to conduct what he could do immediately through the courts and sit back and wait until the credit and criminal come back. The criminal, especially in the state of New Jersey, takes a couple of days. If the subject has anything come up, then the client gets immediately notified. Most of the time they would pull the plug and you would send them over whatever you had and scuttle the rest. It resulted in a lower invoice, which wasn't great, but it ensured that the client would come back and maybe refer you in the future. His company flew under the radar, so there was no Yelp reviews or anything, which was fine, but good word of mouth between personnel managers was well worth its weight….in theory.

After the checks were done Jim logged off and did some puttering around the house when he got a text alert saying that someone was trying to log into the system followed immediately by a call from Gordon.

"Hey Jim, I'm trying to get into the system but I get an error message."

"Yeah, they started a new security item to their login. It texts me a code in order to log on. I have the text here, it's 56734."

"OK, thanks. Crazy day yesterday, huh?"

"Yeah, that was something. Say, Gordon, you free later on today?"

"I can come down around 3, but I have to be somewhere at 4."

"That works. Come by my place."

"OK, see you then." Jim disconnected and went back to work. He was thinking about what he was going to tell Gordon. Should he let on that he knew or would he give him a chance to talk. He decided on the latter.

In the time leading up to the meeting he decided to check up on good old uncle Norm. He had enough info based on the earlier check, so it was time to check his social media to see what was what.

A quick Facebook check found him and his various postings. It was always great when people just put out their entire lives for everyone to see. Sometimes it was too easy.

First he noticed that he was much smaller than he anticipated. Definitely not juiced up anymore, which was nice since there was a good chance they would meet up in the future, and getting his ass kicked by a juicer was not something he looked forward to.

You could have played "Retired Law Enforcement" bingo with this guys' Facebook profile. Deep sea fishing, check, golf outings, check, over-50 softball league, you betcha, foam parrot hat at a Jimmy Buffett concert? Boy howdy. Every other pic had him holding either a Coors Light or a Michelob Ultra. The only thing missing to complete the game is him in some kind of sexist t-shirt. Something to the effect of "Grab a Heiney!" or "Wine 'em, dine 'em, 69 'em!" You could all but guarantee that he was well known at his local strip joint. This was one of those guys who called himself a Patriot when he had no idea what that even meant. And to top it all off, he was a Yankees fan, because.....of course he was.

Jim looked to see if there was anyone he thought he may know in any of the pictures, but there wasn't anything. He was sure there was someone who he knew that knew someone, but that would have to wait for another day.

Norm did post a lot of pictures from what he supposed what was his local bar, Benny's, in Bayonne. He had never heard of the place, but he didn't venture down that far unless it was for an occasion. He did make a note to ask his buddy Tommy about the place. He was a lifer and knew just about everyone.

Checking the dates of the postings he saw that Norm was at the place on Thursdays or Fridays. He would have to head up there, but he would need to consult with Tommy first.

A quick visit to Chemtrail Walt showed no updates since their little visit.

Three o'clock rolled around before he knew it and Gordon was at the front door.

"Hey man, come on in back. You want some iced tea or something?"

"No, I'm good."

"Ok" Jim poured himself an iced tea before heading to the patio.

Before Jim sat down Gordon said that they needed to talk. Jim had heard those words before, mostly from ex-girlfriends kicking him to the curb. Jim himself had uttered those words as well. This time it was a different tone.

"I think I know why the new login procedure is there. When I got home last night I couldn't help myself and looked up my Dad. I just wanted to know. I'll pay you whatever it cost. It was just that the guy from your brother's bar got to me."

"Dude, I get it. That was a lot of shit to lay on you. I had no idea about that guy. Never met him before. He certainly meant no harm."

'Yeah, I get it."

"Did you talk with your Mom about it?"

"No, not yet."

"Man, this is uncharted territory for me. I don't know what to tell you. My usual procedure is to dump the information in the clients' lap and let them figure it out. I don't think I can legally even give advice."

"You can't?"

"I don't know, but sometimes that's what I tell them so I can't get involved."

"Yeah, I mean, at the end of the day I want the people to make their own decisions. I did a few adoption cases where I was pretty sure I nailed the birth parents down. My advice would be to send a letter. A phone call is a shock to the system. An email is too impersonal. A letter gives them a chance to digest the information. I recommended handwritten instead of something printed out. More often than not it worked. After that it was totally in their court. I pointed them to the curtain and opened it. What was behind the curtain was anyone's guess, and frankly, none of my business. You hope for the happy ending, but we all know that's not how it works.

I once had a case a couple of years ago. Seems an old guy from Ohio whose time was running short wanted to reconnect with his daughter. Apparently his ex-wife had turned her against him and they haven't spoken in over 20 years. I did a check and found her about 20 miles away. He wanted her contact information but I wasn't going to give it to him without her consent. The information I found was readily available through an in-depth Google search, but this guy was not computer literate. I ended up calling his daughter a few times and never heard back. Two weeks later I get a call from the daughter. She started in on me, but I had to cut her off, letting her know that I was hired by his father and would not give him any information without her consent. She calmed down a bit and then went into a ten-minute story about what an asshole he was. Broke my heart. The guy wasn't physically abusive, just split and never offered any support that apparently they desperately needed. At the end of the conversation she said sure, give the cocksucker my information. I thanked her, said goodbye, and called the client with the information. Never heard back. Never expected a call back, and there were times that he was dying to call the daughter to see how things went, but that's not in the cards. Had to let it go and move on.

Let me just say I'm with you to the end on this one. Whatever you want, I'll help you out. You're a good kid and you and your Mom deserve to know. I can't imagine what you went through the last couple of years not having your old man around. And the fact that the whole thing could have been avoided is the reason why I drink wine by the gallon."

"Thanks Jim. I appreciate it, and I want you to charge me for that check."

"Not happening."

"I'm afraid I have to insist."

"Dude, it was only about nine dollars. Don't sweat it."

"Nine bucks, that's it?"

"Yeah."

"Oh, I thought it would be at least like 30 of 40 bucks."

Jim raised his finger to his lips. "Ssshhh."

"Oh, got it."

"Yes, it's how I make money."

"I see."

"Look, I don't know what kind of timeline you're looking at here, but I wanted to guess your sense of urgency."

"I mean, I don't want to do anything like, right now, but I would like to do something sooner rather than later."

"Gotcha. Talk it over with your Mom. Sit down and hash it out. Whatever your decision is. I'm in. Just do me one favor, let your mother know in no uncertain terms that this was all your idea. You took it upon yourself to do this. You went behind my back. Please don't get your Mom pissed at me. I hate that.

"OK."

"Cool."

A fist-bump ensued and Gordon was headed to the door.

"Oh, shit! Hold up a second dude. I have something for you."

Jim skittered up to his little office and scanned through his CD collection before returning.

"Here you go."

"What's this?"

"It's a Devo CD. Freedom of Choice. It's their third album, and the one I'm most partial to."

"Why are you giving this to me?"

189

"I saw you were getting down to the Devo a little bit on our road trip."

"No I wasn't"

"Ssshh, ssshh. Yes you were. We're all friends in here. Don't deny it."

"But I don't have a CD player."

"You have a computer, right?"

"Oh yeah."

"Just take it. Who knows, you just might like it. Tell you what, you listen to this and we'll call ourselves even on the whole looking up your dad thing."

"OK, thanks I guess." Gordon put the disc in his backpack and headed out.

It was only 3:30. Time to check the emails before calling it a day. Some puttering around the garden and back patio followed by a quick shower and a walk to PJs.

On his way over to meet Doug he felt the vibrations of his phone for an incoming call, 404 area code......Shit. Let it go to voicemail. He didn't want to hear from this guy right now. He wondered if he somehow found out about the Randy Olson incident. He didn't think he would be ratted out by the guy. Why would he? He saved the guy like, $13 grand. That's a lot of giant truck tires. Was it though? How much did they cost? Who fucking cares? No way the solid Jim sent his way would get back. Even if it did, what could he do? It would be one word against another. Jim didn't make a Nickel off the deal (if he did then that would be another issue), so he was good to go. Plus, Jim was feeling the need to tell this guy to fuck off.

He waited until the little tape recorder thingy icon appeared and checked the message.

"Jim, this is Lamar Gibson, from Prime Asset. I'd like to talk to you about any updates you might have. Thanks and have a blessed day."

Blessed day. Fuck him. Who was he to tell me that?

Jim decided that a couple of drinks were in order before calling him back. Plus, he could look tougher by leaving the bar, but keeping in full view of everyone while it went down.

"Doug"

"Jim."

Doug was immediately given his gin and club soda and conversation turned to work.

"So you're telling me you went down there and just told the guy that he has the money and informed him to bypass your client?"

"Yeah. Is that wrong?"

"Existentially no, but I do have to advise as an attorney that you're an idiot."

"I just can't take these assholes anymore man. They're predators and don't give a flying fuck about the little guy."

"I get it."

"Can they come after me?"

"I don't know. What kind of contract did you sign?"

"I didn't sign anything. I had them sign one for me."

"Then you're good. If you took any money then that would be a problem, but you didn't. I wouldn't worry about it."

"Just do me a favor."

"What?"

"Do not tell Lee about this one. She would get pissed that I went all the way down there and just gave the thing away."

"You know she would be right to be pissed about that."

"I know. I just got more satisfaction that these fuckers aren't getting their cut. What's $500 at the end of the day?"

"$500. I get what you're saying and the conversation goes no further than here."

"Thanks man."

Shortly after the bar started filling with the usual cast of characters. In walked Mike and Chris, followed by Richie. With Richie coming in it was only a matter of time before the talk turned to football.

"Hey Jimmy! What do you think about the Eagles do this year? They gonna be any good?"

"I like what I'm seeing, but who the fuck knows?"

"That kid Wentz, think he's got what it takes?"

"I hope so." It was always better to talk in terms of 'how the hell am I supposed to know?' rather than say anything they could use against you in the future. It only took Jim about 35 years before realizing that.

"Big things from the Giants this year! Big things! I think they're going to take the division."

God bless Richie.

"We'll see, Richie."

Soon it was all the usual suspects and when Lee walked in Jim gave her his seat. It was then Jim thought it was time to call the guy back. He stepped outside but made sure that he was still in view of everyone when he got him on line.

"Jim?"

"Yeah, Lamar?"

"Yeah. How are you? I just wanted to reach out for any updates."

"I'm good. Not much to report. How are we doing with the two I gave you, the women from Toms River and Bridgeton?"

"I have to get back to you on that. I'm not in my office now. I think we have them though. I wanted to talk to you about how you're going about this. I think you need to be more aggressive. You have to close the deal."

"Do I?"

"Yeah. You have to sell them on what you're doing for them! Gotta get in there. Don't take no for an answer!"

"Is that so?"

"Yeah man. You have to get your numbers up."

Numbers up. Fuck this guy. "Look man. I do what I do. I'm not a fucking salesman. I find people and do background checks. Pretty much all I do. If you wanted a salesman you should have hired one. Oh, and I don't work for you. I'm acting as a temporary agent. I get what you're saying. You have a business to run, but I'm not going to a song and dance routine. If I was we wouldn't be having this conversation."

"So tell me how you go about this."

Sigh. "I locate them and cross-reference them through a couple of databases. From there I see if there's any direct contact information, phone numbers, etc.. I don't gather email information because it's pointless. Too many scams. If I can't get them on the phone I send them a notice on my letterhead with my contact information. If I don't hear from them in a week or so I check them for relatives and see if there's anything there.

If they're within 20 miles I then take a ride out to the property and leave another letter.

I don't know how many of these people you're had contact with, but the majority of these people are fucked up, broken. Either through bankruptcy, drugs, gambling, or all the above."

"I don't care what you say to these losers, just tell them anything to get them to sign."

"Yeah, I'm not going to do that!"

"You gonna get back to work on this?"

Jim raised his voice a bit and asked him if he even listened to what I told him. He looked in the window of the bar to see if anyone was noticing. Nope. They didn't give a shit.

"Look man, all's I'm saying is that the more people you bring over to us, the more money you make."

"Yeah, about that. I only get paid when the money finally comes through, which is proving to take months. Not the most efficient way to do this."

"Our hands are tied on that. When we get the money, you get the money. That's that."

"Yeah, that's that. Listen, I gotta run." Jim didn't wait for the response before cutting off and walking back in the bar.

"What's going on? Everything OK?"

"I guess. Just dealing with that client that hired me to track down all those people."

"Did they cheat you out of money?"

"No, they came through on their word. It's just their practices that I'm having a hard time with. Proving to be quite distasteful. I think I'm gonna take a step away from them. Put it on the back burner."

Jim decided that he would just let it go for a bit. He did what he did, but there was at least a couple of thousand in revenue for him out there. If they decided to sign on the dotted line he wasn't going to stop them. One time was enough to give him a little satisfaction.

"It's cool. All good. What do you want to get to eat tonight?" Jim was willing to go anywhere. No more arguing.

"You want Saigon?"

"Sure." He ordered another and settled in for another drink.

On the way to the restaurant he got a call…his brother Rob.

"What's up?"

"Ah, nothing. Hey, can you cover a shift tomorrow?"

"Hold on…..Lee, mind if I bartend tomorrow night?"

"I think I'm meeting up with Eileen in the city. Yeah, go ahead. That's fine"

"Yeah, I can do it. Do I have to close?"

"Yeah, but you can shut it down early, like 12:30. School's not in yet so it dies down early."

"OK. So six?"

"Yeah. Thanks."

Cool. It was nice that he could shut the place down early. 10-15 years ago staying til three and getting up at 7 wouldn't have been a problem. These days, no fucking way.

Dinner went without any hitch and soon they were home having a nightcap.

"So, what time do you have to work til tomorrow?"

"Not late, Hopefully I'll be back by one. School's not in yet, so I don't have to deal with the kids, so there's no real point in keeping it open til 2."

"Oh, Ok. So how long are you going to keep bartending for?"

"I don't know. The older I get the more of a pain in the ass it can be, but it's nice to jump behind the stick every once in a while to let myself know I still have it. Plus, it's good to practice every once in a while."

"I just don't want you to make a habit of it."

"I get it. It won't."

Truth was, Jim enjoyed bartending. Plus the fact that his brother was in a bind made it a no-brainer. Thursdays was a decent enough crowd. The pro was that he could close it down early. Plus, maybe that guy Jerry would be in, so he could dig for a little more information, but how much more could he get? Anyway, it was always worth a shot.

Lee decided to call it a night while Jim went and checked the baseball scores before checking out.

Thursday arrived with little fanfare. Jim had a couple hours of background checks before he had to head to the county clerk. He decided he would give Gordon a spell and do it himself. Then he would head off to the bar.

After lunch and tending to the garden Jim showered up and was ready to head out before he decided to change from shorts and a t-shirt to khakis and a polo. Better to be dressed a bit professionally before bowing to the god that is the clerk of courts. He hoped he might get lucky and run into the same person that knew Gordon's granny.

By 2:00 Jim made it to the entrance of the court clerks building. After a small sigh and deep exhale, giving up all hope, he went in and up to the office.

It looked to be the same woman at the desk, but you just can't tell anymore. The faces were all interchangeable at this point.

After filling out the paperwork Jim went up to the window and offered a hearty, "Good Afternoon! How are you today!" which was met with barely a glance before he was told to sit down.

Jim waited 15 minutes before he got the copies of the judgments and he was out the door. Damn, that was easy.....too easy. He took a second glance at the paperwork and it all seemed to be in order. Damn, it was better to not question things and accept the fact that he got what he wanted without having to beg for his soul.

Jim walked around Journal Square for a bit before heading on the Path to Newark. At this rate he would be over an hour early. Which gave him enough time to grab a burger and prep up for the night.

Upon entering the bar he saw the usual Thursday lineup. There were the Doctors from Rutgers and NJIT, the NJ Transit boys, and an assorted lot of people.

Immediately upon entering the Doctors called him over and were ready to order him a drink before he let them know he'd be working.

"Oh, damn, well that sucks mate." Corey said.

Corey was a neuroscientist from Australia who came to Rutgers on post-doctoral fellowship. On of his first day in Newark he had the misfortune of stopping by the Alehouse and sitting next to Rob. Within two weeks he was one of the guys with a new apartment in Jersey City. He was also the smartest guy in any room he walked into, but never let on about it. Jim and Rob brought him into the fold of being an Eagles and a Phillies fan. Poor bastard.

"Yeah, Rob's a bit shorthanded and asked me to pull a shift. You guys going to be here for a bit?"

Rob came by and Jim asked if he saw Jerry from the AOH.

"Not yet. If he comes in it's not until about 6 or so. Why, you need to talk to him about your kid?"

"Yeah. I don't really want to get involved, but this is kind of weird. I think this kids father may have been railroaded, tarred and feathered and kicked out of town."

"Really? That sucks."

"Yeah. What's getting me is the fact that his Dad didn't seem to put up a fight about it. Lost everything."

"You know where he is?"

"Yeah, and now his kid does too."

"You told him?"

"No, I checked his search history on my database. He figured it out."

"So this guy has had no contact with his family since this shit went down?"

"Yeah. From what this guy Jerry said I think he may have been set-up by his wife's family, namely her mother and brother. Apparently her mother had some real juice in Hudson County and her brother seems to be her hired thug on the inside. Hard to wrap your head around something like that. How some people can sleep at night is beyond me."

"But you don't know for sure."

"No, but it looks to be that way. What I'm thinking is that in order for that to go down, they would have to make the father believe that he did it. Imagine this poor fucker going through life thinking that he hurt his daughter while he had a load on. The guilt he must go through every day. How this guy didn't eat a bullet is beyond me."

"But, you don't know Jim."

"I know, I know. I'm getting ahead of myself. I gotta shut the fuck up about shit like this. You expecting any type of crowd tonight?"

"Don't know. The Rutgers kids don't get back til next week. NJIT the week after that. These are the worst couple of weeks in the summer."

"So I can shut it down early?"

"Yeah, give it at least til 12:30."

"OK. 11:30 it is then."

"I gotta run. Me and Michelle are going out to dinner. I'll talk to you later."

"Later."

Jim had a burger before going upstairs to change before taking over. Rich gave him the rundown on the tabs before making a break for it. If Jim was given his druthers, he would have preferred an opening shift. You may have not made as much as the night guys, but at least you knew when you were getting the hell out of there.

Most of the faces were familiar, so it was an easy transition.

68 Mike came in shortly after and asked why he was there.

"I guess Rob had to can the new guy."

"You mean the guy who drank a bottle of Tully on his first shift last week?"

"What? Didn't hear about that."

"Oh yeah. As soon as Rob was out the door he poured himself a rocks glass of Tully and chugged it."

"Damn. At least I have the decency to wait until the kitchens closed before I do that."

"I know, right? And that's not even the reason he left."

"Rob said something about this place being beneath him."

"Oh, yeah. He was better than us."

"Christ." Jim had seen dozens of these types through the years. They work in one place and think they develop a following. After that they start thinking about how this place would go under if they left. What they don't know is that people go to a place because it's convenient for them. Either it's on the way home, close to work, or in the neighborhood they live in.

Jim got Mike the usual, a bottle of Bud and a small glass of Yukon Jack with a couple ice cubes. Mike was a building engineer who could answer just about any question that involved electric work, plumbing, and heating and cooling.

"You see Ed today?"

"No. Haven't seen him. Not even his rape van. Must be out on the farm....feeding the hogs."

"Dude, I don't want to even know."

"It's just better that way. Where's Rob?"

"He had to split. I guess him and Michelle had a thing going on."

"That's cool. How's work?"

"Not bad. Keeping busy. It's nice to have someone I can pass off the grunt-work to, which frees me up to pursue the better jobs......In theory."

"Seems like a good kid."

"Yeah. Total nerd that puts his head down and gets it done. Just happy to be on the job. Trying to get the kid out of his shell, but at the end of the day that's not my job. I try to nudge him a bit, but not too much."

'Yeah, best not to get involved on that level."

Jim refilled his Yukon Jack before taking care of the rest of the bar. Hopefully the night wouldn't drag on, but it never did.

By nine o'clock the bar was half-filled with a manageable crowd, most of whom he knew, which was nice. Bub and JoJo were watching the Yankees win, which made for a happy audience. Jojo drinking shots of Bacardi Limon and Bub with his Fireball. Another hour and the kitchen would be closed.

By the time midnight rolled around it got sparse, which was perfect. If nothing happened within the next 15 minutes he would shut it down. Bub and Jojo were paying their bills and getting a couple six packs to go, and the remaining people were just having a quick pop before calling it a night.

At 12:15 Jim gave last call as the skies opened. Fuck, Uber would be prohibitively expensive with this shit. He rang out last call and closed the til. By 12:30 it was still pouring and an Uber back to Jersey City was $45. It was normally $12-15, but the weather algorithm comes into effect when it rains.

He was lamenting the fact out loud when one of the regulars, Johnny, offered him a ride to Penn Station, which fine by him.

Jim managed to make it to the PATH platform at 12:40, five minutes before the 12:45 to the World Trade Center.. Not bad, he thought. He could get home at a Christian hour, have a couple pops to unwind before hitting the shower and calling it a night.

The notification read the train would arrive in six minutes, so he found a place to lean to kill the time.

About two minutes later Jim heard an audible, "Mmmm, mmmm, mmmm," and not in the, hey this tastes great tone, but rather filled with consternation. Jim ignored it and went back to his phone. A minute later he heard it again, only with more urgency. Jim looked up to see an older black lady, arms akimbo, staring directly at him.

"Let me aks you a question! What kind of man is coming home at 12:30 at night, carrying a briefcase, with his shirt on inside out?"

Wait, what? Jim looked at his shirt and noticed he threw his polo shirt on inside out at the bar.

"A Cheatin man! That's who! You a cheatin man!" She had the hole finger waving and head nod going on.

Jim turned his shirt back right-side out and approached the woman.

"Maam, I can assure you that this is not the case."

"Oh no, honey, you a Cheatin Man! A Cheatin Man is what you are!" All while pointing the accusatory finger right at him for all to see.

"Maam, I can assure you that I am much too lazy to carry on an affair."

This was true.

The lady calmed down and they entered the same car. Two minutes into the ride Jim saw the hilarity in the situation and couldn't help but to bust a gut, which agitated the otherwise kindly looking old woman.

"You go ahead and laugh, I know what you did!"

"Again, maam......oh fuck this. You know what, you can believe whatever."

"Oh I will, honey! You're gonna have to answer to the Lord for this!" she said as she defiantly crosses her arms.

"Great." What was the point in arguing? Where was this going to get him?

Jim thought for a second about the woman in front of him. Maybe she was on the receiving end of something like this. Maybe she was just a fucking busybody who didn't know how to mind her own business. Either way, fuck her. She would be permanently out of his life when the train pulled into Grove Street.

On the walk from the station to the apartment Jim couldn't help but to start crack up about the Path experience. Thank God he took the Path home instead of a boring old Uber.

When he made it home he immediately woke up Lee to tell her about the interaction. She was not amused, mostly due to the fact that it was 1:00 a.m, so Jim retreated to his headquarters, had a glass of wine before taking a shower and calling it a day.

Lee got her revenge at 6:30 a.m. sharp, when she shook him awake to ask him about it. Jim was a little rankled about it, but quickly realized that she was right. He quickly explained the go-between and she seemed to be satisfied before going back to her daily ritual. As Jim nodded back off to sleep he took great satisfaction that his wife actually trusted him. He knew there were plenty of other people where there would have been follow-up questions followed by further interrogation. Trust was a cornerstone in their relationship, and there was no way he was going to fuck this one up. Shit, they didn't even know each other's phone passwords. It was a nice thing and he wouldn't do anything to jeopardize that.

Jim woke up an hour later to a text message and an empty house. Gordon reached out to see if there was any work for today.

He grabbed a cup of coffee and doddered out to the garden before tending to the days business. Nothing yet, but is wasn't even 9. He texted Gordon back to let him know and went back to the yard to enjoy the morning.

After ten o'clock Jim got a call from Gordon.

"Jim, hey listen, I'm not going to be able to help you out today, or the next few days, probably."

"What's up?"

"My grandma, she had a stroke and hit her head. It's pretty bad. She's in the hospital. We're headed down now."

"Oh man, that sucks. Go man, I got this. You need anything let me know. You good with money?"

"I'm good, thanks."

"OK, take care man. Best to your Mom and your family."

"OK, thanks."

Damn, that sucks. A stroke was one thing, but hitting your head as the result really sucks.

Jim could pick up the slack for the time being. Since it was late summer things were slowing up anyway.

Later in the day Jim got to thinking about the Grandmother and Uncle. All the evidence found as well as what Jerry had to say about her made for a compelling argument that she was a colossal bitch. Maybe this was the end of the road for her. Jim bet that the Uncle would be down at the hospital today as well. After all, she funded his existence. He wanted to think that he would be down there for the simple fact that his mother was in bad shape, but a part of him in the back of his head had the notion that he was hoping to cash in on her demise. He's seen it too many times.

Maybe today would be a good day to trek on over to that bar in Bayonne where Norm hung out. Actually, today would be the perfect time. From what Jim could tell the place was a solid local joint. News there tends to travel fast. Maybe hop over there around happy hour to hear what they're saying.

He did a quick check on the bar's location and saw that it was a short walk from the light rail. Perfect. He could get there in about 20 minutes. That would be the plan then.

He told Lee that he would be meeting up a little late, but didn't tell her why, which was never good. She needed to know. All Jim could say was that he would let her know later. He cut her off as soon as she started raising her voice. It was better to just turn the phone off at this point.

He hopped on the light rail headed south and was in Bayonne in 15 minutes. Benny's was definitely a neighborhood joint. Working class patriots. Looked to favor the Jets over the Giants. This was why his friend Tommy liked the place. Jim was also advised to try the wings, but this wasn't in the plan. A couple of buds, maybe a shot of Jameson, and then get the hell out.

Jim dressed as unobtrusive as possible. His cap just read "Florida" emblazoned with an American flag. A blue t-shirt (no team preference, don't want to start a conversation about your team's chances) and shorts. Coming in from a bright day, it was hard to adjust to the darkness of the joint, but he did make out about four to five necks craning towards him to see who it was.

He didn't say a word and took a seat as far away from everyone as possible. The bartender, a slightly overweight woman in her mid-50's wearing a black waitress apron with a pen behind her ear, asked him what he was having.

"Just a bottle of bud, thanks." He put a $20 on the bar and turned his phone on. Fuck, two missed calls and three texts from the Mrs. This was going to be a fun night.

He settled in to hear the scuttlebutt. Maybe there would be some nuggets of information. Information that was none of his damn business, but needed to find out anyway.

The bartender made some small talk. Jim just told her that a friend from Jersey City recommended the place and that I should try the wings. He mentioned that he was looking at new neighborhoods because he's getting priced out of Jersey City.

"Oh yeah, the prices there are ridiculous. I remember back in the 80's you could buy a brownstone down by Van Vorst Park for less than $80 grand. Now, forget it."

"Yeah, it's getting stupid, the rents they want."

"Who's your friend who told you about this place?"

"Tommy Mac?"

"Oh, Tommy. He usually stops in here when he's on his way back from the track. How's he doing?"

"He's good. I was wondering why he recommended this place, then I saw you guys are a Jets bar. That will do it."

"Oh yeah. We meet up with Tommy sometimes at the Meadowlands to tailgate at Jets home games.."

Fuck fuck fuck. If this was the spring it wouldn't be a problem, but it was less than two weeks before kickoff. He would have to get to Tommy first and tell him he fibbed a bit. Shouldn't be a problem. He just had to remember to do it if he ever wanted to come back down the road.

"Yeah, Tommy's a good man."

Two men at the end of the bar chimed in. "You know Tommy?"

"Yeah. I try to keep up with him every once in a while. Try to. He really makes the rounds."

"Yes he does. He's hard to keep up with sometimes"

The last thing he wanted was to draw attention to himself, but this was mostly harmless. Could even be beneficial. These people weren't in Tommy's inner circle, but rather tertiary people in his life, of which there were many.

Jim made some small talk for the next hour, and tried to listen more than talk. At around six another patron walked in, sat down, and was immediately handed a Miller Lite and a shot of Jack Daniels. Yep, this was a neighborhood bar.

The man, around Jim's age, white male, grey temples, decent shape, wearing a Jets t-shirt and a cap with some kind of fish logo on it, drained his shot and asked the bar "Did you hear what happened to Norms' Mom?"

"No, what?"

"She apparently has some kind of brain injury. In the hospital down by Asbury Park. May not make it."

"Oh dear, that's horrible."

The two men at the end said nothing out loud, but whispered to each other. There was something there, not that Jim would ever find out.

"Yeah, it sucks alright," fish hat said before motioning for another shot of Jack.

Jim said nothing and looked down at his phone. Sometimes shutting down and staring at your electronics could be a good thing. 20 years ago there would have been a conversation. Now he could just stare into the abyss of a three by six-inch screen.

"He was down there all day. On his way back now."

"Oh Boy. How is he?"

"How is he? He's an asshole! everyone knows that. It's just a matter of what kind of asshole we're going to get today." He looked over at Jim and raised his glass. Jim instinctively raised his and nodded his head.

"Who are you? New to the neighborhood?"

"Maybe. I'm looking at new places because Jersey City has gotten ridiculous."

"He's a friend of Tommy Mac!" shouted either on of the two at the end of the bar.

"I know Tommy. Good man."

"That he is. I don't think I've ever heard anyone say a bad thing about the dude."

"My name's Joey."

"Jim. Pleased to meet you."

"This is a good neighborhood. You looking at any place in particular?"

"Nah, this is my first stop. Heard about this place and the wings, so I had to check it out."

"The wings here are good" said the bartender, "You want I should get you an order?"

'Yeah man, you have to try the wings."

"Next time. I'm meeting my wife for dinner in about an hour. Can't overdo it."

"So you get to pick out where your next move is?"

"No. I just do a scouting trip, I have a little more time on my hands than her, I can offer a suggestion, then get told I'm wrong and do what she says. It's just easier this way."

"That's why we never got married. No broad is telling us what to do!" rasped one of the twins at the end of the bar before going outside for a smoke.

Jim was going to leave on that, but decided to have one more. He texted Lee that he would be there in about a half hour with an explanation. She texted back that she was at PJs and had some company, so she was good. Jim just hoped that Norman would make it back before he left. Get a good bead on the guy.

After draining the last of his third Bud, Jim called for the bartender over to change a $20 so he could leave a decent tip. As she was at the register the door opened and in he walked.

"Hey guys."

"Norm! How you doing?"

"Been better. I bet you know by now. My Mom's stable at the moment, but other than that they can't tell me too much. I spent all day down there and need a fucking drink."

The bartender finished getting Jim the change and rushed over to get Norm his Michelob Ultra and shot of Jack Daniels.

Jim looked lost on his phone for another minute before heading out.

"How come you're still not down there? Doesn't she have a big house down near Asbury?"

"Yeah, I was going to do that, but my fucking sister and her stupid kids are staying there. No way I'm staying in the same place."

Jim took a look at the guy and noted that this was definitely not his first stop on the way back to Benny's.

Jim left a fiver on the bar, said a quick "Later" to the regulars, and got out the door. He got some pretty good intel on this guy, mainly that everything he heard about him being a grade-A douchebag was spot-on. He was not a let-down in that department.

He decided to call Lee on the way home to diffuse her anger.

"Where are you? Why did you hang up on me?"

"Honey, I couldn't talk at the moment. I thought the fact I told you as much when we last spoke."

"You didn't!"

"I'm sure I did. Look, it's not a big deal. I just had to do something that I'll tell you about when I get there. It's not a big deal. It's not even seven for Christ sakes!"

"Where are you now?"

"On the light rail. Coming back from Bayonne."

"Why are you in Bayonne?"

Christ. "Didn't I just tell you that I'll explain everything when I get there in 20 minutes."

"Oh, right. Michi and Joe are here."

"OK, great. I'll be there in a few."

Jim was certain he never told his wife that he had to hang up because he couldn't talk, but it just came out. Sometimes it was better to cloud her mind. It was a skill he acquired after eight years of marriage and he was getting better at it by the day. The trick was only to use it in certain circumstances, where it was either that or a night on the couch.

He got to the bar by 7:30, still a half hour to go for happy hour closed out. Lee was talking to Mary down at the end of the bar and Jim took a seat next to Michelle.

"Lee said you were in Bayonne?" Joe asked why the fuck he would he ever want to go to Bayonne of their own free will.

"I had a thing I needed to get checked out. This kid I have working for me may need some help. I'm afraid that this is way above my pay grade if my suspicions are correct."

"What are they paying you?"

"For this? Nothing. This one is on the house."

Lee came back and asked him what was going on. Jim tried to let her know that this was something that should be spoken between them, maybe at dinner. Thankfully she understood and they went back to their respective conversations. Lee sometimes had a habit of needing to know immediately, regardless of who was around. Jim wasn't a fan of making a scene where it wasn't warranted, but she had absolutely no problem with it.

A couple of drinks later and they agreed that tonight would be a burger night, so Left Bank it was.

"So what's going on?"

"Not sure, but I think that this kid Gordon's dad may have been railroaded."

"How do you know?"

"I don't know, but I have a feeling. I went over to Bayonne today and got a glimpse of his uncle, who's retired from the Sheriff's Department. Real piece of work, this guy. You would like him. Charming fellow."

"You're going up against cops?"

"What, no. Hell no. I'm keeping my distance. Not going any further than this, I promise."

"Ok. Just don't go crazy."

"I know, I know. I just can't help it sometimes. This kid got the shaft, and if there's something I can do to make things a little better for him, I think I have to. I'm gonna leave things for now. Let it simmer."

"Ok, good.

The next morning Jim texted Gordon to see what was up.

Yo, how you and your family doing? Any good news?

…..Nothing new. Grandmas in bad shape.

How's your Mom and sister doing?

….I guess she's ok.

OK. Take as much time as you need. We're all good up here. Take care of your Mom and sister. Reach out when you're ready to go again.

…..OK, thanks.

Jim could use him, but oh well. On the bright side, his payroll expenses were temporarily eliminated.

He got back to work on the days' checks. Only a couple of hours' worth of work. Nothing great, but better than nothing. Sometimes it could be a grind, but it was work like this that afforded Jim the time to look out for other endeavors.

Gordon made it back home a week later. His grandmother apparently stabilized, but it the stroke got her hard and she would need permanent care. Nothing the kid could do down there.

Upon meeting Gordon in the afternoon, something seemed off. Something was bothering him, but he had no idea what it was.

"So what's up?"

"Nothing, I'm fine."

"You are obviously not fine dude. In all my years of existence, when someone says they're fine, they most decidedly are not."

"I'm fine. Can we just get on with this. I have to go home."

"I get it. You're probably under a ton of stress. You want a drink?"

"What? No! I'm not like you. Not every problem is solved with a glass of wine....or six."

"Ouch. That hurt a little. Look man, you're not in a good place right now. I'm trying to help you out a little bit, but you're not letting me. Sometimes some work can take your mind off things. I'm going to let some things slide, but I have a business to run, with or without you. You're a good kid and I like you, but you're being a bit of a bitch right now. Just remember one thing. It's not my fucking fault! You got that?"

"Yeah. I'm gonna go."

"That's probably for the better. Want me to dial an Uber?"

"No."

"OK then. I'll give you a couple days to get your shit together. I'm not going to contact you. If you want to keep working for me then reach out. I'm not going to chase you around. I'd like to keep you on, but it's up to you. Take it easy."

Jim showed Gordon the door and he was on his way. He thought that this could be the last time he saw the poor bastard, but fuck it. Work was work, and in actuality he could save a few bucks by doing the grunt work himself.

Something was really bothering this kid though. He didn't think it was the fact that his grandmother was in bad shape. When he talked about her he may have been referring to a coat-rack for all the emotion he showed. It had to be his Mom. Looked like she was bearing the brunt of this. He should reach out to her, but now wasn't the time. Let things settle. From the sound of things, it seemed like granny had the means where she could easily afford home health aides, but people were particular. Maybe she demanded her daughter take the reins. From what he knew she certainly had the influence over her to do so. Who the fuck knew. *You know who might know?* Good 'ol Uncle Norm. Another trip to Bayonne may be in order. A trip he was most decidedly not look forward to. Put it on the back burner. Wait a couple days. See if Gordon calmed down enough so shit could get back to normal.

A week went by and he never heard from Gordon. Against his better judgment, he reached out to him via text.

"Dude, you good?"

Twenty minutes went by before a response.

"I'm OK, thanks."

"Cool. What's the deal? You still want to work for me?"

"I don't know for sure. I'm taking three classes and I have to take care of the house while my Mom's gone."

Oh fuck this.

"Just give me a call when you get the chance. I'll work with you."

"OK. I'll call later."

Over dinner he brought up the topic with Lee.

"I don't know what to do with this kid. He just completely bailed on me. I know that he's going through some shit, but come on."

"You know you're a jerk, right?"

"What? Me? No way!"

"Jim you idiot. He's going through a rough time and has no one to lean on. He's lashing out at you because he's in a bad place. At least that's what I think. His world is shit right now. Let him settle down. He'll come around. You just can't put any more pressure on him."

"I get it."

"He needs a little space."

"I get it."

"It's just......"

"OK, I GET IT! Holy shit honey! Stop!"

"He needs...."

"What the fuck Lee? I said I get it. You made your point, loud and clear. Do you have to hammer your point home anymore? Christ!"

"I'm just saying..."

"Oh holy fuck. Check please!"

"You know what? I'm not going to say anything anymore when you ask."

"I'd appreciate that. I asked your opinion on something. You gave it, and it helped. You just kept hammering the same point home after I said you were right. Can you stop? I mean, what the fuck? I get it. Please stop. I'm begging you."

"OK. So what are you going to do?"

"I'm gonna let it sit for a couple days. See how things go. Unless things ramp up and a really need him. If he begs off, I'm going to have no choice but to hire someone else. Another young mind to mold in my image. Someone to mentor. A new Padawan, so to speak."

"What?"

"A Padawan."

"It's from Star Wars. Oh Christ, why am I even telling you? You've never even seen the movie. I forgot who I was talking to. You have to get your nerd on every once in a while."

"You never got your nerd off."

"Come on. You have to try it sometime. It's fun. Losing yourself in the nerd. It's quite refreshing."

"I'm good with my literature, thank you."

Jim knew his next words would probably get him banished to the couch for the night, but five glasses of wine usually tends to loosen the lips.

"Your novels are not literature. Beach and in-transit reading, sure. But not exactly works of art."

"Oh, and you read the classics?"

"I've read many of them, yes. You've seen my books."

"I see that you never read them."

"I've read them….most of them. I just like to keep 'em around. They look good. I might read them again sometime."

"OK, right."

He could sense this going to another level, so it was time to pull back. This would be another pointless argument that would only lead to a night on his couch, which would suck. He saw the server come near the table with the bill.

"Thank you. So what do you want to do this weekend/"

Lee knew what he was trying to do and dialed it back as well. It was a positive sign. Stand down and start over. If you didn't it just meant a protracted shouting match where feelings got hurt. Nothing good could come from it going the other way.

"I don't know. Are you working at the bar?"

"Not that I know of. I would have heard by now. If there's nothing going on and he asks I'm not going to sneeze at it."

"Let's do a bike ride. Go somewhere."

"You mean like a trip around Liberty State Park followed by Sangrias at the Liberty House?"

"Yeah, something like that."

"Works for me. You ready to go?"

Lee drained the last of her glass of Pino Grigio. "Yeah."

It was a nice walk him in relative silence. Could have gone either way there for a moment, but cooler heads prevailed. Go home, have a nightcap, and hit the hay.

It was another couple of days before he heard back from Gordon.

"Hi Jim. Sorry I didn't get back to you. Things were a bit crazy."

"That's cool. How you doing?"

"OK I guess."

"How's your Grandmother?"

"Same. She's going to need constant care from now on."

"Well that sucks."

"Yeah. The worst part is that she wants my Mom to do it."

"Really? She has a life up here. She has you and your sister."

"I know. She wanted my Mom to move down there with us, but she said no. They compromised so she doesn't have to. She'll go down a couple of days a week and the rest of the time she'll be taken care of home health aides."

"Good for her, and you. What about your Uncle?"

"He shows up every now and then. He mostly goes straight to the attic. He says he's looking for some old pictures. We don't talk too much. Which is fine by me."

"Probably for the better."

"Yeah."

"So what's the deal? You coming back to work?"

"I have classes in the morning Monday through Thursday, but I'll be available in the afternoon. Friday I'm off."

"All I need is about ten to fifteen hours a week. You can do it when you get around to it, but I will be needing it to get done. Think you can handle it? If you can't I understand."

"No, I can do it."

"Ok, great. You free later today? Feel like grabbing a burger?"

"Thanks, but I can't. I'll reach out later about getting back to work."

"Ok, great. Later."

So with that all was good in the universe. At least for the time being. Gordon was back in the fold and that was good.

The next few weeks were uneventful. After Labor Day things really started to amp up work wise. He even got a few Nanny checks. It was a decent revenue source courtesy the local Indian community. Lot's of word of mouth work on these. That revenue stream was quiet for a year or two. He guessed that they were getting busy with the next round of kids, but it didn't matter. As long as the money was coming in.

The matter of Gordon's family seemed to settle down. He still bristled when the subject came up, so Jim just let it go. The issue with his uncle was still simmering on the back burner, but just our of curiosity's sake, a trip back to Bayonne was still on the table.

One late September morning Jim was greeted in the morning by an email from one of his old clients. It was a building management company that hired him to do some penetration audits in their apartment buildings. A solid Job and they paid on time from what he could recall.

The job required entering the buildings at various parts of the day to see if the front desk people were doing their job. You were given a letter that you were to tape to a designated apartment on the top floor of the building. The letter basically stated that you were there on official business and you got through. Most of the time you were stopped at the door, but there were some times that he made it to the top. He felt pretty bad because it usually meant that someone would most likely lose their job, but he realized that maybe they weren't that good at it in the first place.

It was a great gig. Got to spend a couple weeks sneaking into buildings and monitoring the results. It was hourly too, which was gravy. Even for what he was paying the kid, this would turn out to be a solid job.

This would be the perfect fit for Gordon. It was almost unfair.

Jim forsook the text and reached out to him directly. He picked up on the second ring.

"Hi Jim. What's up?"

"Hey dude, how are you fixed this weekend? I have a special job for us. No heavy lifting."

"I think I'm kinda busy this weekend. I think I...."

"I can pay you $20 per hour. How's that sound?"

"I'm not too busy. What's up?"

"I thought that would get your attention. Meet me at Exchange Place Saturday morning, say ten?"

"OK. No problem."

"Great. Meet me at the Katyn monument."

"The what?"

"The statue of the guy with the bayonet in the back."

"What?"

"You know that big statue? The one with the guy with the rifle coming out of his back?"

"Oh yeah. The army guy statue. I know that!"

"Yeah, the army guy statue. Meet me there at 12."

"Ok. What should I wear?"

"Casual but not sloppy. Khakis and a collared shirt will do."

"What will we be doing?"

"I'll fill you in when we meet up. It's easy work. No surveillance or anything. Actually I think you might find it fun."

"Ok. I'll see you then. See you later."

"Later dude."

Later at the bar, Jim was going to tell Doug about the new job, but he thought the better of it. Even though he knew pretty much everyone in the immediate vicinity, he didn't want anyone to overhear about the new job. Who knows, it could be a worker or a friend of a worker at one of the locations. Didn't want anyone tipped off.

Problem was that there was not much to talk about at the moment. The Mets and Phillies were both playing out the string before their respective seasons drew to a merciful conclusion. Doug didn't talk football. It was only the Mets for him. Everything else be damned. While Jim had a hard time grasping that, he had to respect it.

Sports were a year-round thing for him. Spring begat the Phillies, which lately would take him through at least July, by which time they would be firmly entrenched in mediocrity. July meant the beginning of Eagles training camp and eventually the football season, which would take him to hopefully January. Next up would be the Flyers, which would bring him back to spring. It was the never-ending cycle of futility. Such is the life of a Philly fan.

Saturday was one of those great late September days that were a harbinger of Fall. Low 60's, a little chill in the air. He opened up the closet for the first time since early April and saw his favorite leather jacket. Soon, my pet. He grabbed a windbreaker and was headed out the door with the tools for the day. A letter stating their reason for trying to bypass security, some scotch tape, and an envelope. Before leaving Jim thought it would be wise to make some extra copies of the letter and grab a few envelopes. He knew that Gordon would kill this one.

Jim walked down to Exchange place and got to the Katyn monument at 11:30. Gordon arrived ten minutes later and Jim filled him in.

"OK, here's the deal. There are a couple of condo units in the area that hired us to do security penetration audits."

"What's that?"

"Sneaking into buildings through the front door. They hired me to see if their front desk staff are on their toes. What you need to do is to walk into the building and head straight to the elevator. If you get stopped by the staff just turn around and leave. If you make it to the elevator hit the button to the top floor. Once you get there look for the closest security camera, acknowledge yourself, and tape this envelope under the call buttons on the elevator. Take a picture of the envelope and get out. There are a couple of buildings around here."

"That's it?"

"Pretty much, yeah."

'What if I get caught?"

"In the envelope is a letter explaining what you're doing. I'll be close by so if you need my help send me a text. I'll be right over. How about this. Type in HELP as a text to me, but only hit send in case shit gets weird. That way all you have to do is hit a button. Nothing bad is going to happen, trust me. Let's take a walk."

They shuffled down to Greene and York Street in front of the Iron Monkey bar. Jim pointed out the first stop. 99 Hudson Street.

"OK, here's the deal. Like I said. Don't try to be sneaky, just walk right in. If they turn you away, then they did their job. Wait a couple of minutes and try again. If you see a group walking in, try to piggy back in with them. Don't kill yourself though. I'm going to be in here."

"What are you going to do in there?"

"Drink beer and watch college football. What else would I be doing?"

"Got it."

"Great."

"Now, go get 'em young buck!"

Gordon went on his way and Jim walked into the Iron Monkey. It was a little after 12:00, so the college games have already started. It had been a while since he was in the joint, but he did recall that they had some really good beers on tap.

After perusing the taps his memory was confirmed.

"I'll have a draft of Franziskaner."

The bartender, a bubbly 20-something young blonde, easy on the eyes, nodded and went about her duties. Jim was pleasantly surprised when she presented the draft. Nice pilsener glass with about an inch and a half of head. Perfect.

"Do you want to see a menu?"

"No thanks, er sure."

Jim handed her his credit card, she responded by saying she didn't really need it as it wasn't busy.

"I get it, but I may have to split at any moment, so I just want to make sure you know I'm not running out on you."

"OK, thanks."

Jim scanned the tvs and settled into an SEC matchup, Florida playing Tennessee. Since Jim had no allegiance to any particular college team he could just sit back and enjoy the game.

20 minutes later Gordon came in.

"How'd it go?"

'OK, I guess. I made it to the top." Gordon showed Jim the picture of the envelope taped to the elevator, just as instructed.

"So what happened."

"I walked in, trying not to make any eye contact, and just walked over to the elevators like you said. The elevators there take a long time. That's why I was a little late."

"Totally cool man. So I have a couple others if you're up to it."

"OK, sure. This is fun!"

"Yeah, it is. I did the same in Manhattan a couple of years ago. Spent two weeks in the summer dicking around the city. Got to wear shorts, which was a big deal to me."

"Nice."

"Yes it was. Something like this doesn't come along too often, so when you get it you have to get right on it. It's a job like this that makes the grunt work of pre-employment investigations a little less tedious."

"I bet."

"So, you hungry? Want to grab a bite before the next job?"

"I think I'd rather just go right back out there."

"My man. Let's see here. Next up is 70 Greene Street, right down the block." Jim informed the bartender that he would be right back and walked him down the block."

"Ok, same drill. Take your time." Jim walked back to the bar.

"Will do."

Jim made it back to the bar and finished his beer.

"Another one?"

"Sure. I find it refreshing that you actually know how to pour one of these."

"They make it very clear to us as to how each beer needs to be pulled from the keg."

Pulled from the keg. Nice.

"It's a dying art form. Most people now, especially your age, either don't care of don't know how to do it."

"Thank you! My names Kelly!"

"Hello Kelly."

"Is that your son?"

"What? Him? Oh hell no! Wait, that came out bad. No. He just works for me. You caught me off-guard with that one. I can see why you asked."

"What do you guys do?"

"He's just delivering some letters on behalf of my client."

"What do you do?"

Ugh, the question. Time was that Jim would gladly answer that he was a private eye, but over the years he was worn down having to answer the same fucking question. "Oooh, to you spy on people?" *Not really (not in that sense anyway).* Do you carry a gun? *No (as far as you know).* It was better to provide a vague answer to that one.

"I have a due-diligence company. I do background checks and the like."

"Oh, cool." As much as she was easy to ogle, Jim was a little relieved when she turned away.

There was a time that Jim would have tried to flirt a little bit, but that was a long time ago. He was pretty good at it back in the day, but now he was just happy with some pleasant conversation. He had no delusions that this young woman would ever find him remotely attractive, and that was fine with him. The last time he noted someone had a remote interest in him he just grew tired of the back and forth and just left.

Jim glanced back and forth between the game, his phone, and the menu. Some bar food sounded pretty good right now. Better to wait for the kid to get back though.

He took time to relish the fact that here he was, sitting and sipping a nice Weiss beer, watching college football, and getting paid $55 per hour for it. Yessir, this certainly made up for all the grunt work, calling references and tracking down old employers.

Gordon came back again 15 minutes later.

"How'd this one go?"

"Not good. An older lady stopped me before I could get on the elevator. I left and did what you said. A group of people went in and I tried to mix in with them. I guess she had her eye out for me because she yelled over. I just left and came back. Sorry."

"Don't be sorry dude. You did a helluva job. Apparently, she also did her job well. Just take quick note as to what the lady looked like, the time you went over, and what you did. Better to write it down now before you forget the minor details."

Jim handed Gordon his little notepad that he always kept on him for instances such as this.

"Just jot the important stuff down. You want a soda or something?"

"No thanks. Do you have another one?"

"You want to get right back out there. I like that. Let's see."

The last one was Liberty Towers, two high rise condo units.

"OK, last one and that will be it."

Jim motioned to the bartender that he would be right back, which was met with a nod.

They walked down Greene Street to Liberty Towers.

"Ok, this last one is pretty large. It's two high-rises, but I think there's only one lobby. What I want you to do, after you try the front door, is to see if there's any alternate entrances. Looks to be a parking lot attached to the building. Try that."

"Ok, got it."

"You da man. After this meet me back at the bar for some snacks."

"Ok."

"Cool."

20 minutes later Gordon came back in.

"I was stopped at the door the first time. The second time I tried going in with an Asian family."

"I'm guessing that didn't work out to well."

"Not really."

"Oh well. Good job today man. You want some wings or something?"

"Sure."

Jim motioned for the bartender. "A couple orders of the house wings and a sarsaparilla for my partner."

"What?"

"A coke."

Gordon chimed in. "Actually, I'd like a rum and coke please."

As the bartender checked his ID Jim looked over at Gordon. "Rum and coke? You madman."

"Well, I don't have anything else to do today. I'll pay for it."

Jim recalled that he said he was tied up later today and was going to bring it up but thought the better of it. Hey, plans change. Leave it at that.

"No it's not." Jim motioned for the drinks to be on him.

Jim tilted his drink to Gordon's and they toasted the day.

"Good day today. Not even 2:00 and things are all wrapped up. What I am going to be needing from you are your notes."

Jim got out his notebook and transcribed the times, who was manning the desk, a description of the lobby, the weather, and how he made it up to the top. After a couple of minutes Jim was satisfied with the information and didn't even notice that Gordon drained his first drink and was well into his second.

The wings came shortly after and as Jim situated himself, he heard the unmistakable sound of another cocktail coming to its' end.

"I'd like another one please."

"Yo dude, slow it down a bit."

"It's ok." Gordon took his fresh one and stared intently at his wings.

Jim thought, *let it go.* This kid could use a few pops. These last few months were hard on him. He needed to blow off a little steam, and the good people at Bacardi were providing a release valve.

"Sorry man. Didn't mean that. You do what you do. Fuck it. Make it a double if you want.

They ate in relative silence and Gordon was true to his word. He slowed down on the rum and cokes, but they were already taking effect.

"So how you doing dude? You had a helluva month or two."

"This whole thing just sucks. My Mom's gone half the time and even though my sister is almost 18, I still have to stick around to make sure she doesn't run around."

"Does she?"

"No, that's the thing. She pretty much stays home and studies."

"Dude, that's not too bad."

"I know. It bothers me more than it should."

"I get it. Hey, if you don't mind me asking, how's your Mom?"

"She doesn't talk about it much. She's pissed at my uncle, who's not helping out. I mean, other than rummaging through my grandmothers' house."

"What's he looking for?"

"He won't say."

"I don't want to talk out of turn, but I think your uncle is a bad dude."

"Ya think?"

Jim didn't let on what he know about him, but he wanted Gordon to add another layer to what he already knew.

"This guy never helped us out at all. Not even once when my Dad left."

Gordon drained his drink and Jim motioned to the bartender to back him up. He was getting closer, it was just a matter of leveraging the dosage. Too much and he would have to pour him into an Uber. To little and he would clam up. Jim's years of being on both sides of the bar told him that he was getting close to the zone in between.

"That sucks. What does your grandmother think of him?"

"He's such a suck-up to her that he can do no wrong in her eyes. That's what pisses me off. My mother is probably one of the few people that ever stood up to her At least she tried to anyway. My uncle just kissed her ass. Now when she needs help the most, she ends up doing the right thing while my uncle rummages around the house. It's not fair."

"I'll say. I'd like to throw out an adage like, what goes around comes around, but that's horseshit. One of the things my father used to say was that 'as long as you can lay your head on your pillow at the end of the night knowing you did the right thing, then you've done well.'

"He said that?"

"I don't know. Probably not. He said a lot of things."

"My Uncle keeps on asking me questions like if I ever got laid. He wanted to take me to strip clubs. Said 'He'd take care of it.'"

"Figures. Did you go?"

"I went once. He didn't give me much of a choice. Just picked me up one day and said we were going for a ride. Took us to some place in Union. I didn't like it."

"Strip clubs are some of the most depressing places. Look into the eyes of the customers and the dancers. They're dead inside."

"Why do they go?"

"I don't know. Don't get me wrong though. When I was your age, I thought they were the best. Went there many times with friends. It got tired real fast. I liked going to placed where you actually met women that you might have a chance with. Throwing someone a $20 for a three-minute lap dance is just sad. If you ever go there again, just look around the bar. A bunch of 40-60 something men with a stiff drink and a pile of ones in front of them. Pathetic."

"He offered to take me to a prostitute, but I just told him to take me home."

Christ, fuck this guy.

"Of course he did. I don't want to speak out of turn about your family, but your uncle is a douchebag."

"Oh, no argument here!" Gordon motioned over to the bartender for another one. She came back with a fresh one and placed it in front of him."

"Thanks"

"You're welcome sweety." She winked and sauntered back to the other end of the bar, adding a little extra ass-shake on her way. If Jim was religious, he would thank the lord for bestowing the gift of yoga pants unto the world.

"You see that?"

"Yeah, she's pretty."

"I think that's an understatement. You see her………..…, wait what were we talking about?"

"Not sure, I forgot."

"I think it was your douchebag of an Uncle."

"Oh yeah, right."

"So tell me something, was he in the picture after the whole thing with your father went down?"

"Why?"

"I don't know, just curious."

"Well, it was pretty crazy then, but I do remember him stopping by a few times. I remember that he told me that he would be stepping in for my Dad, but he never did. He stopped coming by altogether, which was fine by me."

"Yeah, I get you. Can I ask you something? If you don't mind me asking, did your father ever try to contact you?"

"No. Not at all."

"You ever try to reach out to him?"

"Kinda. Every time I brought it up though Mom shut it down. I asked my Grandmother once and she freaked out on me. Said we were all better off without him."

"That's kind of fucked up. Who the hell is she to tell a kid that he couldn't look up his old-man? Well, you're a big boy now. Do whatever you feel is right for you."

"Thanks."

They sat in silence for a couple more and watched the early football games unfold. Neither of them had much interest as their minds were on something else.

Gordon was noticeably fired up after a while and let loose.

"You know what? I'm going to find him. I don't care what my Mom says. And my Uncle can go fuck himself."

"Be careful what you wish for dude."

"I need answers!"

"Yes you do. Just tread lightly is all I'm saying."

Jim looked at Gordon and noted that while he was good and stewed, he was nowhere near the point of blackout.

"I get it."

"OK, good. If it's anyone that deserves to have some questions answered it's you. I got your back."

"Ok, cool. We'll put a plan together and set it in motion. Maybe a little trip to see our guy in Pennsylvania too. See what he's up to."

"OK, but no costumes though."

"OK, got it."

They sat in silence for another round when Jim heard the bar door open behind him. Not two seconds later he heard a familiar voice "How about them Eagles? They doing it this year or what?"

Christ, it was Mick, a local loudmouth who while harmless, never met a conversation he didn't immediately jump into. He also had the unfortunate penchant for injecting any current movie cliché he could think of at any given moment. He was incapable or original thought and made up for it with other people's quotes. Thank God he didn't know him during the Austin Powers years.

"Hey Mick, what's going on?"

"You must me psyched, huh?"

"Yeah, the Eagles are off to a good start!"

"Just wait until they have to play someone good."

"OK, sure." Mick was a Giants fan and never let Jim forget that the Eagles had never won the Superbowl while the Giants had won four. It was like some form of personal accomplishment for the guy. Like he actually had a hand in it, other than sitting his fat-ass on a bar stool and chugging Coors Lite.

"Who do you like today? I put a hundred down on Alabama giving 25."

"I don't bet the games." Gambling was one vice that passed Jim by. Years of living in Atlantic City had cemented that. What he did enjoy, however, was watching people who did bet on the games losing their shit on a last second field goal or a botched extra point.

"What brings you down to this neck of the woods, Mick? I thought you were a Healy's loyalist."

"I'm meeting Steve here, then we're going to make our way back up the hill."

Shit. Steve. He should have known. Steve was a good guy, but whenever you saw him it always boiled down to dueling shots of Jameson. He would buy a round, then you would be obliged to get another one. It was a duel that Jim was up to the task for most times, but this was a Saturday afternoon. Maybe he'd go easy this time.

"Steve, huh?"

"Yeah. He had something going on so he asked me to meet him."

"That's cool. Who's the kid?"

"This is Gordon. He works for me. Gordon, this is Mick, a local legend."

"Nice to meet you."

Kelly greeted Mick when he pointed to us and did a quasi-wave, which was a signal to back them up. Jim thought that this could get ugly. He hadn't even spoke to his wife about tonight's plan, which may be in serious jeopardy.

"Thanks Mick." Jim raised his glass and tilted towards him.

"No problem, fly Eagles fly, amirite?"

"Right again."

There was only one option. Even though the bar stools were feeling like he could sit for another four hours it was time to make a move.

"We gotta split after this one."

"Why? I was just starting to feel pretty good."

"I get it. We don't have to call it a day, we just have to leave this place. You have to trust me on this one."

"Ok."

Jim and Gordon drained their drinks and asked for the check. He instructed Kelly to back up Mick and gave her his card.

"Where you going? I just got here."

"Sorry Mick, but I gotta split. I have to meet up with the wife soon and if I sit down with you and Steve for any significant amount of time, I'll be a mess. I'm halfway there right now, but at least I think I can fake it a little bit. Next time."

"OK, take it easy."

As they were putting on their jackets to leave Steve walked in.

"Hey Jim, where do you think you're going?"

"Hey Steve, how are you?"

"Good, why are you leaving. I just got here."

"I gotta meet with the Mrs." Jim would have added the 'you know what I mean,' but they didn't. Most of these guys were lifelong bachelors and would remain so for obvious reasons.

"You're not leaving before we do a shooter of Jamo!"

Christ.

"Hey, sweetheart. Three shots of Jamo. This kid with you?"

'Yeah."

"Make it four shots."

"No, I think he's good."

"You want a shot kid?"

"Um, sure. I guess."

Oh, this was not going to end well. Kid had about six rum and cokes and he's going to top it off with whiskey? Fuckin A. He wasn't going to stop him though. He was a big boy.

What the bartender failed to hear in the initial greeting was the word 'shot' because she was pouring them all two fingers of Jameson in a rocks glass.

Each glass was placed in front of them and Jim raised his and took a sip. He turned to look to see that Gordon had drained his in one gulp. This was going to be messy in a couple of minutes. Jim hesitated before emptying his glass and getting out of there.

"Thanks Steve, I'll catch you next time, but we really have to go."

"Ok man. Take care. Best to Lee."

"Thanks man. Take it easy boys!"

And with that they left. A good walk would do them both good. Jim had to monitor Gordon because the next 15 minutes would be crucial to see if he could keep the toxic stew brewing in his belly down.

"You know, I feel pretty good! I know I shouldn't but that shot of whiskey made me feel all warm inside."

"That's what it does, but be careful. How you feeling? Queasy at all?"

"Nope. I'm pretty good.

"Cool."

They walked in silence for a couple of blocks before Jim was sure that Gordon wasn't going to yak.

"So how come you never moved to the suburbs and had kids and stuff?"

"I don't know. I guess I had the chance once or twice, but I torpedoed it. Not sure if I did it consciously or not. Maybe I wasn't done yet. Sometimes it doesn't work out. Can't complain though. I'm pretty happy here. Lucky to have married a great woman, have a nice place to live, I'm in relatively good health. Now that I look at it I think I'm better suited for city life. Not sure the burbs would have worked out for me. PTA meetings, homeowner associations, car pooling, Applebees...fucking gender reveal parties. Holy hell.

That shit is all well and good, but it wasn't for me. Gossiping about neighbors and mowing lawns? I don't think that I'm cut out for that. Maybe if I got married earlier that would be me, but not now. I can't complain. City life has agreed with me."

"Yeah. I think you're right. I don't think I could do it either."

"So you think it's up to you?"

"Isn't it?"

"That's funny."

"How do you like being married?"

"Being married is pretty cool I guess, but you have to deal with some shit, on both sides. Believe me, she has to put up with my epic bullshit and I'll never be able to thank her enough for it, but damn, you just never fucking know how she's going to handle things. I could blow off our anniversary to hang out with some old college buddies and it would be no big deal, but I leave a spoon in the sink and I won't hear the end of it for a month. Go figure."

"That's weird. You want to get another drink?"

"I think it's about ants. She hates ants. What?"

"Another drink."

"What the hell! I'm already up shits creek with the Mrs., so I better make it count."

They were in the vicinity of Jersey City's best dive bar, the Golden Cicada. Lee absolutely hated the place, which was perfect because she would never look there. The trouble was that it was most likely closed. You couldn't tell until you got there. The place was a bunker.

"I know a place close by."

Walking down Grand Street to their destination they passed the best dive bar in Jersey City, the Golden Cicada.

"Oh man. Check the door. See if that place is open!"

"This place is a bar? Looks like a Chinese restaurant. And a shitty one at that."

"Exactly."

'Door won't budge."

"That's what I thought. I was hoping to get you in there, for at least one. That place is a spectacular dive. Really amps up at night with the hipsters. My wife absolutely hates the place, so I like to go there on occasion."

Jim told the story of when he first moved to Jersey City. Lee went away for the weekend, leaving him to his own devices. He wandered around downtown for a bit and poked his head in the place.

An older Asian man was sitting at the bar by himself. "Hi! You're just in time! Come on in."

"In time for what?"

"Patton!"

Jim looked at the screen and saw that the movie had just started. He sat there for the next three hours with the owner, Terry, knocking back beers and some whiskey talking about WWII with a complete stranger. Couldn't have been a better night. After the movie Terry rummaged through the back before bringing out the karaoke equipment.

"You want in? I have every song!"

Jim thanked him but declined. He came to the realization that he was going to like it in Jersey City on his short stumble home that night. No way Lee would have put up with that place for more than ten minutes.

It was a good weekend.

A block away from Zepp Hall he got a call from Lee and realized he never responded to her texts. If he answered it he knew there would be some yelling, but if he didn't answer it, well. Boy howdy.

"Hey hon, what's up?"

"Where are you."

"I'm with Gordon. We just finished up for the day and we had couple of beers to celebrate a job well done."

"You said that you would be done at two o'clock."

Correction. He told her he would be done at one, but he'll take it.

"OK. I just stepped out of the shower. Meet me at PJs in 20."

"OK."

Jim hung up the phone and looked at Gordon.

"I have time for a quick one but then I gotta split."

"You know what? I think I'm good. I should go home."

"The whiskey hit you, didn't it?"

"I don't know. I don't feel too great."

"You gonna yak?"

"I don't think so, but I think I should go lie down."

Jim started to dial up an Uber for the kid, but he declined.

"I got this one."

"You sure?"

"Yeah. It's only like, nine bucks."

Jim thought of the $250 cleaning charge for someone chundering in their ride.

"OK dude. Sure you're good? You get carsick."

"Never have."

"Cool. Just send me a text to know you made it back ok. Good with that?"

"Yeah."

The Uber showed up two minutes later and he was on his way.

Jim then set upon heading to PJs.

The Saturday afternoon crowd was different from the other days, but Joe and Michi were there, which was always a welcome sight. Before Jim sat down his drink was already in front of him. He was going to just have a beer, but he wasn't quick enough. A couple of glasses of wine would put him on the floor, and it was still light out. Oh well.

"Hey Jim. What's up?"

"Nothing. Just did a job today and brought along my protégé. This kid is something. He looks like a dud, but there's something in there. A diamond in the rough, if you will."

"Is that the little chubby kid I saw you with here?"

"The very same. Good kid. His family is a bit fucked up, but whose isn't?"

"How so?"

Jim went on and gave an intro course into what he knew. While talking he looked down the bar to see who was there on the slight offhand chance that uncle dickhead wasn't there. The odds were slim to none, but you never knew.

"Oh man, that sucks. Poor kid."

"Yeah, and for the first time in my life I think it's something I can really help out with. I'm walking the tightrope over whether it's none of my fucking business or this kid deserves to know the truth."

"Tough decision."

"I'm struggling. I mean, I know I'm going to end up in the middle of this whole shitstorm, and there's a good chance I could get my ass kicked. Actually, there's a very good chance I could get my ass kicked, but fuck it. I know that I'm right. Besides, chicks dig scars, right?"

Michelle rolled her eyes. "Depends on who it is and the type of scar."

"The thing is, I have a sneaking suspicion that deep down everyone kinda knows the truth. I think that the grandmother has such a fear stranglehold on the family that they don't dare to speak up. I'm gonna have to be the one."

"You need any help let me know."

"Thanks Joe, but I think I have to go this one alone. Besides, there's no way I can pay you anything, seeing that I'm not getting paid for anything."

"I don't need anything like that. If I can help you out give a shout."

"Well that sounds better."

Here was a guy who Jim knew for less than four years and he was willing to just jump right in to the fire for him. Now that's a friend.

"I have to think about how to do this."

A minute later Jim got a text from Gordon. "I'm home. Thanks for today."

"OK, cool. Talk later. You're a good kid, don't let anyone tell you different. P.S. You're Uncle is a douchebag."

"Who are you texting?"

Jim turned around to see Lee as she was taking her rightful seat next to him.

"Just some broad I met earlier today. We were making out for a little bit, but she had to leave because her husband was returning from deployment later today. I guess it wasn't meant to be."

"Funny."

"No, it was my protégé. We went out for a couple earlier today and he got lit up. Just wanted to make sure he got home OK."

"Looks like he wasn't the only one who got lit up."

"Me? I'm OK, I guess." He had been drinking steadily for the last four to five hours, but he felt pretty good. Just stick to beers for a while and he would be cool.

And with that the bartender refilled his wine glass without him asking.

"So what are we doing tonight?"

"To tell you the truth, it will be an early night if I have a couple more glasses of wine."

"How much did you have?"

"About five or so Weiss beers and two glass of wine here.... Oh, and a giant shot of Jameson. It was thrust upon me and I had no recourse but to have it. Would have been bad form if I didn't! Joe knows, right?"

"Don't get me involved in this one."

"Michelle?"

"Nope!"

"Of well. Look, I'll be fine. We ate some food as well so it'll be good."

"Why did you go out in the first place?"

"Look. I'm not going to get into it too much, but let me just say that Gordon wanted a couple drinks and blow off some steam. It was the first time I saw him drink alcohol. He normally just has diet cokes, but today he was all about the rum. Here, I'll show you."
Jim rummaged through his pocked for the receipt and was about to present the evidence for the defense when she relented.

"OK, fine."

Jim loved his wife, but every time he stepped out without her, she acted like he was going to Vegas for the weekend.

"How did it go today?"

"Great. He performed well above expectations. Everything I hoped it would be."

Michelle asked if that was a good thing or not.

"He's perfect for the job. He could walk by you ten times and you would never notice. So what are you guys up to tonight. You're out a bit early."

Michelle responded that they were going to a birthday party and were pre-gaming it at the bar.

"Good idea."

"I know. We're probably not going to stay there late."

"No, we're not. We're going to go there, get something to eat, hang out, and get the fuck out of there as soon as possible" said Joe as he returned to address his bourbon.

"You guys have a sign? Like touching your nose or something?"

"No. I just say, let's get the fuck out of here! You can stay if you want, but I've had it with dese blowjobs."

"That works."

"I get it. That being said, I'm sure you'll be there late. That's the way it works with these things. Look forward to a party and you'll be back at the bar by 9. Go to one grudgingly and you'll stay all night."

"Not tonight."

Jim turned to Lee and asked her what she wanted to eat, thus beginning the dance.

"I don't care. Where do you want to go?"

"How about a burger?"

"No."

"Italian?"

"No, I don't really want Italian. We had it like three days ago."

"I'm not feeling up for Saigon tonight."

"Me either."

"So where do you want to go?"

"I don't care. Whatever you want is fine with me."

And the dance went on. After some wrangling Lee decided that maybe she wouldn't mind a burger after all, so Left Bank after all.

Jim asked the bartender to keep the tab open as they would be back after dinner. It was easier that way. They said their goodbyes and as they were leaving through the front he noticed Steve and Mick come in from the side door.

Meeting averted for the moment, although it would be inevitable that their paths would cross again. And with that, another round to be had. It was inevitable

It was still relatively early so there was no problem getting a seat.

"So. How'd it go today?"

"I told you. It went swimmingly."

"No, I mean with your assistant."

"His name is Gordon."

"Fine. Gordon."

"Good, I guess. He really needed to get some stuff off his chest. He was pounding the rum and cokes. When he hopped into the Uber, he said he was grateful and that he needed that." It was a slight embellishment, but it wasn't a complete fabrication.

"I'm just torn on what to do. I think if I could jus get some decent intelligence I could really get somewhere."

"I think you've done enough. Remember, you're not getting paid for this."

"I know, I know. But this is the right thing to do. Don't you at least agree with that?"
"Yeah. Just don't stick your neck out too much."

He agreed and made a note not to mention this to her again if he could help it.
By the time the fried pickles came Jim was starting to slide. He knew he was on the downside of today's

bender and it all hit at once. All he had to do was keep it together through dinner and they could call it a night. He stared at his hall-full glass of Malbec with contempt before taking a gulp. Oh well, this is how it's going to be.

It wasn't like he found himself in that position before, far from it. It was just that they were getting further in between now that he had gotten up in age.

"You know, you should consider yourself fortunate that you married a humanitarian like me."

"Oh, really?"

"Yeah. And another thing. This kid will not be referred to as 'my assistant' from henceforth. His name is Gorgon…No wait. His name if Gordon. And don't forget it!"

"Why not? You already did." She glanced at him and saw the signs that he was beginning to fade. Not that it mattered in the least to her. She was just starting out, and that meant that Jim was going to be along for the ride. Even if he would need a car seat and a sippy-cup.

By the time they were finished their burgers and paid the check Jim was on cruise control. Normally, in this state, Jim would just opt to head home and call it a night. But not tonight.

"Let's take a look to see who's at PJs. If there's no one there we'll head home, OK?"

"OK. You good?"

"I guess."

"You're fine. Don't be such a wuss. Besides, you started this by going out drinking at noon."

"I guess that's my punishment? That doesn't seem fair."

"Well, we're going anyway."

"I guess we have to go since we have a tab still open."

"That too."

"They popped their heads in and saw all the familiar faces; Mike and Liz, big Joe, and his boy Doug. That settled it."

'Hey guys. What's up?"

Lee went over to talk to Liz while Jim sidled next to Doug.

"Hey man, what's up?"

"Nothing, you?"

"I'm pretty tuned up. Been out since about noon. Had a job earlier today and I ended up having a few with my assistant. Seems to have snowballed from there."

"You seem fine."

"Well thank you then. You have any trips coming up?"

"Yeah, Hawaii…..again."

"It must be tough being you."

"You going to the Gilligan's Island dock again?"

"Yep. I'll send you a pic. Hey Mike! What's going on? How ya doing Joe?"

"Hey Jim."

"Hey Jim."

"Mike motioned Jim over "I may have something for you."

Jim sidled over to Mike and leaned in. "What's up?"

"I remember you asked me if I knew anyone from the Sheriff's Department that I might know. Didn't think of him at the time, but I do know a guy."

"Mike, you know everyone."

"I guess. I went on a couple golf outings with this guy, Mike Jenkins. He's retired from the Sheriff and has his own contracting company."

Mike peered into his phone while Jim pulled out his notebook.

"Here it is. No, it's not a contracting firm, it's a landscaping company. Here's his number."

"So this guy knows you? Can I throw your name in so I can get him to talk to me?"

"Sure. I paid for his round the last outing."

"OK, cool. Thanks."

"Do you know if this guy hangs out anywhere?"

"Not sure. I know he lives around here, but I've never seen him around."

"OK. Can't hurt. Thanks man. I owe you."

"You can pay me with a Jameson."

Ugh. "You mean like, now?"

"Sure."

"OK, what the hell." Jim motioned for two Jameson, which were promptly poured. As Jim was raising his shot glass, he met Lee's unapproving stare. Fuck it. Too late. Besides, they were on the down turn of the night anyway. Even though it was still relatively early, he wasn't much long before packing it in."

"Thanks Mike. Appreciate it."

Jim then went back to his seat next to Doug and it was back to the usual talk.

20 minutes later and Jim had felt like he had said all he was going to say for the day and he wanted out. As he was asking for the check Michelle and Joe

came walking back in, which meant that bedtime would be delayed.

As they settled into some silence Jim fumbled for his phone and did a reverse search on the phone number for the lead.

MJ Contracting, LLC. 133 Bright Street, Jersey City, NJ. Not too far away at all. Maybe it was worth a shot, but then again, maybe it was best that he keep this at a minimum. Ask too many people questions and it's only a matter of time before shit gets out of hand. Best to put it on the back burner.

Doug asked how business was going.

"Not too bad, but to tell you the truth, I'm getting tired of it. When I started this thing up it was the understanding that if things weren't going as planned I'd go back to the workforce in a couple of years. Well, it's been over seven years now. Sometimes it's real good, but sometimes it sucks. The good part is that I'm my own boss. The bad part is that sometimes my boss is a fucking idiot."

"Ha, I get it!"

Jim and Doug set about commiserating about the stooges and didn't even notice his friends walked back in the bar until he saw a shotglass of Jameson pushed under his nose.

"Oh No! Well, OK." Jim looked up to see Michelle and Joe waving at him. They also had shots in front of them."

"You guys trying to kill me?"

"Sure, why not?"

"Just make it as painless as possible, that's all I ask."

"No promises."

Jim raised his glass, downed it and exclaimed "Nighty night!"

The rest of the evening faded into an oblivion of laughs and bar banter before Lee had finally had enough to call it a night.

They talked on their way home, but nothing of consequence as far as could be remembered.

Jim opened his eyes the next morning and immediately regretted it.

"You're awake. It's about time."

Jim looked at the clock and saw it was 8:30. Time was he could have slept til noon on a Sunday. Not anymore. He rolled around in bed for ten minutes and contemplated drifting back to sleep, but the overwhelming urge to empty his bladder won they day.

Upon exiting the bathroom Jim noted that his notebook was on the kitchen island. He must have jotted something down, but at the moment he had no recollection of what it could be. It must have been important that he left it out.

Jim leafed through the book and found the page:

Future Jim
Moe—didn't do it
talk to Dad
Lancaster tapes
Go B ids!

Lee asked what he was looking at.

"Not entirely sure. Maybe you can help. What was I talking about last night."

"You and Doug were talking about the Three Stooges."

"That explains Moe. Anything else?"

"You were talking about something about rare footage. I don't know. Why, you don't?"

272

"No. I know exactly what I wrote."

"Yeah, right."

Jim grabbed his coffee and stepped outside on the front porch. Still a little warm, but not for much longer. Days like this are fleeting. He could see a nice bike ride in Liberty State Park......And he wanted to hear how good a time his wife had because he would be spending the afternoon in PJs because today was the Eagles-Giants game. No escaping that. Not that he wanted to anyway.

He thought of reaching out to Gordon but thought the better of it. Let him have a day with no contact. If Gordon chose to reach out, then fine.

Jim looked back at his cryptic writings from the night before to see if there was anything Saturday night Jim was trying to tell Sunday morning Jim. *Lancaster, cheese*? What the actual fuck? *Moe-didn't do it, talk to Dad.* He then remembered the gist of the conversation. It was the missing Moe film footage of him playing baseball with Honus Wagner. "Spring Fever," or something like that. The dad thing was explanatory, but would have to wait.

Monday came with a start at 6:30 sharp when Lee started her morning routine. He turned to look at his phone and to read todays sports page. It was always nice to head there first thing when the Eagles won, especially over the Giants, leaving them at 2-1. He even won a dollar from Richie on the winning field goal.

He never heard from Gordon, so a text would be in order, but that would be later.

"What do you have planned for today?"

"Work, and lots of it, hopefully."

"So you'll be busy?"

"I have work to do, but I hope more comes in, as always."

Jim worked himself out of bed, grabbed some coffee, and stepped outside to enjoy the morning sun. He brough the laptop outside and popped up the Philly news on the game, followed by the New York news on the game. Benigno and Roberts was going to be a good one today.

"Oh, you're enjoying this aren't you?"

"Yes, I'm quite enjoying it."

"You're just doing this despite me."

"What?"

"Since I'm a Giants fan."

274

"Oh please. You can't name three people on the Giants. Don't act like you're upset about the game. You don't give a shit."

"I'm kidding."

"Then make it funny. That's all I ask. Here's a hint, if you're making it a joke, have a punchline. That's how it works."

"I know how it works!"

"I don't think you do!"

"I'M FUNNY!"

"Listen, honey. You are a lot of things. Smart, beautiful, generous, and insanely tolerant of my bullshit. But funny is not on your list. You're at your funniest when you're not trying. Then you can be pretty good."

"But my Mo…"

"No, your mother doesn't count. My Mom thinks I'm the most handsome man in Jersey, but it doesn't make it so. Top 20, maybe."

"You're an asshole!"

"That I am honey. That I am."

Lee went back to the morning routine and Jim decided to start the day.

Another dozen or so checks came in at 10 and Jim forwarded them to Gordon. At 10:30 another nanny check came down the pike. Jim noted that it was a previous client, so no need for a retainer. An addendum at the end was a note asking to speak directly later this afternoon. No problem there.

Jim sent a follow-up text to Gordon and waited for a response. Fifteen minutes went by with no response, which was unusual, so he called him. Straight to voicemail. He would give it another half-hour before starting the work on his own. He checked the search database and saw that he hadn't logged on, so something was going on. This kid was usually automatic.

At 11:00 he got a call.

"Gordon, what's up?"

"Sorry, was tied up helping my Mom out. What's up?"

"No need to be sorry. Can you put in a few hours today?"

"I'm sorry, I can't. My Mom needs my help. We're going down to my Grandmothers."

"Ok, no worries. I got it. How'd you do on Saturday? Did I get you in any trouble?"

"What? No. I went home, ate some hot dogs, and went to bed."

"Atta boy! Go do your thing with Mom. I won't bother you with this. I'm not too busy so I can handle it. Just let me know if you'll be available later in the week."

"OK. We're moving my Grandma out of her house and into one of those homes."

"Oh, that sucks. Sorry to hear that. I've been there and I can tell you it is not fun."

"Definitely. I gotta go. I'll reach out later."

"OK dude."

After disconnecting Jim's thoughts turned to Uncle Norm. This guy would probably go into overdrive down there now that gramma was out of the way. A trip to Bayonne this week was suddenly on the table.

In the afternoon Jim got a call from Sal.

"You Sal, what's up?"

"Hey Jim, what's doin?"

"Just slugging it out over here in Jersey City. You?"

"Good, good. So, I got a job for you. It's kind of a rush. You got the time."

"Sure. I'm listening."

"Great. Remember that auction house we had as a client?"

"Yeah."

"So, they called me in a panic. Apparently, they misplaced one of their pieces and they need to get it back, like fast."

"I don't know what I could possible do to help, but I'll give it a shot."

"Apparently they gave it to some guy to restore and he disappeared. The owner of the painting wants it back, so I'm going to put them in touch with you. This could be a good payoff if you play it right."

"I get it."

"Now I want a cut of this."

"Ten percent of the net work?"

"Yeah, that works."

"OK. Shoot me over the information and I'll reach out."

Jim wrote down the contact info and called them immediately after. No answer, but he left a message. Jim thought that their desperation would be measured by how quickly they responded.

Two minutes later he got a return call.

"Hello James? This is Ted Page from Savoy Auctions."

"Hello Ted, I spoke with Sal and he gave me a quick rundown. Can you elaborate a bit?"

"Sure." Ted then went and explained how they turned over a Diego Garcia painting to a guy to restore. Apparently, he checked himself into a mental health facility shortly after and no one had heard from him since. The more he talked, the more Jim was sure he could be of immediate service."

"So, no one has been able to contact him in over a year. Now the owner is asking around. I can't tell you how important this is to us that we get this done as immediately as possible."

"I got it." Jim jotted down some numbers in his book and doubled them.

"So here's what I can do. I have access to systems that aren't available to the public. They have more information than you can get on line. What I want to do is start out with the person. What information do you have on him?"

"I have his name and last address."

"I think I can work with that. Do you have an age range for him? What about his old contact information?"

"He was about thirty-five when we conducted the transaction, and I do have his old number."

"OK, I can run with that. Here's what I propose. I'll start out by running him for any current addresses. I'll also look up any possible relatives and get their contact info. You said that he checked himself into a facility. I'm afraid that those records aren't available, even for me. It's a felony to run up that tree. But that's neither here nor there. If I can't find him I'll reach out to the relatives and forward your sense of urgency to them. Maybe they can provide some information if they can't find them. As soon as I get any information, I'll get it over to you and we'll come up with a proper plan."

"He's in the Los Angeles area. Do you have anyone out there? We would have to send someone by.....if you can find him."

"I do have someone out there." He *had* someone out there. Herb O'Keefe, a retired California State Police Officer. Nice guy, was usually ready at a moments notice, but that was about eight years ago. Regardless. He could get it covered. "So here's the deal. $350 for the locate report for him and his possible relatives, plus $200 per hour. Per person.

Four-hour minimum. If that's ok with you I'll send you an email so we can confirm. I won't ask for a retainer since you were a former client."

"That's fine." When can you start?"

"As soon as I hang up with you."

"OK. Send the email and I'll confirm your price before sending you over an email with all his information."

"Great. I'll send it right over."

Sweet. This was shaping to be a good day. Within three minutes of sending the email he got the response.

Rudolpho Torres-Soto (approximately 35 y/o in 2014), 220 Sierra Street, El Segundo, CA. Address last updated in June 2016. This was something to run on.

Jim input the info to the search engine and got a current address in Long Beach, with a land line and everything. This could be all the information he needed. Usually the land lines were dead-ends, but what the hell. It was registered to him, so it was worth a shot.

He picked it up on the second ring.

"Is this Rudolpho Torres-Soto?"

"Who is this?"

"Pardon. My name is James O'Neill. I'm a private investigator hired by Savoy Auction house to locate you regarding the Diego Rivera painting they loaned out to you a few years ago. Do I have the right person?"

"What was the name of the person from Savoy who hired you?"

"Ted Page."

"Ted...yeah, that's him. Yeah, I have the painting right here. I'm looking right at it. It's been ready to go for over a year. I would have reached out, but I went through a tough time. I don't want to talk about it."

"Sorry about that. Listen, it's none of my business what happened to you. Can I have Ted reach out to you directly at this number?"

"I guess."

"Is this a good number for you or would you prefer another?"

"This number is fine."

'Great. Rudolpho, glad to hear your doing better and expect to receive a call shortly."

"OK, thanks."

Holy shit. This was the quickest caper he's ever been involved in. 'Old Jim solved a missing classic art case in 15 minutes. Had to be a record. Now the conundrum begins. If he immediately called the client, they would start asking about why they were charged so much for something that took less than half an hour. But at the same time he knew that time was of the essence and things needed to be expedited as quickly as possible. He looked at the time. It was less than a half hour since he talked to Sal. Instead of reaching out to Ted first he decided to reach out to his contact in L.A. He called Herb and left a message. Herb and Jim worked in conjunction on several white-collar investigations and had developed a solid rapport. He was an easy-going guy, but knew how to turn on the cop when needed. It was amazing how easy your job could be when you weren't dealing with assholes.

Hal returned the call in five minutes because, well, that's how this day was going.

"Hey Jim! How you been? Didn't recognize the number, but I remembered the voice. What's up? You start up a new shop?"

"Yeah, I branched out on my own about five years ago. How's things? You still up and running? I may have some work for you. It's in Long Beach."

"Yeah, I'm good to go. You caught me at a good time. I'm headed up to my hunting cabin in Montana tomorrow."

Jim filled him in on the information and Herb said he could be out at the address within an hour.

"What are you charging these days?"

"$75, four-hour minimum. I won't charge for mileage."

"Great. I'll reach out within an hour regardless."

Jim hung up and did a bit of rejoicing. It wasn't often that you got a case like this, and it was even rarer that things could be buttoned up as timely as they were today.

He decided to have a quick lunch before reaching out. Right before he was about to enjoy a pickle, he was struck with the idea that if this guy may have still had Ted's contact number and if he called him first it would not look good. Fuck it.

"Hello, Ted."

"Jim. Didn't expect to hear back from you so soon."

Jim eyed the pickle on his plate. God, he wanted that pickle. Now it would have to sit there, beckoning him until he finished the call.

"Well, I have some good news. I found him!"

"That is good news indeed! Thank you."

"He said that he has the painting in his possession and is waiting your call. Now I have a guy ready to go out to his place. I was thinking he could go there and send you some pictures of the painting."

"That's great, but let me talk to him first."

"No problem. Just let me know when you can so we can get this wrapped up."

"Absolutely, no problem."

After downing the pickle Jim set about doing other work that was neglected. This was why he put a timeframe on these checks so he could give himself an extra day. He set upon running the checks when Ted called back.

"Jim. Hi!"

"Hi Ted. How'd it go?"

"Great. I would like to send your guy over just to make sure before I send a team out to collect the painting. I'll take care of the latter."

"OK. Do you have any special instructions?"

"Just tell your guy when he gets there that he is there to inspect Lot #7425. Rudolpho will know."

"Ok. No problem."

"I can believe you did this so fast. Can't thank you enough!"

"Yeah, well...." Jim leaned back in his chair and checked his fingernails "That's what I do. Glad to help."

Jim then reached out to Herb and gave the green light. He casually mentioned that going over the four-hour minimum would be no big deal.

"If traffic is a bitch, which I know it can be, then by all means don't rush things."

Herb knew what he was talking about and said he was on it.

"Great. Seeing that this is a one-shot deal, get me an invoice over ASAP. It begins and ends with this. Just give me a call when things are wrapped up."

"Will do."

"OK, man. Good luck."

Jim gave himself a couple of minutes for a victory strut. It wasn't often that a job like this comes around, and it's even rarer to wrap things up so neat and quick. A call to Sal was in order.

"Hey Jim, what's doin?"

He proceeded to fill him in on how the job went.

"If only something like that came down the pike more often."

"Yeah. I seriously doubt that this will ever happen again."

"You're right on that one. Did you deal directly with Ted?"

"Yeah."

"Good. We did a couple of jobs for him in the past and he would always add something out of gratitude if we did a good job. For something like this, it's all a matter of keeping it all out of the papers. If this had been leaked to the media their reputation would be ruined. One time they sent us a nice gift certificate for Peter Lugers."

"I'd take that. If they send one, I'm taking you with me."

"That's not necessary, take your wife."

Lee didn't really enjoy steak and Peter Lugers was not a place you took your wife for romantic Dinner. Peter Lugers was an old-school meat fest. Cranky 70 year-old waiters, giant slabs of dry aged porterhouse beef, creamed spinach, and hearty red wine. Sure there were women scattered about, but they didn't necessarily look happy. By the time you walked out of there you would have walked through the essence of a thousand cows.

"With all do respect Sal. It's the best steak I ever had, but it's not exactly a date-night place."

"OK. Good job. Let me know how things go. They pay pretty quick if I recall."

"That's always good to hear. Thanks Tone."

He saw it wasn't even 2:00 when he disconnected.

"This, is going to be a good week!" He thought as he tended do the days other tasks.

Work slowed to a trickle for most of the remainder of the week because the cosmic balance seemed to be shifting in Jim's direction. Karma looked down and said "Fuck this guy," because, well that's how it goes. No biggie. When things tipped in the other direction Karma also said, "Let's give this fucker a break, but not a big one. Just enough to get his hopes up. That's when the fun starts."

On Thursday he got a call from Gordon.

"What's going on dude?"

"Hey, sorry but I may be down here for a bit longer."

"It's cool. I really don't have much for you anyway. Things kind of dried up."

"OK."

"So what's the word? How's Mom? You're Uncle bothering you guys?"

"Mom's good. There's a lot of stuff here, so it's taking time. Uncle Norman comes down every other day in the afternoon for a couple of hours and storms through the place. It's better when he's not here."

"Is he down today?"

"No. He'll be down there tomorrow."

"OK. Hey man, best to your Mom. You get back when you get back. No worries up here."

"OK, thanks."

And with that Jim was left to his own devices. Everything was wrapped up, all the billing was out, and that was that. All by 3:00. He had some time to dick around, but a trip to Benny's would be in order later.

He hopped on the light rail and was on location within an hour. The local happy hour crowd had gathered and there was no room at the bar. Jim found a side table and ordered a bottle of Budweiser and some wings. No sign of Uncle Norm, but he was in no hurry. Jim tried to tune in on some of the conversation going on, but he couldn't focus on anyone in particular.

The bartender remembered him, which was fine. "You were here a couple weeks ago, weren't you? You were looking at places around here, right? Any luck?"

"Not really. I was looking at different neighborhoods rather than places."

"Well, you could do worse. It's a blue-collar neighborhood. Everyone looks after each other here." She placed the wings on the table and she returned to the bar.

Whenever people say that people around here look after each other it means "Everyone is going to get into your business." No thank you.

He took a bite of the first wing and was un-flattered with the lack of heat. He saw a bottle of tabasco behind the bar and stood up to ask for it. Right as he got her attention the door opened and in walked Norm.

"Norm!" everyone shouted as he scanned the bar for a seat. Jim could see that he was annoyed by this and he understood why. As long as everyone remembered 'Cheers' it was going to be a thing. Poor bastard.

Jim got the tabasco and retreated to his seat. Norm shoehorned in between two patrons he was familiar with and ordered a Mich Ultra. He ate his wings in silence and stared at his phone. It was a good thing that this guy was easily the loudest one in the bar. Made his job easier.

He made some small talk about the Giants blowing the game on Sunday, which made Jim smile. He would have to wait for this guy to settle in for a couple and let his lips loosen up a bit.

After he finished his wings and ordered another round from the bar Jim noticed an empty shot glass in front of Norm. Looking at the time he figured he had time for one more. Jim sat back down and buried his head in his phone, trying to keep his profile as low as possible.

As he was settling his check 20 minutes later, he started hearing some choice words. "Fucking bitch sister!" and "goofy fucking kids" were a couple of the lesser bon-mots strewn about, but nothing of substance. Jim decided that this exercise was horseshit. Even if he got any nugget of information, what would it be? What the hell was he thinking about going up to a complete stranger at this guys watering hole and start asking pointed questions? Oh well, there were other avenues.

When he got off the light rail at Marin Jim decided to take a right and do a waterfront walk. He called Lee and she agreed to meet in Paulus Hook. The Light Horse it was. He was still full from the wings, but he could fake it.

After dinner they walked along the promenade on their way home. The north side marina was half-empty, with most of the larger boats headed south to warmer waters for the winter. Lee suggested a stop-off at PJs, but Jim pulled a rare veto and stated that he would prefer if they just headed home, which she agreed to, which was odd for a Thursday.

Saturday morning he got the text from Gordon:

My Grandma died

Oh shit. It was over. Being disassociated gives an air of practicality on the matter. At least now they could move on. For all intents and purposes she was a horrible person. He was sure that there were a lot of people out there thinking the world would be a better place without her.

Oh man. Sorry dude. Tend to your Mom and sister. Give me a ring when you're ready. Don't worry about your job. Take as much time as you want.

OK. Thanks.

You need anything reach out.

Got it.

At least now there was no mystery about it anymore. Jim wondered how long it would take Uncle Norm to make a B-Line down to the house and tear it apart. Maybe he should go to pay a visit in Bayonne. He said he wasn't going to do it, but this was a game changer. Instead he reached out to his brother.

"Hey, what's up?"

"Nothing much. What are you doing for the game tomorrow?"

292

"Not sure. Haven't thought about it. It's a late game, so I'll probably stay local."

"Ok. Cool. Hey, that guy Jerry, the AOH guy."

"Yeah."

"When does he usually come in?"

"He's all over the place, but it's usually later in the week."

"Do me a favor. Next time he comes in, start him a tab under my name and give me a call and I'll be over there within the hour."

"OK. Any reason for this?"

"I need to talk to him about the kid who works for me. His grandmother kicked it this morning. Jerry seems to know all about her and I'd like to pick his brain a bit."

"OK, no problem. I have his number if you want it."

"No. That's cool."

"You have any shifts that need to be covered?"

"No. I'm good right now."

"OK. Cool."

They disconnected and Jim went back to his routine. October would be upon us before he knew it and time was getting near to shut the backyard down. Always a somber occasion, but necessary. Hopefully they could push it back until November.

Lee was tending to her rosebushes and Jim inspected his pepper and tomato plants. Another mediocre harvest. Next year he wouldn't half-ass it. Go big or go home. Jim recalled that he said the exact same thing in March. It was like when he was a kid on the first day of school. "This year I'm going to do my homework every day right after school and get straight A's." That lasted about a week.

Lee reminded him that she had a hair appointment later today, so he was left to his own. A text to Tommy Mac would be in order. Some college football at Healy's sounded like a good afternoon.

Tommy texted back that he was tied up with his family, so that was out.

The more he thought about it the more he thought that a trip to Benny's was in order. Fuck it. What does he have to lose? It was all but certain that uncle Norm would be gone, and there definitely would be chatter about the old lady.

Lee asked him what he was planning to do with his free time.

'I dunno. Maybe head over to PJs later on, watch some of the games."

"OK. I'll meet you there. I should be back around five or so."

"OK."

He kissed her goodbye, grabbed an iced tea, and retired to the backyard. Maybe he could get someone to go with him on this little jaunt.

He texted Joe, but he was out of town.

Fuck it. He would just go solo and get it over with. He would head over about three. He had two hours of puttering around the house and tending to the garden. Looking at plants that on first sight healthy, but still haven't produced any crops of notice.

He realized he was starting to become a familiar face at Benny's when he walked in and the bartender immediately gave a warm welcome rather than a suspicious stare.

"Hey Hon! How are you? Bottle of Bud?"

"Yes please."

Jim took a seat at the bar and took a quick glance around. One of the tandem was in his regular spot, no doubt waiting on the arrival of his partner. Jim nodded hello and buried his face in his phone on the hope that he would just slide into the background and they could continue their conversation. It didn't take long before he got what he came for.

"So, do you think he'll get the lion's share of the inheritance?"

"With all the stuff he said he did for her, you would think so. Personally, I think he's full of shit."

"He does tell stories, but something went down. After all, he did have to quit his job....I mean, retire."

"Asshole sold his soul."

Oh, this was good stuff. Too bad he couldn't ask for them to go into detail. He had to let it come out organically.

"Yeah, she was an evil bitch, but it's a sin to speak ill of the dead."

"If that guy did half of the shit that he said he did, he should be in a jail cell right now. That woman kept his ass off the hot seat so many times, he should be eternally grateful."

"Hudson County politics. It's the gift that keeps on giving. Can't wait to see the handjob of a tribute they give her in the paper."

Two minutes later the duo was reunited.

"I guess you heard by now."

"Yeah."

"Did he even go down there?"

"Yeah. He went down this morning."

"No doubt tearing the place apart looking for anything that would incriminate him."

Jim couldn't help but to look up and take it all in. The two looked at each other like they had been caught in the act, so Jim just asked for a menu to send them back. Even though he wasn't hungry, some wings were in order. He desperately wanted to ask, but he had to be the indifferent one. They sat in silence for a minute before returning to their conversation.

"If his mother left him with nothing I'd laugh my fucking ass off."

"Yeah. That kind of comeuppance would be great. The way he's been shooting his mouth off for all these years."

The conversation turned silent before shifting over to the state of the Giants and Jets, two teams having less than stellar years.

Jim ate his wings in silence in the hope that someone would come in and re-start the original conversation. Two more beers and he lost hope. That conversation was far in the rearview mirror. It wasn't a total loss. He did get some good intelligence out of this trip, even though if it was just enough to reinforce his opinion that this guy was garbage. A little bit in the back of his mind felt sorry form him, though. With a Mom like that he probably never stood a chance. The fucker was probably groomed for this since he was a kid. The only thing he knew about was how to fuck people over before you get fucked. It was the mindset of the criminally self-righteous. He wondered what kind of person his father was, if he was even in the picture at all.

After paying his bill and saying goodbye for hopefully the last time another patron walked in and the original conversation was rejuvenated. If he stayed for another one it would have aroused suspicion, so he acted indifferent and set off.

"That, is definitely the last time I go to that place!" He thought. Pretty much every time he walked out of the place he came out with more questions. It didn't help matters that he couldn't ask the questions, even if he wanted to. Fuck it. Maybe some news would come down the pike in another form.

A week went by with no word from Gordon. Jim would reach out, but it was time to give this kid as much space as needed.

It was Wednesday he got the call he was hoping for from Rob.

"Hey man, that guy Jerry's here."

Jim looked at the time, 4:30. This was going to be an issue.

"OK. I think I can get there in about a half hour. Does it look like he's going anywhere?"

"I think you're good. He just ordered some food."

"Great. I'll be there in a bit. Thanks!"

Jim dialed up an Uber and he was picked up in five minutes. On the way over he called the Mrs.

"Hey hon, what's up. You working late?"

"No. I should be out by five. You at PJs already?"

Fuck.

"No. I had to head into the city to take care of something. I'll be there a little later, like after 6."

"What do you have to do?"

"Nothing big, just meet a client is all."

"OK. Who's the client?"

"Just a client. He wanted to meet and talk about doing some more work."

"What kind of work?"

Oh Jesus Christ.

"Masonry work. Come on! What do you think?"

"OK, OK. I'll see you later."

Sometimes, just sometimes, Jim wanted to make her listen to some of the questions she asked him.

The fact that he was lying to her notwithstanding, it was a bit infuriating at times. Well, it wasn't really a lie. He was going to a city (Newark), and he was going to see an old client (that would be Bub, who would most likely be there anyway), so there was that.

When he got to the bar it was a little after five. Jerry was seated, alone, looking at the news and finishing off his wings. Jim greeted him as he sat down.

"Hey man."

"Jim, right?"

"Yeah. We met a while back. You used to work for Jersey City, right?"

"Yeah. You were with that kid. The thing with his father. Yeah. Heard about the old lady checking out.

Sucks for the kid, but in all honesty, fuck her. Hope she's rotting in hell."

"Yeah, that's the sentiment going around."

Jim ordered a beer and asked the bartender to back Jerry up.

The conversation drifted back and forth for a bit and Jerry asked about how Gordon's mother was.

"Great tits, that one."

"Agreed. Say, can I ask you a few questions?"

"Sure, what's up?"

"So the kid was telling me something that's making me curious. He said that his Uncle, the guy from the Sheriff's Office has been tearing apart the old lady's house and each time he leaves empty handed. Do you have any idea what he could be looking for?"

"Beats me."

"OK. Thought I'd ask. Thanks though."

Fuck, and he was picking up the check for this guy too. Oh well.

"Maybe it's got something to do with the tapes."

"What?"

"Well, the rumor was that she secretly recorded every conversation she had and used to blackmail people left and right. Scuttlebut was that was how she got to where she was. Maybe that's it."

"Do you think she would blackmail her own son?"

"Fuck yeah. Apparently, she didn't give a shit."

"Damn, what a cold-hearted bitch."

That was what he had to be looking for. If he wasn't looking for them himself it was for someone else. Someone who could have been hurt bad.

"She must have put them somewhere for safekeeping. Her house would be the first place they would look."

"I'm sure there are a lot of fuckers looking for that!"

"It's hard to imagine, how you can be so fucking conniving. How do people live like that?"

"Pretty well, actually. Looks like she had her place at the shore and a nice chunk of change. Probably laid her head down at the end of the day on one of those California King sized beds."

"This asshole tore the place apart. The fact that he's still looking makes me think that either he's an idiot or there not at the house." Whoever gets a bead on this McGuffin is has a hell of a head start. Right now there seems to be only one person on the job. An idea popped into Jim's head and he wrote it down in his little notebook for future reference.

"You still use those things?" Jerry said, pointing to him as he scribbled it down.

"Yeah. I find it easier than using my phone."

"That's cool. Old school."

"Thanks."

Jim looked at his phone and noted that it was hitting six. The wife would be getting impatient and the texts would start any minute now. Fuck it. This was a bit more important.

"Can I get you a shooter? A Jameson perhaps?"

"Sure, why not?"

Jim motioned the bartender for a round of shooters. Just one though.

After the shot Jim excused himself and went about the bar to mix with the regulars. 68 was deep into conversation with Mueller, who was about nine drinks in. You could tell with Ed how much he had by how grabby he got. He had stubby hands, but they were vice grips. Years of construction and punching made them a formidable duo. When he put his mitts on you there was no letting go. His next step was biting, which hasn't happened in a while, but it was always on the table. Mike had the 'help me' look that warranted intervention.

"Hey guys, what's up?"

Ed looked up and reached out, grabbing Jim by the crook of the elbow. He was going to be 'goon handed' by a 70-year-old man. Mike took that as a cue and took off. "He's all yours.

"Have you ever shot someone?"

"You mean today? Not yet, but it's still early."

"I have."

"I'm sure you did. Was it for fun or did they have it coming?"

"Both." He followed that with his hearty, high pitched laugh. More like a squeal. Pure delight. He was also not lying about it.

"OK, um, cool."

He felt the grip loosen a little and Jim pulled away. Ed retracted to his seat and turned to his drink. From behind the bar Rich saw what was going on. This wasn't his first rodeo with Ed. He leaned over and grabbed his keys, which meant that he would be driving him home shortly. Ed was the master of the Irish exit and he would slip out without notice. Grabbing his keys was not only a reduction in liability, it was just what Rich did.

Jim went over to the server station and was approached by Rob, who was holding his glass of Franziskaner.

"So you get anything?"

"Yeah. Before I forget, let me pay this guys' tab."

Rob told him not to worry about it as it was on him.

"You know I hate it when you do this, and one day I'm going to say no. Today is not that day though. At least let me pay for his food."

"Ok." Rich was standing by and heard the entire conversation. Jim handed him his card and closed it out, giving Rich a $20 on top of everything. If only this is how everything worked.

Rob was a couple of beers in, and was on the cusp of greeting everyone as,"Bitch." Had all the makings of a good night, which was dangerous. He had to get the hell out of there.

Jim said goodbye to Jerry, who now had an interest in how things were going to work out.

"So what are you going to do?

"Dude, I wish I knew. I don't think I can stand back and watch this thing just fade away."

"Well, don't get me involved, unless it's with Mom. Did I tell you she has great…."

'Yes, I'm aware. The fact that she has a great set has been well-documented. Thanks again dude"

Jim gave him his contact info before heading out and was waiting outside for his Uber when Bub and JoJo came walking in. Damn, this had the fixings to be a good session, which would have been fun, but the payback would be overwhelming.

"Later, fuckers. Bub, this is the best way to see you. Just as I'm leaving."

"Oh Jim. You say the nicest things."

"Next time, dude."

"Got it."

On the car ride back to Jersey City Jim pulled out his notebook and called Gordon. He picked up on the second ring.

"Hey Jim, what's up?"

"Nothing. Just wanted to see how things were going."

"Nothing much to report."

"How's the family?"

"Ok I guess."

"Hey, is your Uncle still sniffing around the place?"

"He comes down like, every other day. Doesn't say much. Each time he comes down it seems he gets more pissed off."

"I think I have an idea what he's looking for. Where did your grandmother keep her mail?"

"Right here, on a little nightstand by the front door."

"If you get a chance, go through it and see if there's anything from a storage company, like a bill."

"Well I can't do it now since we're headed out in a few. I'll check later. Why?"

"Just an idea. I'm probably wrong, but fuck it. Can't hurt to look."

"Ok. I gotta go."

"Alright. Later."

Jim made it back to PJs before seven, so Lee was only simmering and not full-on pissed.

He kept mostly to himself with his little conundrum, keeping the conversation to the usual football and local doings.

"Eagles going to win this weekend?"

Ugh, he hated that question. How the fuck would he know this one. It was when his wife asked him if it would be windy next Wednesday. How on earth would be know this? He got it though. It was just small talk.

"Not sure. They had a squeaker against the Chargers, so you never know against the Cardinals. They should win, but it could be a let-down game."

Richie turned his glass of wine and added a cube. "I don't know. I don't think Wentz is the real deal."

"Who knows. He's playing lights out right now."

"Yes he is."

Lee had nothing to add to the conversation, but motioned that she wanted to get something to eat. Jim mentioned Saigon and she eagerly agreed. Seared tuna and banana leaf rainbow trout it was then.

Jim was mostly silent over dinner and was going over various scenarios in his head.

"What are you thinking about? Tell me."

"Honey, you don't want to know. I have so much shit rattling around in my head right now I can't make heads or tails of things."

"What is it?"

"Just work stuff. Gordon's situation."

"I don't want you getting involved in this, especially since you're not getting paid. It's really none of your business as well."

She was right, but he was in too deep now. Better to keep her out of this, at least for the time being.

"You're right hon. I'll just keep my distance on this one."

"Good."

Two days later he got the payment for the art caper and just as promised there was a $250 gift certificate for Peter Lugers. A call to Sal was in order.

"Hey Sal!"

'Hey Jim, what's doin?"

Nothing much. Hey, I got that gift certificate to Lugers. Up for a porterhouse?"

"You sure you don't want to take your wife?"

"Absolutely sure. That place would be wasted on her. She would order the fish. We can't have that. When is a good time for you?"

"Let's see. Next Wednesday or Thursday works for me."

"OK. Let me see what I can do." Jim hung up

He called the Brooklyn location and was informed that they could get a table for two next Thursday at 6:45. He texted Sal back and confirmed.

Jim then texted Gordon to see if there were any updates, but got no response. Checking his text history with the kid he noticed that he hadn't replied to any of his texts for the past couple of days. He brushed it off, thinking that he had larger family matters to tend to, but he would have to call him to see if he acted on his hunch.

An hour later he got a call from the kid.

"How you holding up, dude?"

"I guess I'm ok. I don't think I'll be able to help you out with the company for a while though."

"All good. When you're ready to come back I'll be here."

"OK, great. Thanks. Oh, hey, I still haven't gotten the chance to go through the mail. I'll be back there in a bit and I'll check it out then. What was I looking for?"

What was he looking for. Jim had forgotten it himself. Oh, right.

"Just any bills or receipts from storage companies or anything like that. I have a feeling that what your uncle is looking for is not in the house."

"Oh yeah. That's right. The place has been crazy lately. A lot of people coming in and out. They looked like important people. They all seemed to know my Uncle, they were all huddled in a corner the other night."

"I bet. If you find something just let me know."

"Got it."

He got to PJs later that afternoon along with the usual cast of characters the horseshoe. Mike and Chris had apparently gone on a golf outing earlier. Mike would go on at least of dozen or so through the course of the year. Jim was the 'emergency' fourth on the rare occasion when they absolutely couldn't find anyone else to go.

He tried golf, but he just couldn't get into it, mostly due to the fact that he was so god-awful at the sport that he just gave up. He supposed some lessons would have helped, and there was a time where he was looking to sign up, but he decided that he just didn't want to invest the time and money on something that he would do maybe a handful of times a year.

"Hey guys. How'd you hit 'em today?"

"Not bad."

"Which outing was it for today? Cops or Firemen?"

"Cops."

"Got it."

Chris downed his drink and said goodbye.

Big Joe looked up from his phone to say hello.

"How about them Eagles!"

"Yeah man. Three and one. Not bad. I'll take it."

"How you been?"

"Good. Things are pretty good. Can't complain."

Doug came in shortly after and they made small talk until Lee showed up.

"Hey hon, how was your day?"

"Not bad. Not bad at all. Going to dinner with Sal next week at Peter Lugers."

"Oh, that's nice."

"Yes, yes it is."

Ten minutes later he got a call from the kid.

"Jim, what's up?"

"Hey man. Forgot you were going to call. Give me a minute." Jim reached into his pocket and grabbed his notepad and pen before stepping outside. "OK, what's up?"

"I'm going through the mail. There's a ton of it."

"I bet. Are you alone? Is your Uncle anywhere around?"

"No. He went home."

"Ok, cool. You see any letters from self-storage companies?"

"Let me see. Man there are a ton of charities hitting her up. Retirement homes, life insurance. Here's something, Metro Storage."

"Really? Holy shit! Is it a bill? What's the address?"

"I don't know if it's a bill. 276 Tonnelle Avenue, Jersey City."

"Open it."

"But it's not mine."

"Dude, I don't think your Grandmother is in any shape to do it right now."

"Yeah, I guess."

"Just see if it's a bill?"

"Hold on. Looks more like a statement. Says here it's for a unit there. It says something that if she wants to renew for another year, she can get a deal if she does it now."

"Does it say when the year runs out?"

"Hold on. Looks like January."

"So we have a couple of months. Do a favor. Tuck that away somewhere. See if there are any other things from the same company and do the same. Good work you magnificent bastard!"

'What?"

"Nothing. Give me a shout when you come back."

"OK, thanks man."

This was something else. His hunches usually never really panned out. He strutted back into the bar and sat next to Lee and Doug.

"Who called you?"

"Oh, it was from Gordon. I asked him to check something out and he came through. He's a good kid." Jim tucked away the notebook. He would check out the address later on. Now the question was how to find out what the hell was in those units. From the looks of things, it seemed like Jim and Gordon were the only ones who knew about this little nugget. Next step was to get the keys. He had time.

Jim met Sal at Peter Lugers the next Wednesday at 6:30 on the dot.

"Hey, Sal!"

"Hey Jim, what's doin?"

Sal was dressed in a collared shirt and sports jacket, which is exactly what Jim was wearing.

"Nothin much. You ready to get your steak on?"

"Yeah, let's have at it."

Jim noticed Sal take note of the clientele as they were ushered upstairs. There were a couple of knowing nods and even a "Hey Sal!" before they were sat down.

"You know those guys?"

"Some of them. You see that gray haired guy with the mustache?"

"Yeah."

"That's Vinnie Conigliardi. He used to run with the Gambinos back in the 80s. I had him locked up for racketeering. The other guy is an associate who runs with the same crew. Never locked him up, but he knows who I am."

"Seems like there's some kind of grudging respect going on there."

"Yeah. I'm retired now so it's none of my business anymore. They respect me because I was an honest cop, doing my job."

Jim's head immediately sorted to the old Warner Brothers cartoon of Wile E. Coyote and the Sheepdog. How they would walk in to work together making small talk, then clock in and beat the shit out of each other for the next eight hours. At the end of the day they clocked out and walked home together.

"That's pretty fucking cool. Twenty years ago you probably would have been at odds, but now I guess you're both out of the game."

"Well I am, that's for sure. Those guys probably still have their noses in a couple of ......enterprises."

They ordered a bottle of wine and didn't even have to look at the menus before ordering. Fatback bacon and wedge salad with blue cheese dressing as an appetizer, a 48-ounce Porterhouse for two (medium rare), creamed spinach, and two baked potatoes.

Over dinner Jim told Sal about his dilemma with Gordon, his dad, and the whole fucking mess he was about to get into.

"Sounds like the Uncle is no-good."

"Yeah. I think he was under the direction of his mother. She was calling the shots, that's for sure. He was just the lap-dog. In a way I feel almost sorry for him.....almost."

"There were plenty of weasels like that on the force. Guys who were only there because Daddy knew a Senator. Some of these guys went out of there way to prove themselves to us. Others didn't give a shit and knew there was nothing anyone could do about it. We did our best to make life hard on these guys."

"I bet. I'm thinking about sticking my neck out and reaching out to the kids father. I think he at least deserves to know that it wasn't his fault that his life was completely fucked over."

"Be careful with that. I'm not sure I would do that."

"Why not?"

"Maybe you should just tell the Mom and leave it up to her."

"I think this guy needs to be in the loop. I think I have to do this. You know what? I don't even really care if this kid never talks to me again because of this. Everyone needs to know."

"How did you find this out again?"

Jim explained about Jerry from the alehouse, who worked in the same department, the fact that the guy was a tea-totaler, how Uncle Norm was at the same party the night it went down. How very convenient the timing was when he was run out of town on trumped up bribery charges that magically went away when Granny got what she wanted.

"Well Jim, you gotta do what you gotta do."

The rest of the meal was filled with general small talk, with almost total silence as they consumed the main course.

As they patted their stomachs and worked a toothpick for the remnants of the steak Jim contemplated an aperitif. Jim gave the suggestion but Sal declined, which was fine too. It wasn't even 8:00, so he knew where he would be heading next.

He checked what Uber was charging to get back to Jersey City. $65. Suddenly the aspect of riding two trains back to Jersey City seemed reasonable. Besides, he could use the walk.

Jim said his goodbye to Sal and set about getting on the L train. A couple of stops and he'd be at 14th street where he could hop on the Path. Yeah, this was probably better.

The only thing going on in his head was how we was going to go about getting dad in on the news.

Another road trip was in order.

He said he had a surveillance job about an hour away and he would follow that with a visit to Mom. It was just easier this way, the half-truth. Besides, it wasn't that he was going to see another woman or anything. Well, not in the biblical sense. Going to see your Mom doesn't count.

He made it to Enterprise at around Noon and picked up the car at the location in Jersey City so he could just drop it off when he came home so he wouldn't have to worry about going to Newark the next morning.

No black Impala, but a gray Ford Fusion this time, which works as well. Jim went casual as he didn't expect to take a quick trip over to PA to see what his buddy Walt was up to, but he didn't want to rule it out.

Driving down the Turnpike listening to Benigno and Roberts had a zen effect on him. It wasn't often that he got to drive alone, without fear of repercussion of listening to sports radio was quite the tonic. *"The pain, bro!, the pain!"* as a Philly fan Jim could relate. He stopped off at the Vincentown Diner and enjoyed another thing that he rarely got to do anymore....have lunch in silence while he read the paper.

He reached out to his sister to let her know he was coming to town shortly after. He didn't want to startle the old lady. He picked up his usual bottle of Prosecco and scratchers and made it to the house at 2:00.

Jim walked in and saw his mother dozing in her chair. At her advanced age it wasn't a great look to sleep with your jaw agape.

He backed off a bit before waking her up. It took a minute to gather her senses and she focused on him.

"Oh, Jimmy, what are you doing here?"

"I was in the neighborhood and thought I'd come by." He handed her the tithe in the form of scratchers and presented the Prosecco.

"Oooh, what's the occasion?"

"I dunno.....Wednesday?"

"OK. What time is it?"

"2:00. Brought some bubbly. Work for you?"

"Why not? I'm not going anywhere. You having a glass with me?"

"Sure, why not." Jim went in the kitchen and poured two glasses before returning. When he came back in the room, he saw that his mother had a puzzled look on her face. He knew that look before, saw it in his grandparents when they were in full-fledged dementia. It was a look where they were trying to make heads or tails of things. An almost empty look. He didn't understand it well as a child, but it was heartbreaking to see it coming from his mother.

"Who are you? Do I know you?"

"Mom, it's me, Jim. Your son?"

"My son. I don't know you. Should I know you?"

Jim came over and grabbed her hand as he sat down.

"Mom, it's me, your youngest son!"

An agonizing moment passed before he saw the lights go on again.

"I know who you are. Good one, huh?"

"Damn woman, you got me. Damn you're good!"

"I know, I know. Shut up and give me some champagne."

"Can't say you didn't earn it."

For the next twenty minutes they sipped away and talked about how things were going. All Jim could thing of was how he was got by a 94-year-old woman. God bless her.

Driving up the turnpike Jim got a call from Sal. He put it on speaker and answered.

"Hey Jim, what's doin?"

"Nothing much Sal. How are you?"

"All good. Thanks for dinner. Good time. Hey, I have something for you. Remember that missing persons case we worked on a while back?"

How could he forget it. "Yeah. I remember."

"They have another one. I'm thinking you should charge hourly on this one. You took the stand the last time."

"Yeah, I remember. I got it. Hey man, I'm driving at the moment. Could you email me over the information and I'll get on it when I get the chance."

"OK. Great. Did you follow-up with the kid and his father?"

"I'm doing it now. Wish me luck."

"Ok then, be careful. I'll send you over the email. You're going to want to call this guy as soon as you get the chance."

"Got it. Thanks Sal."

Jim remembered the case well. It was a solid job, and the first time he was ever presented as an expert witness.

The case was an investigation into a woman who walked out on her family.... in 1969. They had her legally declared dead in the 1980s and the properties they owned were put in the name of her husband. All but one property. A little piece of land in the Hamptons. Fast forward 20 years and the husband checks out. The property was still in the wife's name, so they had to go all over again to get her declared dead. The day of the trial he met up with the client and was introduced to the state attorney. "Don't worry, this is just a formality. We're just going to ask a few quick questions so we can close it out".....they said.

The proceeding next half hour can only be described as a bludgeoning on the part of the state attorney. He dissected every paragraph of his report, questioned his methods in the investigation, his degree of expertise, and belittled him to the point of agitation. He was almost to the point of crying "Cut it out!" but he held the urge down. He held his own, for the most part, and the matter was settled in the clients favor.

After the hearing the state attorney explained that this is what he had to do because the judge was a stickler for details. Jim was commended for his work and he was on his way. That was the day that the seed was planted that he should open up his own shop. Why did he spend the past three hours of his life getting beaten down in a courtroom so someone else could make a buck? Fuck that. Ten years later here he was.

He would have to reach out later. Now wasn't the time. They can wait.

Jim pulled up to the most recent address that he had for Max. The place was a simple cape-cod type house that you used to see at the shore, before the McMansion monstrosities became the norm.

The house looked well-maintained, but there was no one home. It wasn't even five, so he supposed that he had some time before he came home.

Jim promised he wouldn't do it, but he was just across the river from Easton, PA, and 'ol chemtrailz, conspiracy theorist extraordinaire. He questioned himself if it was the right thing to do. After all, after the last visit he really kept his banter to a minimum, at least on the forums that he could monitor. It was only a ten-minute drive away, so fuck it. Why was this even a question?

He made it over in under that and took a slow drive by. Nothing in the lot and no activity that he could see at the moment. Jim found his spot right where he camped out the last time and said he would give 15 minutes, tops. Jim just let the car idle, just in case he had to get the hell out of there and he spent the remainder of the time with his head on a swivel.

20 minutes later he called it and went back to the job at hand. Oh well, goodbye Walt, I'll miss your hackneyed ideas and bat-shit insanity

Jim made it back to dad's about ten minutes later. Still nothing. He found a little vantage point a couple of houses down where he thought he'd be good.

The problem with this neighborhood was that it was a little on the edge of upper-middle class. The lawns are well manicured, houses maintained in a tidy manner. A car like his would immediately be pegged as an 'outsider,' and met with immediate suspicion. In a small town like this everyone was in each other's business, and the topper was that he could guarantee that at least one cop lived on the block.

The protocol in a situation like this in a small town was to notify the local PD that you'd be sitting on a residence, just in case they were called. The problem was that in an insular community there was more than a solid chance that the subject of the surveillance would be tipped off, nullifying the job. Four hours later the client would call off the job and you would spend the next eight months chasing them down to pay the fucking bill. No thank you. Also there were the dog-walkers. The fucking dog walkers. They were the eyes and ears of the neighborhood. Good for the neighborhood, bad for surveillance.

He hit paydirt at 5:30, when a brown Camry rolled into his driveway. A thin middle-aged male, mid 40's balding, got out of the car and headed into the house. He had no prior description of this guy, so he just had to assume. He got out of his car, checked his phone, and went inside. Jim thought he would give him some time to get settled before knocking on the door. Trouble was, how was he going to approach him? What was he going to say? Jim hadn't even given it an inkling of a thought until now.

"Hey, remember that time when you were run out of Jersey City on a rail ten years ago? Well I think you were set up. Let's talk," would be the most direct approach, but Jim had a wonderful way of stumbling over his words in a situation like that.

He milled it over and thought, fuck it, the most direct was the best. He got out of his car and was headed over to the house when the door opened and out stepped the subject, who walked to his car and backed out.

Jim was put into a situation where if he sprinted back to his car he would be noticed, so Jim just pulled out his cell phone and did a hurried walk. By the time he got back to his car he was at the end of the block, at a stop sign making a right-hand turn. By the time Jim made it there he could see the car on the same street about 200 yards away. With a little luck he'd catch up with him shortly.

He had to run a yellow light, but it was worth the risk. By the time the Camry was on the main road Jim was right on top of him.

He didn't travel long before he made it to his destination, a local restaurant/bar/packaged goods spot by the name of Henry's.

Jim pulled into the lot and saw him exiting his car and heading in. Now the trouble was what to do now. If this guy was going in for just a six-pack, he'd be caught flat-footed. He decided to give it ten minutes before going in.

The time passed agonizingly slowly as Jim rolled scenarios around in his head. Some came to the conclusion where he left with a handshake and contact information. Others were getting his ass kicked. He always had the tendency to overthink this shit and he had to right his mind. Just go the fuck in, state who you are and just ask a few questions, you fucking idiot.

He walked into the bar and was met with the sign for the special of the night.

"Tonight! Wings and Trivia!"
"25 Cent Wings and $1.50 domestic drafts
For trivia players"

Not a bad deal. Jim could have made himself at home in this place. He used to be pretty good at this shit, but he got tired of some of the people it brought in. People who just couldn't enjoy the game. They had to win

Jim stepped passed the package goods area and stepped into the bar. It was early so there was plenty of room. A station of the NCR video game boxes was available to anyone who wanted one. These things must have been 20 years old, but they proved to be durable. The contests were up and running and Jim noted there were about four people already in the game. The main board showed rankings of all the bars in the US and Canada that were involved. Invariable it was usually someplace in Moosejaw Saskatchewan that was in the lead. Guess there wasn't much else of anything to do up there, so what the hell.

Jim picked his place at the bar two stools away from Dad. To Jim's right was a borderline obese, sweaty man. Balding with glasses and a black t-shirt and jeans. When he stood up to go to the can he saw his shirt, a cartoon of Wile E Coyote and the Road Runner with the caption "*Chasing Tail.*" He most certainly was, he thought. This guy must be getting laid all over town.

He looked over and acknowledged Max before going back to the game. He had what Jim assumed was a rum and coke next to him. The bartender tossed a cocktail napkin in front of Jim and asked what he wanted.

"Just a bottle of Bud, thanks."

"Will you be playing any trivia tonight, sweetie?"

"No thanks. I hung that up a while ago. I'm strictly a spectator now."

"Ok, but it's .25 wings if you want to play."

"Great. I'm just passing through though, thanks."

She presented the Bud in front of Jim and he placed a $20 on the bar.

"Thanks!" Jim said as he raised his beer. "It's been a long drive. Just had to stop off for a quick one before completing the journey."

"Where's your destination?"

"Jersey City."

Jim noted that Max turned his head and studied Jim for a moment before going back to his game. The bartender even made a look over to him. Well, he had the right guy, no doubt about that.

Jim drank his beer in silence while he pondered his next move. He decided it would be better to wait for a break before he made his move.

About five minutes later Max was delivered a plate of wings. As Jim recalled, these games had 15–20-minute breaks every once in a while, so people could recalibrate. Looked like Max had times his wings to coincide with that. Would be best to do it then.

"Just fucking do it Jim. Don't overthink this shit!"

The voice in his head was right. Best to just do it and let the chips fall where they may.

When the break came Max dove into his wings without hesitation. He pushed his drink towards the bartender to let her know he was ready for a refill.

"Another diet coke, honey?"

"Sure, thanks Marie."

So no rum and coke for this guy then. Jim sized him up and figured he could be no more than 5'8", maybe 170 pounds. If things took a turn for the worse it would seem that Jim would have the advantage. Seem.

Fuck it. Time to do this. Jim leaned over and introduced himself.

"How's it going? My name's Jim."

Max instinctively reached out his hand before realizing it was covered in wing sauce and pulling back. He then nodded. "Max."

"Pleasure." Jim retreated back to his beer for a moment before plowing ahead.

"Max Peralta, right?"

He dropped his food and took a closer look at Jim. He was about to get his haunches up before Jim tried to talk him down.

"I'm sorry to bother you in this matter, but I have some information that I think you would like to know. You see....."

"You one of Norman's goons? You tell that motherfucker I did everything I was told to do to keep my family safe. Tell him thanks for ruining my life. I heard that the old bitch died. Glad to hear it. What is it you want? You want some fucking blood? Come on, motherfucker!"

Max got up and slammed his stool into the bar before heading straight to Jim.

"Hold up dude. It's nothing like that! Just give me a sec...."

It was too late.

Max came at him with his head down and in a bullrush. Jim hadn't been in a fight or thrown a meaningful punch since St Patrick's Day 1993, and the was such a distant memory that he couldn't recall whether not he actually won. The one thing he counted on in such a situation was that his opponent didn't know that. Jim had only one real advantage which, was that he outsized him by a couple inches and 50 pounds. Jim absorbed the initial onslaught before Max backed up and threw a wild fist that missed the mark by a wide margin. Jim popped him in the nose with an inadvertent elbow before the fight was broken up by the cook, a slightly obese, long haired-bearded guy who looked like he was no stranger to brawling. As far as fights go, this was pathetic.

"Get the fuck out of here! Both of you! Now!" Jim took a quick look around the bar and saw "Chasing Tail" dude guarding his beer and wings.

"This isn't what you think!" Jim protested before being given the bums rush by the cook. Right behind him Max was being shown the door as well. He was holding his nose, which, happily wasn't bleeding. Max looked up at Jim with a defeated look.

"Happy now? This was the only place I could come and actually sit in peace! You took that away from me too." He sat down on the cement stairs and buried his head in his hands.

Oh fuck. This was bad.

"Look man, I came to help. I wanted to let you know that I may have some information that would prove that you were innocent! I'm fucking sorry about this, and I'll make it right. I promise. But first you have to hear me out."

Jim looked up to see a bunch of eyes peering out towards them, hoping for a round two that would never come.

"First off, my name is Jim O'Neill and I'm a private investigator. Your son works for me." He gave him his card. Max took a glance and inserted it into his pocket.

"Gordon works for you? You have him doing this shit?"

"No, not at all. Fuck, I don't even do this shit. I just got kind of in this mess. He just does some computer work for me, background checks and the like. He's a good kid."

Jim took a seat next to Max and explained the situation. Things calmed down and he became more receptive the more he spoke. He talked about Uncle Norm, the mystery recordings, and their possible whereabouts. When Jim was finished, he stood up and offered his hand to Max to help him up. Max took the hand and held on for a moment.

"I'm sorry man. I thought you were one of his fucking thugs."

Thug. He was never called that in his life. Jim recalled that he was also called a 'goon' earlier. Two words that were never directed at Jim directly in his life.

"No man. This is all my bad. Hey, stay here for a second. Let me make things right."

Max nodded and Jim went back in. The bartender had her arms folded and the cook stood at the ready.

"I meant absolutely no harm when I came in here. This was a pure misunderstanding. I just came here to try and help him out and he thought I was after him. This is purely all my fault."

The bartender let her arms down and the cook returned to my kitchen.

"Look. I was a bartender for a long time myself, and I know that most places have a policy about fighting. Please don't 86 this guy. I delivered some news that was upsetting and he reacted. I guess it was my delivery that sucked. Again, all my fault. I see there was no damage done, but let me make it right anyway."

Jim reached into his pocket and found two 20's. That along with the $16 already on the bar would make $56. Not a bad night for a local bartender.

She told him he didn't have to do that, but kept it anyway. Jim would have done the same.

"Honey, I've known Max for the last five years. I've never seen him even raise his voice. You must have told him something serious. Who died?"

"Well, it was actually his.....you know what, can I let him tell you? Can he come back in?"

"Sure. We're good."

"Thank you very much."

Jim stepped back outside the bar and motioned for Max to come back in. "Come on dude, we're good."

Max, still checking his nose, entered and sat back down at his seat.

"Sorry Marie, I don't know what came over me."

"I've never seen you like that, honey. Here, let me get you some fresh wings!"

Jim knew that look she was giving him. It was the 'do something manly in their presence' look. He'd has this happen to him a few times before, usually after breaking up a fight or standing up for someone. No doubt about it, Marie was horned up and if Max played his cards right he would be on the receiving end of it.

Jim approached Max on his way out.

"We good?" Jim reached his hand out.

Max reached his hand out "We're good."

"You have my card?"

"Yeah, I think I do. Hold on a minute, before I forget." Max took the card out and dialed the number. Jim's phone rang immediately after and he pulled out to look at the display.

"Now you have my number."

"OK, great. Look man. I'll be in touch."

Marie placed a new order of wings in front of Max and laid a glancing touch to the top of his hand. "Here you go, honey. These are on me."

"Thanks Marie." Max looked up and their eyes met. He knew. Hell, he was married once, and had a couple of kids. He knew the deal.

"OK then. Well, thanks for having me everyone! I have to run."

The *Chasing Tail* shirt guy raised his hand. "Thanks. Best Tuesday night we're had here in a while!"

"Glad I could help! Take care everyone!"

Jim left and headed towards his car. $60 bucks for one Budweiser in the outer reaches New Jersey. Oh well. Hope it was worth it.

As he got into his car he noted the time. Not even 8:00. He could get back before nine, drop the car off, and stop off for a quick pop before calling it a night.

The night crowd at PJs has different faces from the happy hour crowd. Deadhead Bill, who was always good conversation, was sitting with a friend as well as Mike and Sandy, a local couple that were always good company. The only issue he had with Mike was that he made it nearly impossible for you to buy them a round, or leave without his consent.

Jim had his pick of the seats and chose to sit in between them. Lee had already packed it in for the night, so he had a window where he could just sit and take it all in, just enjoy the banter. Bill had his finger on city politics and it was always good to pick his brain for a bit. Tonight the topic was the schoolboard, a seemingly endless treasure trove of corruption. After 10 minutes you wondered how the hell could they betray their positions like that. After 20 minutes he had decided to run for the schoolboard himself.

Three drinks later and he called it a night. He looked at his phone, 10:30. Not too bad. When he made it home, he saw that Lee was sound asleep. She left half the last glass and a half of Malbec for him, which was always appreciated. He retreated to his little office and caught up on the days' events before retiring.

The memory of his encounter with Max had become an afterthought in the ensuing days before he got a call Friday afternoon. The number wasn't stored, but it kind of looked familiar, so he picked it up on the second ring.

"Apollo, this is James O'Neill."

"How fucking dare you!"

"Excuse me?"

"You fucking asshole! Who the fuck do you think you are?"

He was trying to get a line on who the hell he was talking to, but when the voice on the other end-stopped shouting, he figured it out. Oh, shit. This wasn't going to be good.

"Oh, Rose. How are you?"

"How am I? Fuck you! That's how I am! How the fuck could you do this?"

"Do what?" He knew the answer, but he wanted to know how much she knew.

"You know what the fuck you did. Going to see my ex-husband and filling his head with lies."

"Lies?"

"Yes, fucking lies! Now you have his hopes up! He reached out to me and told me about your 'meeting.'

Now he thinks that he was set up. Why would you do this? Why?"

"Well, because I think he was."

"What? Were you there that night, Mr. O'Neill? Were you there when he broke my daughters' arm? Were you there when the cops took him away kicking and screaming? Were you there? Fuck you!"

If Jim knew one thing in life it was never tell a woman to "Calm down" when they were worked up. Having four older sisters, being married for ten years, and numerous failed relationships prior to that had mandated that rule. The only problem was that sometimes Jim wasn't very bright.

"Calm down."

"Calm down? Calm down? Fuck You!"

Oh yeah.

"Rose. Please listen to me for a second!"

"You have one second."

"First off. I never intended to get involved in this. It's not what I do.

A couple of months ago I ran into Jerry Feely. Do you know him?"

"Not offhand. No. Wait. Did he work with Max?"

"Yes. He said he met you on the odd occasion. He was there the night everything happened at Casa Dante."

"I remember him now. He couldn't take his eyes off my chest. What about him?"

"He knew Max, well enough to not believe the turn of events that evening. He saw Max only have, maybe three drinks that night."

"OK."

"He noted it wasn't shortly after your brother showed up and quickly left that he got blotted."

"Are you saying my brother had something to do with this?"

"I think so. Look. I know this isn't going to be easy to hear, but I think that he was working in conjunction with your mother to get a building project passed. There were several well-heeled people who had great interest in that project, and from what I could tell Max wouldn't sign off on the permit because it didn't meet the standard code."

"Can you prove this?"

"Well, no. But I think I'm on the right track. Your mother was apparently known to keep meticulous records of all her conversations. Maybe to keep herself insulated, but also to hold over people's heads."

"Yeah, that sounds like something she would do. My brother too. That fucking asshole."

"Look. I'm sorry that I went where I did. I overstepped my boundaries and ventured into something that was none of my business."

"You sure did."

"But what I came across is a colossal wrong. And if I at least didn't try to see if I could see if it could be righted, then I think that would mean a lot. Rose, I've spent a lifetime sitting on the sidelines looking at other people stick there necks out for less. I didn't see this as an opportunity. I have absolutely nothing to gain. Hell, I'm half-expecting to get my ass kicked once your brother finally gets wind of what I did."

"Yeah, that's probably going to happen."

"Yes, I visited Max. This guys' entire life has been destroyed. He's living a marginal existence out there, from what I can tell. To be brutally honest I'm a little surprised that he hasn't tried to do himself in. I'm also sure that it's too late for any type of reconciliation."

"You got that right."

"I get it. Ialso get why you're pissed. I had no right to do what I did. I apologize. But I'll take your derision and whatever else you have in store for me. If you don't want Gordon to work with me anymore that's fine as well. But if I'm right about all this....well."

"Well what?"

"What?"

"Well, what are you going to do?"

"I have no idea. Nothing, I guess. I never honestly thought this would be ever taken this far."

Jim heard an audible laugh some through the other end. He thought he may be coming out in the clear.

"Mr. O"Neill."

"Jim, please."

"Mr. O'Neill. I see what you're trying to do, and I get it. The bottom line is that even if you could prove the charges against my husband were false, there is still no way in hell that I would ever take him back."

"I get it. I just hate to see an innocent man get hosed like this."

"I see. Is he paying you any money?"

"Not a cent. In fact, I've done all this on my own time. Gordon has no idea about this. He mentioned Max a few times, but it was nothing more than in passing. It had to be hard on your kids, not to mention you. I'm not looking for anything more than to help to make something right."

"Thank you. Look. I have a lot of shit to process. I'm sorry I yelled at you earlier."

"No apologies necessary. I would have done the same."

"Jim, my son really looks up to you."

"He does?" That may not be a good idea."

"Yeah. You think he didn't?"

"No, well, I guess not. To be honest I've never really thought about it much. I was just trying to do right by him. When I hired him, I thought that he could have used a break."

"I think you mentioned that."

"Probably. I do that a lot."

"I can see. I also don't think it's a good idea if he keeps working for you. I don't want you filling his head with the idea that everything is going to work itself out."

"I get it, but I think that should be his decision. He's a grown man, kinda."

"Look. Just do me this and we'll be good."

"OK, got it."

And with that they disconnected.

Man, that was an earful, but he wasn't the least bit surprised. He knew that it would be coming down the pike one way or the other. Jim was just grateful she was willing to just listen for a second. Actually, he was quire proud of himself at how it turned out. He got it that she didn't want Gordon working for him, at least for the time being, but he was a big boy now and could make his own decisions. He would have to reach out to him later today. He figured he had a couple hours to go before he could call it quits and call it a week. Fridays were always a good happy hour at PJs, and today should be no exception.

An hour later Jim got the urge to reach out to Max. He hadn't saved his number, but he went back to the night they met and checked his call log. He picked up almost immediately.

"This is Max, who is this?"

"Hey Max, this is Jim O'Neill. We um, met the other night."

"Oh yeah, you."

"Hey man, my apologies for the other night. It was something I definitely could have handled better."

"It's OK. I see where you were coming from."

"So we're good?"

"Yeah, we're good."

"OK, great. Heard from your ex-wife Rose a couple hours ago?"

"How pissed was she?"

"Oh, she was hot. But I understood. I was surprised that she actually listened to my side of the story."

"Really? Wow! She's changed."

"That's a good thing. So I just wanted to reach out to keep you in the loop."

"You sure about that? Rose will kill you."

"Yeah, I'm aware and I'll take my chances."

"OK, up to you."

"So, since the old lady died, things are starting to move. Your former brother in-law has been tearing up her house looking for something. It had to be the recordings. This guy is freaking out about it a bit. I think they're somewhere off-site, like in a storage locker or something. Now, we found a possible one, but we can't be certain. You know what? I have to go. I wanted to keep you in the loop."

"Got it. Thanks."

Three hours later, on his way to PJs, Jim got a call from Gordon.

"Hey man, what's up?"

"Heard my Mom went to town on you. Sorry about that."

"No worries, it's cool. So what's the fallout?"

"She said that I can't work for you any time soon."

"Yeah, she made that perfectly clear to me. So is there a solution to this?"

"I dunno. You?"

"No idea, well, I kinda do. Say, remember those storage unit statements you found? I asked you to put them somewhere safe."

"Yeah, I remember. I put them between the mattresses in the guest room that I stay in when I'm there."

"Good man. What's the deal with the house?"

"Not exactly sure, but I think that I overheard that she left it to the church."

God, what a fucking bitch. Give the church a shore house instead of her kids, who could obviously use it more. Trying to make up for your sins and give your assets to the earthly representatives of sky-daddy.

"You planning on going down any time soon?"

"I'm going down with my Mom and my sister on Sunday."

"Is your uncle coming down?"

"Yeah, I think so. Ok, great. Let me know when you make it down. Thanks dude."

Jim looked and saw it was time to officially call it a day. This was nice. Everything wrapped up nice and tidy. No pressing issues to tend to. Eagles weren't even playing until Monday night, so Sunday was wide open. This had some potential. First things first was to tidy up and meet Doug at PJs to kick things off.

He took his usual seat at the bar and awaited the Friday lineup. 20 minutes later Doug was the first to appear, followed by Mike and Chris, then Bob and Mary. McNeil then came right in front of Michi, who took a seat next to Jim.

"Hey, what's up?"

"Nothing much, yay Friday." Michi ordered a Miller Lite. "I have a date tonight. Some guy I matched up with on Bumble. I don't have high hopes for this one, but what the hell."

"Gotta keep plugging away. I had some of my best times when I was active in the dating scene. When I lived in Brooklyn I used to do what I called 'the circuit.'"

"What was that?"

"Initially I would take them to places that I never go to. Never to my regular haunts. Luckily it was Brooklyn, so that wasn't a problem. I'd take them out for some drinks and if things went well, we would meet up again for dinner. The better things went the more you moved them into your comfort zone. Worked pretty well for me."

"Oh yeah. Never take them to your local. If things go south, you never want them to know where you hang."

"You have to keep hopeful. When you give up that's when you just become a bump on the log, check out, and start collecting cats."

347

"So how was your week?"

"Oh, it was interesting. I created a bit of a shitstorm I did." Jim then went into detail about his adventure in Philipsburg and the predictable backlash.

"Damn Jim. You really got yourself in the middle of something."

"Boy howdy."

Michelle motioned for a shot of Fireball before heading out on her date. Being the gentleman that he was, Jim ordered a shot of Jameson as well, which turned into five more for the Friday boys. Oh well, fuck it.

They all raised a glass to welcome the weekend and just like that, Jim was out $50 bucks. All good though. These things were usually met with reciprocation.

"So, do you have a plan to get things right?"

"I think so. I mean, I'm pretty sure. Well, kinda. Maybe."

"Well, good luck with that, Jim. Maybe I'll see you guys later."

"Have fun!"

After Michelle left Jim turned his attention back to Doug, who was buried in his phone arranging his next trip.

"Where you going?"

"Just down to Wilmington to see my Mom."

Jim remembered something that he wanted to mention to Doug.

"So I was reading more about the missing Moe shorts."

"The one's we were talking about the other night? I looked it up. It would be a miracle if they were ever found. 'Spring Fever' I think they called it."

"Wow, that would be something."

"So, you up for a road trip?"

"What?"

"Thing about it. If we find the missing footage, we would be Gods! Well, at least in the Stooge world. Which I must have to speculate is a dying lot. I mean. I don't see the next generation picking up the torch any time soon."

"Yeah. That's true. Hate to say it, but I think it may die out with us."

"But you never know. They are still on TV, so there's that. So what do you think?"

"About what?"

"Going to find them. Come on! It would be fun! What do you think?"

"Are you crazy?'

"I bet those shorts are sitting in someone's attic right now, begging to be discovered. Now hear me out. We would have to find places in Lancaster that would have been boarding houses in the 1920s. How many could there be?"

"I don't know. A lot?"

"Maybe. From there we cross-reference from newspaper archives, get an address, and see if there's any estate sales going on."

"Sounds like a plan. You can take Lee."

"What? No. This is all you and me baby. You have the zeal and passion for something like this. Besides, Lee's a girl. She just wouldn't understand. She shouldn't understand. Some things are just meant to keep the sexes apart, and I think the Stooges are probably the kings of that hill."

'Yeah. I'll have to pass."

"I'll let you think about it."

"So, it sounds like you're in a bit of a pickle, what with the family."

"Yeah, it's a tough one. I could have let it lie, and I usually do with something like this because, at the end of the day, why should I give a shit?"

"I think what you're doing is the right thing."

"Thanks."

"So, what did Lee have to say about all this?"

"About what? What is it?"

Jim turned around and saw that Lee had stepped inside. She was quite the stealthy one, for good or bad. This time, not so good.

"What?"

"What are you talking about?"

"Oh, well that. Yeah. Well, Doug and I are going to go out on a road trip to Lancaster Pennsylvania to look for lost Stooge artifacts. I didn't tell you because, you know, it's the Stooges."

"Great. Have fun with that. I guess I won't be going on this one?"

"Honey, would you want to?"

"I guess not."

Lee took her seat at the bar and settled in. Bullet avoided. Jim planned on discussing it later over dinner anyway, but this wasn't the forum to hold the conversation. Better to catch the heat over this in a calmer setting.

After a couple more drinks and the nightly debate of where to eat, Jim got a text from Gordon.

Hey, came down early. What do you think I should do with the mail I hid?

> *I was thinking to just lay them out where the mail usually goes. Mix it in there, but make sure it's on or near the top.*

Ok, got it.

> *You're Uncle do down any time soon?*

Not sure, but we came down early because they moved up the time frame for turning over the house.

> *Got it.*

I'll be down here til Wednesday, I guess. We'll keep an eye on things and see what happens.

> *OK, cool. Take care Dude.*

"Who are you texting? And why are you doing this while we're getting ready to eat?"

"Sorry, it was Gordon. Things are going down soon and he's keeping me in the loop."

"What do you mean?"

"OK, here goes." Jim drained his wine and ordered another. This was going to be a long one.

She never said a word when he gave her a blow-by-blow account of what happened earlier in the week and what was in the near future. When all was said and he laid it on the table, she provided a two-word response.

'I see."

She took a last bite of her salmon, carefully chewed it, swallowed, gently wiped her lips with the napkin and placed it on the table.

"Godammit Jim! Why can't you mind your own God-Damn business for once!"

"I tried, but in this instance I just can't. You're going to have to trust me on this one."

"Why on earth would you do this?"

"I told you before. I think this guy was the victim of a major crime, and I think I can prove it. This kid lost his father because of these pieces of shit. If I sat back and let it go, then what the fuck kind of person would I be?"

"I see, but the main goal here is to make some money, right?"

"Yeah, but if I could spread some goodwill along the way, what's the harm in that?"

"Sounds like this Uncle would kick your ass if he found this out."

"I know, I know. It's a risk I have to take."

"What about me? Am I going to carry you if he puts you in the hospital?"

"I sure hope so."

"I'm getting a bit tired of pulling the major share here. I let you start this business when we got married. It's been about what, seven years?"

"I think."

"And how are you doing?"

"Well, you have to admit that this year's been pretty good. I've put every extra cent I've made into the mortgage account."

"Yeah, but how long is that going to last?"

"My numbers are up."

"They are. And the moment they are you go out and try to save the world and go out on your road trips to god knows where."

'Well, I did see Mom. She says hi. Actually she didn't."

"Great. Seriously, Jim. You're going to have to grow up sometime and let all this shit go."

"You know what? I'm doing well, well enough that I hired someone. And that kid needs some fucking help, even if he doesn't want it. Nobody has been in this kids' corner for a long time. His Mom is doing her best, but he needs more than that. I can't not do anything. I just can't."

"I get it honey, but how much longer is this going to go on for?"

"Hopefully not long."

"After this, no getting involved in shit that you don't get paid for. Can we agree on that?"

"Sure. You got it."

Jim paid the check and they walked home in relative silence. As much as he hated to acknowledge it, he knew she was right. This was it. It would be strictly business from now on.

Like that was going to happen.

Sunday shaped up to be a great mid-fall day. Temps in the early 60's, sun, and just enough crispness in the air that you knew colder days were ahead. But not today.

After making breakfast Jim suggested that they take their bikes out for a final ride before they go in storage. She was surprised that he would give up a football Sunday to be outside, even though Jim had mentioned that the Eagles don't play until Monday. He was going to remind her, but thought the better of it. Why would he tell her and ruin things? Besides, now wasn't the time to remind her. He had to pick and choose when to use her forgetfulness to his advantage, and this wasn't one of those times.

A nice ride through Liberty State Park, a stop at the far end to view the harbor, with the Statue of Liberty, Ellis Island, and New York harbor all in their full glory. It really was a sight, something that never got old. They reminded themselves how fortunate they were to have something like this in their backyard.

On the way back they didn't even have to bring it up to each other to stop off at the Liberty House for Sunday Sangrias.

They were always welcomed with open arms when they entered the place, which was nice. Carlo, the maître d, was always there with a warm hello and a round on the house. Jim liked to think it was because they were such wonderful people, but he knew that while true, it was the fact that they were married there was the main reason. Yep, spending $35,000 in one night does do the trick, and hey, they get a free drink every now and then.

It was the age-old problem with these drinks, however. They packed a wallop. One wasn't enough and two was too many. Aahh, who gives a shit. It was a wonderful day, and autumn can quickly turn into those sullen dank days before you know it. Today it was just about enjoying some warm sunshine on your face before it becomes a fond memory.

They decided to just go straight home as they navigated the pathway at Liberty Harbor. Better to drop off the bikes and hoof it for the rest of the day.

After putting the bikes away they instinctively just started walking to PJs. They didn't even suggest it anymore. It was a given. Plus, the Giants were playing the Seahawks too, which was a bonus.

They got there with time enough before kickoff to grab one of the better seats at the horseshoe end of the bar. Mike was already there in his Giants jersey, as was Richie, who had given up putting up motivational signs around the bar. They were 1-5 and going nowhere. At this point it was just about meeting up and enjoying the time.

A familiar face appeared that he hadn't seen in a while, but was always a welcome sight. Manny, an always impeccable dressed Welsh gentleman. Always impeccably dressed. Shit, even his sweatpants were classier than anything Jim had in his wardrobe. He was always good for a laugh and solid conversation. He had gotten in one of the last rounds of golf of the season with his buddies in Long Island before stopping off to enjoy the game before calling it a weekend. They brought each other a whiskey and had some laughs. Sundays were a good day at the watering hole. The gatherings were organic. No one really made plans to go out, it just turned out that way.

It took until the latter part of the game, but it became apparent that the Giants would soon be 1-6, and while Jim couldn't be happier about that, he almost felt for his friends......Almost. Oh, screw 'em. They've seen the Giants win the big one four times, while the Eagles were still in the 'haven't done it' category. Someday, maybe. He just hoped he would still be around to see it.

After the game the conversation turned to dinner. Earlier in the day there were plans on making something elaborate, but as per the usual with a Sunday during football season, it ended up with a pepperoni and mushroom from Buon Appetite. Not a bad way to kill off a weekend.

It wasn't until Tuesday that he heard back from Gordon. Nothing much to report. He had put the billing information from the storage company among the other mail, but uncle Norm was nowhere to be found. Mom had settled down a bit, but the aspect of him coming back to work was not looking good.

No worries. Reach out if you need anything.

    K. Thanks.

Jim went through the daily machinations of the day and headed to ShopRite to figure out what was going to be on a plate for dinner. He passed by PJs and gave a passing glance. Some familiar faces, but nothing that would draw him in on a Tuesday. He had to draw the line somewhere. Give the place a rest every once in a while.

He came to find the pickings at the seafood aisle barren. Nothing but Halibut for $25 a pound, some tilapia, and catfish. The counterperson said that they would be expecting a shipment tomorrow. Not much help tonight. He ambled down to the meat department when he got a text from Lee.

I'm at PJs, come here.

    At Shoprite. What do you want for dinner? Seafood pickings are pretty slim.

I could do with the leftover pizza.

    OK. See you in a bit.

Perfect. Looks like he wouldn't be laying low after all. Fuck it. He wasn't too keen on cooking anyway.

He made it back and grabbed his seat between Lee and Doug, who was finishing up his last gin and soda and cashing out. Jim offered to buy him one more and he accepted, settling back down in his seat.

Mike and Richie came in and the conversation turned to the Eagles, who were now 6-1. Frankly, Jim got tired of talking about it, but at least it was a conversation point. Sports were a nice common denominator, something that allowed anyone to join in.

Halfway through hearing that the Eagles were a hollow 6-1 he got a call. It was Gordon. Jim motioned that he would take up the conversation later and walked outside.

"Hey man, what's up?"

"Jim! I was out with my Mom picking up dinner when my Uncle came to the house. He found the information and took off!"

"Really? Holy shit! Wow! It actually worked! So what's the deal? How long ago did he leave?"

"About a half hour ago. I was out and my sister was home when he came in. She didn't hear him come in, but she saw him take off in his car. She told me when we came back."

"OK, great."

A half hour, and with the kind of car he drove means he should be there in 20, maybe 30 minutes tops.

"OK, look. Here's what I'm going to do. I'm gonna hop in an Uber and head over there. I suggest that you guys get up here too. I don't care how mad your Mom is at me. If she wants to slug me, then so be it. I think it's very important that you guys are there."

"OK."

"Alright, cool. What's the address of the place again?"

"Address?"

"The address of the storage company. What is it?"

"I don't know. I thought you did."

"What? How would I know this?"

"I gave you the address when I found the information."

"You did?"

"Yes, I did. Remember?"

He remembered. It was somewhere buried on his desk, among the 200 post it notes with useless information scribbled on every one.

Fuckfuckfuckfuck

"Yeah, I have it written down somewhere. What was the name of the place?"

"Not sure. Something storage."

"Yeah, that's a given. It was on route one or something. I remember looking it up."

"You mean Tonnelle Avenue."

"Yeah, that's it. Tonnelle. Hold on a second."

He looked up storage and Tonnelle in Jersey City and got three hits.

"Ok, which one sounds the most familiar. Jersey City Storage, City Storage, or Metro Storage?"

"Was it Metro? I think, no wait, it was definitely Metro."

"Ok. I think your right."

"OK. It's at 276 Tonnelle Avenue. I'm going to hop in an Uber to and I hope to see you there."

"We'll be there."

Jim re-entered PJs and was already dialing up a car request.

"What's going on? Everything OK?"

"Yeah, well, not really. Look. I have to go. And by go I mean now."

"Where are you going?"

"This whole thing with Gordon and his Uncle is finally coming to a head. I have to head over to a storage unit on Tonnelle Avenue."

"I want to come with you."

"Absolutely not. Out of the question." Jim looked her dead in the eye. "I know what you're going to say, and I'm in full agreement with what you think, but I started this whole thing and I have to be there to see it through. Now please, I'm begging you. Don't make a fuss and let me go. I'll be back before you know it. Everything will be fine."

Lee heard the earnestness in his voice and acquiesced.

"OK, just go."

He kissed her and said a quick goodbye before stepping outside to wait for the car, which arrived two minutes later. When he hopped in the car he thought that the goodbye kiss should have been more dramatic, but oh well.

The time to arrival at the destination was timed at ten minutes, give or take a couple. With any luck he would get there a couple of minutes early.

In the car he dialed up Max, who picked up on the second ring.

"Hello Jim. What's up?"

"Hey man. What are you doing?"

"Nothing much. What's going on?"

"Well, I know this is short notice, but I have a feeling everything is coming to a head, and I mean soon. Norm found where the tapes may be, and he's heading to the location as we speak. I'm headed over in an Uber to double-check."

"Where is the place?"

Jim gave him the address.

"I'm in my car now. I can be there in under an hour."

"OK. This whole thing can amount to a nothing sandwich, but I don't think so."

"I get it. I'm on my way."

Jim tried to settle down before he reached his destination, but the adrenaline was going into overdrive. It was the feeling you got after sitting on a surveillance for four hours before the subject finally makes a move. Hours of sheer boredom crushed in an instant when things kicked into gear. It was too easy to overreact in a situation like this and the best thing to do was take a few deep breaths and let things unfold.

Which proved to be bullshit. A few deep breaths did nothing. Only kicked his excitement up a notch. As the car pulled into the unit, Jim looked around and came to the conclusion that he had made a big mistake. *What the fuck was he doing here? Are you a fucking idiot? You are way out of your comfort zone you dumb motherfucker! Get back in the car and head back to the bar and sit the fuck down!!*

Jim said his goodbye to the driver and stepped outside.

The front space consisted of several units, with more showing in the back, up an incline. He looked around and saw no signs of Uncle Norm. Maybe he hadn't gotten there yet. Maybe he was in the wrong place. Maybe Uncle Norm decided to go to the local and have a few before taking things up tomorrow. All these questions were answered when he heard some loud bangs and "Mother fuckin cocksucker!"

Yep, that was him.

It was coming from one of the units in the back.

As Jim stepped closer, he could hear what could only be Norm trying to pry open the door to the unit. A lot of jostling followed by a quick slam and more colorful language.

Jim stopped when his phone rang. He was worried that he may be heard, but this guy was being so loud there was no way he could have.

He looked at the number and saw Perth Amboy. While he should have let it go to voicemail, for some reason picked it up.

"Hello?"

"Mmmmister O'Neill?"

"Yes?"

"It's Tracy."

She could barely get that out between sobbing heaves.

Why the fuck did I pick up this call?

"Tracy, this isn't really a good time."

"Please, you have to help me! I'm losing my mind! Please!"

Fucking hell. Jim turned and took a step away towards the entrance.

"What's going on?"

"He's bugged the appliances. I know he did. I can hear them. I know it sounds crazy, but you have to believe me. Please."

Normally he would have hung up, but this woman sounded to be at wits end. She had nowhere else to go. Not that he could do anything about it, but the fact that she reached out confirmed that she was at the end of her rope and needed a knot to hang on to.

"OK Tracy. Listen to me. I really don't think that he could bug your appliances, but I think I can help. Is it your refrigerator that's bugged?"

'Yes."

"OK, is it stainless steel?"

"Yes."

"OK, perfect. Now listen to me. Do you have a radio with an antenna?"

"Yes, in the garage."

"OK, what I want you to do is get the radio, turn it on to the lowest FM frequency, and touch the antennae to the fridge. This will cancel out any bugging device and you should be good to go."

"Will it?"

"When the metal from the antennae hits the metal from the fridge it cancels out any frequency that could be listening in."

"Really?"

"Yes. Now I need you to do that now. I really have to go, but if you have any further problems give me a call. I think that should do the job."

"Oh, thank you. Thank you so much!"

"Good luck Tracy."

After hanging up Jim wondered where the hell did that idea come from. This woman was obviously in a sorry mental state, and other than seeking professional mental help, something like an idea like this can be effective. Fix crazy with a little more crazy. Maybe it was the equivalent of drilling another hole in the bottom of a boat to let the water out, but at the moment it was the only thing that came to mind.

A moment after disconnecting he saw Uncle Norm pull out of the parking lot.

He missed him. Fuck. Now what.

Nothing to do but take a quick lookabout.

He made it up the hill a bit and took note of the units. He saw one that must have been the target. The bottom right part of the door was askew and bent. From the looks of things this was the one. Looks like the thing held up. He may have been able to slide under, but that was about it.

While scoping out the lot a security guard approached.

"Sir, may I ask what you're doing on the premises?"

"Oh, I was just meeting my friend here. Was going to help him out."

"Oh, you mean the cop?"

"The what?"

"The cop. The guy in the Camaro."

"Oh, yeah, him. That's right. Didn't hear you."

"You a cop too?"

"What, me? Oh, no no-no. I'm here on some personal business. We may have some other people coming to meet as well. Is that cool?"

"Well, it's after hours, but the cop said he was on official business, so we're good. I don't want any trouble with the police."

"I hear you. Thanks man, take care."

"Y'all take care."

So Norm was playing cop now. At least it helped get the security guard out of the way, so there was that.

A minute later he got a text from Gordon saying that would be there in about five. Five minutes 'til Mom unloaded in him.

Gordon was true to form in his punctuality and they entered the lot in under five minutes. Jim greeted them and suggested that they park away from where anyone could see the car.

After exiting Mom walked purposefully up to Jim. At least her fists weren't clenched, but she was simmering.

"OK, Mr. O'Neill. What is the meaning of all this? Gordon says that my mother may have stored some important papers here, is that right?"

"Well, not exactly papers, per se. Let's call it, oh I don't know, overwhelming criminating evidence. If I'm right it's all in there right over here.

Jim led them to the shed.

"You see? Your brother was just here trying to bust into the unit. He took off about 20 minutes ago."

"Well, what's in it?"

"Rose, apparently your Mother wasn't the must upstanding of people."

"I know that."

"Well, apparently one of her favorite hobbies was blackmailing people. I hear she was quite good at it."

"I heard rumors, but that's about it. It was none of my business anyway."

"Well, I have reason to believe that she royally hosed you, and especially your ex-husband Max, and I think that your brother was in on it."

"How do you know this?"

"Everything we need to know may be right in there."

A minute later they saw another cars' headlights pull into the lot. Immediately after Jim got a text. It was Max. Now things were getting interesting.

"Who's that?"

"Rose, please understand. I figured that he needed to know."

"Is that Max? You motherfucker! Why would you do this?"

Rose turned and started sobbing. Given his druthers, Jim would have rather been on the receiving end of a punch in the face rather than see her in such a state.

Gordon went and put her arm around her.

"Mom, it's OK. I asked him to do this!"

He did?

"You did?"

"Yeah. I heard that Dad may have been set up. I was the one who asked Jim to put this together."

"Um, yeah, that's right. He did. You guys hang here."

Jim left Gordon and Rose and walked down to greet Max.

"Hey man. You made it! Cool. I think it may all be for naught though. Norm took off about 20 minutes ago. Looks like he tried to break into the unit but couldn't."

"Fuck, really?"

"Yeah."

"Also, Gordon and Rose are here as well. I don't know how you want to handle that,"

"Gordie, Rose? Oh my God. I'm not sure what to do. It's been so long. Fuck. What do I do?"

"Well, maybe start with 'Hello.' Don't overthink it. Just see how things fall out."

"It's just been so long."

As they walked up the incline and passed the corner of the building into view of each other they locked eyes, but before any words could escape, they were blinded by the headlights of Norm's car.

Immediately distracted, they turned their attention to the black Camaro. Norm pulled in and stopped his car directly outside the storage unit he had visited earlier. He kept the car running with the headlights focused on the slightly damaged door. He popped the trunk before he got out and didn't seem at all taken aback at the extra company. Jim would have jumped out of his skin.

"Hey Rose, you come to see the show? I see you brought Gordon. Good for him. The little fat fuck needs to get out. And who's that? Is that Maxie boy? Well, I'll be. Looks like a family reunion here. Isn't that something. And who are you? You look familiar."

Norm pulled out a small flashlight and lit up Jim's face.

"Where do I know you from. I know I've seen you before. Oh well. I guess you're all here for the show. What's behind curtain #1, amirite? I know what Max is looking for."

"Is it true, Norm? Did you set me up? You motherfucker. You ruined my fucking life!"
He took a couple of steps towards Norm, who lifted his shirt, showing the hardware he was packing in the form of a handgun. Norm took another step and didn't stop the verbal assault.

"You think I give a fuck if you shoot me? You took everything else in my life away. At this point, I really don't care anymore." He took another step but was stopped by Gordon.

"Dad, stop! Please. It's not worth it. Please."

Maybe it was the thought of getting his brains blown out in front of his ex-wife and child or maybe it was what was left of little self-preservation senses, but he stopped.

"That's right Max, stand down. It's not worth it. Also, none of this was my idea. It was all the work of 'dear old mom.' You should have played ball, Max. None of this would have happened. If you had just signed off on the building then none of us would be here."

"That place was a disaster waiting to happen. Everyone knew it. Even if I did sign off on it there was no way it would have made it through a final inspection."

"Oh, it would have. Mom had it all set up. But no. You had to be all uppity and do your job."

Rose chimed in. "You mean that this was all over Max doing his job? Did you really set him up? Norm, you're my brother. How could you do this?"

"It's not me, sis. It all came from the top. I was just the errand and clean up boy. In turn, she made sure my life on the force was as easy as possible."

"So, what's in the storage unit?"

"Evidence, Rose. Recordings. Agnes apparently kept quite the list of people she blackmailed. Why she would have it stored here I have no idea. My guess is that maybe she hoped they would just deteriorate over time." Max looked at her for the first time in several years and Jim could see the look in her eyes. He knew that look. It was a good look if you were on the receiving end of it, but now was not the time.

Norm took the time to dig into the trunk and find a crowbar. He then went to the task of opening the unit. He wedged the steel bar on the non-damaged side of the door and gave it a lift. At first it looked like the door would hold, but after another pull the lock mechanism failed, sending the door rattling straight up.

At first sight it looked like any other storage unit. Loads of undescriptive boxes, a couple of lamps, and an oriental rug tossed on top.

Norm quickly set upon the boxes. He opened one, then another, and then another.

"What the actual fuck?" Norm pulled out of the unit and crouched with his head in his hands.

"There's hundreds of these things."

"Of what?"

Norm looked at Max. "What do you think?" and he waved for Max to take a look.

Max walked in and looked down at the open boxes. The lights from the Camaro weren't much help at the moment so he pulled the string to the overhead light.

"Jesus Christ! What the actual fuck?"

"I know, right?" For a moment Max and Norm stood in agreement and had a moment, which was immediately shattered by Rose.

"What's in the fucking boxes? Jesus Christ, tell me!"

"Tapes Rose. There must be hundreds, if not thousands of these things. The few open boxes I saw are full of them, and there's at least another dozen or so in there. So you do the math."

"What's on the tapes?"

Norm started to talk, but Max waved him off. "Rose, how do you think she got to where she was. The official record was that she was a tough, shrewd woman, but the reality was that she liked to blackmail people."

"From the looks of things she really enjoyed her work."

"I was hoping that there would be maybe a box or two, but nope. Oh well, looks like it's going to be plan B."

Norm got up and shooed Max out of the unit, their brief moment together quickly forgotten. He then went back to the trunk of the Camaro and retrieved a container of gasoline. On his way back to the unit Max confronted him.

"Norm, think about what you're going to do!"

"I did. This is the only way." He turned to Max and lifted his shirt again. "Now back the fuck off!"

Max raised his hands and backed off. He took ten or so steps back and almost walked into Gordon.

"Dad, you OK?"

"Yeah, I guess. Thanks buddy."

They were quickly joined by Rose. Max took notice on his way back into the unit.

"Oh, look. You're back together! Well ain't that fucking great. Whoopdy fucking do! I guess I did do something good today."

Norm stopped at the entrance of the unit and took a deep breath. He looked down at the gas can, exhaled, and proceeded to distribute the contents liberally about. It only took a minute or so before it emptied and he tossed the container in as well. He took a couple of steps back towards his car and pulled out a cigar.

Rose pleaded with him one last time. "Norm, think about what you're doing! This is crazy. Please. We can work this out!"

Norm looked at his cigar, then at Rose. "Thanks sis, but it's too late for me. It's over, and to tell you the truth I'm glad. It ends here. Mom gets what she wanted and none of this gets out. A lot of people, important people, are going to be very relieved that I did this! I'm going to be well-compensated to see this through!"

He took a match and lit his cigar, took a deep hit, and exhaled. He looked at the match, which was still lit but running low, getting close to his fingertips.

Gordon spoke out as he tossed the match.

"I wonder if she ever had digitized all those tapes to a thumb drive."

"What?" was the last words that came out of Norm's mouth before the match ignited the gas.

The sound was something between a propane grill being ignited and a jet engine, a loud pop followed by deafening "Woosh" before the fire took over.

The Peralta family were far enough back the be spared the initial onslaught and they retreated from the heat. Jim was standing a bit closer to the side and backed away as well, but not before feeling a brief rush of fire hit the side of his face. He backed off further to the side and put his hands to his face to cover. A moment later the unmistakable smell of burning hair filled his nostrils. He grabbed the top of his head. Ok, most of it was still there, just a singe. Could be worse.

After the initial blast the fire took hold in the unit. Lots of fuel inside that unit. Mostly cardboard and acetate.

After they all assessed that they were still in one piece, they turned their attention to Norm, who was blown back head first into his Camaro, which was still running. At first glance he looked like he was knocked out, but on closer inspection he saw that it wasn't the case. Necks just aren't made to bend like that. He wasn't a coroner, but he could surmise that the cause of death was when his head met the front bumper of his car.

Jim went around the other side of the car and turned the engine off. He dared not to move the car for fear of moving Norm's broken body, so he just left it in park. Jim pulled out a leather jacked Norm had in the front seat and placed it over him, relieving Rose of having to see him like that.

No words were said. Rose had her head in her hands, sobbing. She knew he was gone. It didn't matter that he did it to himself, all that mattered at the moment was that she lost her brother.

Both Gordon and Max came to comfort her and for a moment they looked like a family again.

The moment of silence was quickly drowned out by the approaching sirens. The security guard came around and just started cursing. He had one job.

Make sure no one blows up the place up at night.
One job. He had one job.

The police and fire department were on the site
shortly after and by the time the fire was extinguished
there was pretty much nothing left. At least Norm got
his last job done right.

After taking statements and looking at the security
footage, the police acknowledged that they were
nothing more than bystanders and they were all let go
after taking a statement. Shortly after Jim was dialing
up an Uber to get home. It wasn't even nine o'clock.
When he confirmed the ride he went over to the
Peralta family before he took leave.

"So......that was, well," Jim was initially going to do
what he always did and try to make light of the
situation before he remembered that there was one
less person breathing after this whole shit show. He
looked at Rose, who had gathered herself enough to
speak.

'Rose, I'm really sorry. I had no idea."

"I know. You didn't do anything wrong... and I guess
you might have been right all along." She looked up
at Jim and started giggling. "You know you lost your
eyebrows, right?"

"What?" Jim felt his face above his eyes and felt
nothing.

"Oh, shit."

"Dude, you look like an alien."

"Thanks dude, much appreciated. How bad does it look?"

"It's just kinda weird."

"I can live with that. Look. You guys have a lot of shit to sort out. I'm outta here. Good luck man."

"Thanks Jim. I'll reach out shortly."

Max approached Jim as he was getting into his ride and put out his hand.

"Jim. I don't know what to say."

"Well, not much to say. Looks like anything that might prove we were right was destroyed."

"I know. I don't think it matters that much anymore. We know."

"I guess so. Take care man. Good luck."

He saw them in the rearview and had some hope that there may be a happy ending there somewhere.

Then he saw his eyebrows, or lack thereof. He would definitely have some explaining to do to the Mrs. He was thinking about stopping off for a nightcap but thought the better of it. Just call it a night.

Jim didn't hear from Gordon for another week.   He put it on the kid to reach out rather than pry into what was going on as far as their lives were concerned.

The fire made the news, but it was pretty much buried in a day or two. Apparently, there were a lot of people in high places that were just happy to know that those tapes were destroyed.

Jim thought about what Gordon said about digitizing the conversations. While entirely possible, he didn't think that was the case. If it was, it was probably on a thumb drive out there somewhere.

By the time Gordon reached out Jim's eyebrows had started to come back in, which was nice.

"Hey Jim. You good?"

　　　"All good dude. You?"

"Can I call you?"

　　　"Sure, any time."

"Is now good?"

　　　"Yep"

A minute later his phone rang.

"Hey dude, what's up?"

"Nothing. So that was pretty crazy, huh?"

"Yeah, that was something else. Definitely something I wasn't expecting. How's your Mom. She good?"

"She's fine, I guess."

"She's got a lot of stuff to process. Just take care of her."

"OK."

"So you and your Dad have any kind of reconciliation?"

"Kind of.....I guess. There's a lot of stuff going on. My sister is excited that he's getting back into our lives, but I still need to see what's going on. I don't think Mom is back on board yet."

"Understandable. Just give it some time."

"Yeah. Sucks that all that stuff was destroyed, but I think we all know that he was set-up."

"I guess."

"First off, I just want to say that I'm glad that everyone's OK. Things could have been much worse. Hope your Dad didn't get lumped up too bad. Things will eventually settle and you all can move on. In one way or another. All's well that ends well, I suppose."

"Yeah, all's well that ends well."

"Except for your Uncle. He's dead."

"Yeah, I know. Fuck him though. Couldn't have happened to a better guy.

So, Jim. The main reason that I'm calling is to tell you that I don't think I can come back to work for you. I appreciate all you did, I really do, but I think it's better that I concentrate on school. Plus, it looks like we're got some money coming to us, so we'll be good."

"That's cool man. I get it. Dude, it was a pleasure working with you. I mean that. You've got a solid future ahead of you. You got into this racket for just long enough. Hopefully you picked up something that you can use down the road. Plus you have some pretty good stories to tell the chicks."

"Yeah, totally"

Jim heard his stereo in the background. Jim could easily hear an unmistakable song intro.

"Dude, are you listening to Devo?"

"What? No."

"Oh, come on man. You're listening to Gil-U Want! Who do you think you're talking to?. You getting your Devo on? You magnificent nerd! Let it fly!"

"I don't hate them."

"Listen dude. You're going to be good. You need anything give me a shout. You and your family take care, alright. And if your Mom wants to talk let her know I'll make the time."

"OK, well, take care. Thanks."

"Later man."

Jim put his phone away and went about finishing up
for the day. A little tear came to his eye when he
thought that even if this kid didn't pick up any practical
knowledge from working with him, at least he got
some different music into his head. It was a good
start.

Two minutes later he got a text from Doug.

"PJs?"

"Sure. Gimme 10."

"K"

THE END

CPSIA information can be obtained
at www.ICGtesting.com
Printed in the USA
LVHW020938010322
712307LV00014B/896

9 781942 500773